Bloodlines

SHORTS ANTHOLOGY

BLOODLINES SHORTS #5

SUZAN HARDEN

Bloodlines Shorts Anthology (Bloodlines Shorts #5)
ISBN-13 - 978-1-64918-005-6
Copyright 2020 by Suzan Harden

Published by Angry Sheep Publishing
Findlay, Ohio

Interior Design by JW Manus
Cover Design by For the Muse Design

CONTENTS

'TWAS THE NIGHT
SANTA GOT SHOT

Author's Note: This story takes place ten years prior to the events of *Blood Magick*.

Chapter 1

A peculiar scratching woke Tiffany Stephens from a sound sleep. She sat up in bed. Not her bed at Uncle Duncan and Aunt Philippa's. Their house smelled like pine and peppermint and gingerbread at this time of year. Grandpa Kensai and Grandpa Jamal's house smelled like the exotic incenses they bought in Chinatown.

The odor wasn't wrong, just not right for Christmas Eve. Maybe she'd dreamed the sound. She was cold without her covers. The pretty lady on the Weather Channel said Los Angeles might see snow, but all the grown-ups laughed at the idea. Uncle Duncan had lived here over a hundred years, and it had never snowed in Los Angeles. Up in the mountains, sure, but not in the city. Uncle Duncan told her stories of when he and Grandma Margaret were little, and they often played in the snow on Christmas morning in England.

But it wasn't Christmas morning yet. Uncle Duncan said she couldn't open her presents until the sun was up. She punched her pillow a few times for good measure and pulled the covers over her as she lay back down. She was almost asleep when she heard the scratching again. It seemed to come from the roof, and this time, she knew she hadn't dreamed it. Tiffany's feet had barely touched the icy wooden floor when she heard the noise for the third time.

On the roof. Definitely, on the roof.

She didn't care if Mai yelled at her for investigating without waking her oldest cousin or telling the enforcers on duty. Her stupid cousin thought she knew everything because she was almost sixteen. Well, Tiffany turned eight first, and she wasn't stupid no matter what the teachers said or the therapist thought, and she definitely heard noises coming from the roof.

She eased her bedroom door open and crept down the hall toward Mai's room. A loud grunt froze Tiffany in her tracks. Mai's bedroom door was ajar, so Tiffany peeked through the crack. Mai rolled over and resumed snoring.

Tiffany continued her path to the weapons cabinet Grandpa Kensai kept on the second floor. He'd made her a crossbow in her size for her seventh birthday, much to Uncle Duncan's dismay. But then, Uncle Duncan was dismayed by everything she did. Even when Johnny Tucker deserved that punch for tak-ing Kevin Mercer's Pokémon cards during recess.

No sounds came from the direction of Miko's bedroom, but there was more scraping from the roof. Somebody or something was definitely up there.

The hinges of the cabinet door squealed as Tiffany opened it. She paused, but nothing else stirred.

Except whatever was on the roof.

Counting to ten, Tiffany waited, but none of the enforcers appeared. She retrieved her crossbow and slung it over her right shoulder. The quiver of bolts went over her left. The straps dug through her thin nightgown. Maybe she should put on something warmer. But if she did, that would give the thing on the roof time to escape.

Tiffany raced back to her bedroom, closed the door, and locked it. It wouldn't take her cousins long to pick the lock, but by the time they did, she would have proof of whatever creature was making sounds on the roof. The weres and witches weren't stupid enough to come to any vampire's home with-out an invitation. But the fae might.

Or worse, it could be rogue vampires who didn't like Uncle Caesar being the boss in California.

Why was she spending Christmas Eve here anyway? Grandpa Kensai was Shinto, and Grandpa Jamal was Muslim, and it really made no sense. Except something was going on that the adults wouldn't tell her about. Something big.

She wasn't stupid. It was something bad enough that Uncle Duncan had her spend Christmas Eve with Grandpa Kensai's house rather than taking her to midnight services. Uncle Duncan never missed Christmas Eve church services.

It wasn't the first time he fibbed to her. As much as Uncle Duncan tried to hide the truth, Miko had told Tiffany what really happened the night all their parents had died.

Tiffany hesitated a moment. No, she was being silly. Rogue vampires would have killed everyone already, not fooled around on the roof. So why weren't the enforcers checking on her? The humans like her may not hear her, but the vampires should have.

She crossed to the window, unlocked it, and raised the sash. Cold air swept into her bedroom, and she shivered as she removed the screen and set it aside. A little part of her wished she was a normal kid with normal parents. If she was, she would think it was a reindeer on the roof.

No. What stupid kid believed in Santa anyway? She'd found the stash of presents in the secret compartment in Uncle Duncan's study ages ago.

Tiffany climbed through the open window and grabbed hold of the trellis. In a year or two, she'd be too big to scale the wooden latticework Grandpa Jamal was training his roses to climb. White puffs of steam floated from her mouth as she clambered up and onto the shingles.

Nothing was on this side of the roof. The sound was more pronounced, but it came from her right. Her fingers and toes dug into the gritty asphalt squares, and she crawled to the apex. Peering over the cap shingles, she spotted what was making the noise.

What appeared to be a baby caribou paced back and forth. Its tiny hooves scratched against the gritty asphalt. When it spotted Tiffany, it bleated plaintively and hesitantly approached instead of trotting away from her.

How on earth did the calf get up on the roof? Not to mention, what was a caribou of any age doing in the middle of Los Angeles?

"Tiffany!"

At Mai's shout, Tiffany jerked and lost her grip on the cap shingles. She flailed, trying to find a handhold. Any handhold.

The caribou calf charged over the ridge. Its teeth clamped onto the strap of the crossbow and tried to slow Tiffany's fall. But the pitch of the roof on this section of the house was too steep for the animal to brace itself.

The calf glanced at her as if it was trying to tell Tiffany something before it raced headlong for the eaves. Two stories below, Miko screamed as the caribou launched itself and Tiffany into the air.

CHAPTER 2

Tiffany waited for the abrupt stop and the pain that would follow. Gravity was a constant. Two heartbeats passed. Three. She still hung awkwardly from the crossbow strap, the butt uncomfortably wedged in her armpit.

However, she drifted towards the grass below as if she were a snowflake. Or she did until the caribou dropped her a couple of feet above the ground.

She tumbled across the yard. Crossbow bolts scattered in her wake. When she came to a halt, the first thing she did was pull her crossbow to her chest in order to check it for damage.

Except a furry snout wuffled in her face. The calf's breath wasn't unpleasant. Sort of like rolled oats before they were cooked. It sniffed down her body as if it were checking her for injuries. She wiggled her toes, but everything seemed to be okay.

Mai and Miko rushed over to her.

"What the hell, Tiffany?" Mai shouted.

Miko crouched on Tiffany's left side. "You okay?"

"Yeah." Tiffany pushed herself into a sitting position. "I've jumped off higher picnic tables." She examined her crossbow. One of the sights was bent, but otherwise, it was still intact despite her landing on it.

However, Mai still stood several feet away and stared at the baby caribou. "Have you been fooling around with magick?"

"No," Tiffany retorted. "How could I? I'm not a witch or a fae."

Mai jabbed a finger in the direction of the calf. "I just watched that thing fly down from the roof! Were you trying to sneak it into the house?"

"No!" Tiffany replied hotly. "I crawled up there to find out what was making all the racket on the roof. Why didn't any of the enforcers check on it?"

"All the enforcers are asleep," Miko whispered. "Including the two out in the guardhouse." Grandpa Kensai and Grandpa Jamal's house was an older estate, which meant there were plenty of outbuildings including a little stone shed at the front gate.

"What do you mean they're asleep?" Tiffany frowned. "None of the vampires would dare—"

"They're all out cold," Mai said. "Like they've been drugged."

Tiffany didn't like the accusation in her cousin's voice. "I didn't do anything to them." The caribou wuffled against her hair. She automatically reached up and scratched her chin. At least, she thought the calf was a her. "Do you think it has something to do with all the grown-ups taking off on their secret mission tonight?"

Mai's scowl deepened, but there was an edge of fear in her voice. "We're going to the panic room. Just in case."

Miko and Tiffany scrambled to their feet. There really wasn't much use arguing when Mai used that tone. And Uncle Duncan and Grandpa Kensai were insistent that Mai was in charge tonight. But then, she remembered her parents a lot more than Miko did.

Mai had watched their mom and dad die.

The outdoor security lights around the house helped Tiffany and Miko find all the crossbow bolts. They hurried after Mai toward the closest entrance, and the baby caribou trotted after them.

Mai paused at the side door. "You can't bring that thing into the house."

Tiffany jutted her chin, even though it was too cold to argue in only her nightgown. "It saved my life. If something bad is about to happen, I'm not leaving it out here to be killed."

Mai rolled her eyes. "How do you know it's not a werecaribou?"

The calf bleated, but it sounded like a disbelieving "What?"

"The werewolves would have eaten it," Tiffany shot back.

Miko snickered. "Need some aloe for that burn, sis?"

Mai groaned. "Fine. Get it down to the panic room. But so help me, Tiffany, if it makes a mess, you are cleaning it up."

"Fine," Tiffany growled back. She marched into the house and started for Grandpa Kensai's study. The baby caribou trotted after her. Her hooves made a sharp clicking on Grandpa Jamal's special floor tiles he had imported from Spain.

"What about the enforcers?" Miko protested. "We can't leave them out here defenseless!"

Tiffany paused as did the calf. They both turned toward the Osaka cousins.

"I can't drag them all into the panic room by myself." Mai had never been afraid of anything, but Tiffany could practically smell the terror rolling off her. Even the calf wrinkled her nose.

"What if Bella and I help?" Tiffany said.

Both Mai and Miko turned, stared at her, and said, "Who's Bella?"

"Our caribou." Tiffany lifted her chin. She hadn't thought of the name until just now, but it seemed like a perfectly reasonable name for the calf. After all, caribou were reindeer, and reindeer wore bells on their harnesses.

The calf nuzzled Tiffany's upper arm as if she approved of the name.

Mai groaned. "Fine, but—"

"What's that?" Miko screeched.

Tiffany looked in the direction she pointed. Some sort of powder or smoke wafted toward them. Except it was glittery under the security lights.

"Inside!" Mai bellowed. "The panic room!"

Tiffany scrambled back into the house. The calf matched her strides, and her cousins' bare feet slapped against the tiles behind her. She glanced over her shoulder. The glittery cloud followed them through the house.

Magick. It explained why all the adults were asleep. This was not good. If the witches or the fae were attacking the house, things were very bad indeed.

They raced to Grandpa Kensai's study, and together, they pulled open the heavy bookcase that was the secret door to the panic room. Tiffany darted inside, stuck a bolt in her crossbow, and wound the cables. Miko grabbed a handgun from the weapons rack and slid in the appropriate magazine.

"Lock the dooooooorrrrr . . ." Mai's voice sounded funny. She was surrounded by the glittery cloud.

Heart in her throat, Tiffany watched as her oldest cousin hit the carpeted safe panic room floor with a dull thud. Behind Mai's crumpled form, a tall shadowy figure approached.

"Stay back!" Tiffany warned.

The figure muttered something, as if ordering its glittery cloud to do to her and Miko whatever it had done to Mai. Tiffany raised her crossbow to her shoulder and pulled the trigger.

Chapter 3

The bolt slammed into the shoulder of the figure. A masculine bellow of pain erupted from him, and he stumbled forward. The light of the panic room revealed a large man with a white beard.

Or it would have been white if it weren't smeared with soot just like his blood-red leather jacket and pants. He fell to his knees and sagged against the bookcase that doubled as a door.

"What did you do that for?" he grumbled.

"You cast a spell on my cousin," Tiffany yelled. The faintest hint of sweets filled her nose. Except, instead of honey like the fae, he smelled of peppermint and gingerbread.

The cloud floated to the carpet like someone had released a glitter bomb.

He sighed. "The spell only affects human adults."

"But my sister's not an adult," Miko protested.

"If she's had her period, the fae consider her an adult."

Miko grimaced, and Tiffany wanted to comfort her, but she didn't dare lower her crossbow. Besides, Miko already told her about periods, and they sounded gross. Maybe there was a way to avoid them.

"So why were you putting all the adults in the house to sleep?" Tiffany demanded.

The man winced as he checked the bolt embedded in his shoulder. "I was looking for Frigg."

The word was the same one Uncle Alex switched to when he was about to say a bad word. "What?" she asked.

The man gestured at Bella. "The calf."

Bella stepped behind Tiffany and made a raspberry.

"Don't take that tone with me, young lady," the man snapped. "You shouldn't have run off tonight of all nights."

"Don't you yell at her!" Hot tears welled in Tiffany's eyes. Right now, she wished Uncle Duncan or Aunt Phillippa or Grandpa Kensai were here. They'd know what to do.

"Tiffany, I need to take Frigg home before dawn," the man said gently. "She can't survive in Los Angeles. It's too warm for her here. And to do that, I need to get this bolt out of my shoulder. It's steel-tipped, isn't it?"

She nodded.

"Steel only affects fae." Miko kept her gun aimed at his head.

"I'm human, but I've picked up some tricks from the fae." His smile was barely visible through the massive beard. "Steel won't kill me, but I can't get Frigg home with the bolt in my shoulder."

The baby caribou made another raspberry.

Unfortunately, the man was right. Tiffany couldn't let Bella stay here and get sick. She glanced at Miko. "You get the med kit. I'll keep an eye on him."

"I don't think leaving you alone with him is a good idea," Miko muttered.

"Miko, I swear by Morrigan and Jehovah I will not harm Tiffany," the man said. It wasn't the disparate deities that bothered Tiffany.

"How do you know our names?" she snapped.

Once again, the man smiled. "I know every child's name, my dear."

"Then what's yours?" Tiffany demanded.

"Nicholas," he said.

Miko lowered her gun. "All right, I'll get the med kit, but if he so much as twitches, plug him again." She whirled and marched toward the supply closet at the back of the panic room.

Tiffany's arm trembled. If Grandpa Kensai hadn't made a small version of a crossbow for her, she would never be able to hold it up for this long. She wasn't sure how long she could keep it aimed at the man, but she didn't have a choice. Mai was lying too close to him.

Miko came back with what looked like a small, white fishing tackle box if it weren't for the giant red cross on the top. She knelt beside the man, opened the med kit, and grabbed a handful of white and blue sealed packages. She tore one open, and a medicinal smell filled the small room. With the white antiseptic pad, Miko wiped blood away from the wound so she could see it better.

"Well, it doesn't look like she hit an artery," Miko muttered. "We need to get that jacket off you so I can properly take care of this wound."

"Too thick to cut without special tools." The man sounded like he really hurt, and a tiny bit of guilt whispered in the back of Tiffany's mind.

"Lay down," Miko ordered.

With a series of grunts and groans, Nicholas maneuvered until he was flat on the carpet. Miko tried to pull out the bolt, but his blood slicked her hands. It didn't help that he was jerking around from the pain.

"Tiffany, I need your help," Miko said. "I'll hold him down and you pull out the bolt."

"Me?" Tiffany squeaked. Her stomach rumbled its own objection.

"You're too little to hold Nicholas still."

"But Uncle Duncan said to never touch anyone's blood!"

Miko gave an exasperated sigh. "Then put on some rubber gloves."

Tiffany nibbled her lower lip. What had started as an adventure had become ugly reality. "But what if I can't pull it out?"

"It's a target bolt," Miko said. "It'll slide out if I can keep him still." She cocked her head and stared thoughtfully at the caribou. "Bella, can you lay across his chest while I lay on his arm so Tiffany can pull out the bolt?"

The calf trotted over and performed a belly flop across Nicholas's ribs. The sudden weight produced a strangled half-groan, half-squeal from the man.

Reluctantly, Tiffany laid her crossbow on the floor, well out of Nicholas's reach, marched over to the med kit, and snatched a package of gloves. The plastic package was hard to open, and she resorted to tearing it with her teeth. Once she donned the purple gloves, she said, "Ready."

"On my count." Miko laid over Nicholas's arm. "Three . . ."

Tiffany wrapped her fingers around the shaft.

"Two . . ."

She planted her left foot against his collar bone for extra leverage.

"One."

She yanked as hard as she could. Nicholas yelled. The bolt came free with a sick, wet sound.

And Tiffany toppled over on her butt.

A sharp bark came from the bookcase doorway. A wolf with a pelt of rust and gray stood there with its teeth bared. It stalked slowly into the panic room, but the wolf shifted its form until it stood on two legs, though it still had a wolf's head, tail, and fur.

"Touch one of the children, fae," a lady's voice growled. "And I swear to Mother Wolf, it'll be the last thing you do."

Chapter 4

"I think the children are rather touching me," Nicholas said through gritted teeth.

However, the were's voice was familiar. "Mrs. Lannigan?" Tiffany climbed to her feet. The lady werewolf had always been nice to her and her cousins, but this was a totally different side to Uncle Duncan's friend.

"Are you all right, Tiffany?" Mrs. Lannigan didn't take her eyes off of the injured man.

"We're fine." Tiffany stepped between him and the werewolf, even if blood dripped from the bolt all over Grandpa Kensai's light tan carpet. "Nicholas didn't hurt us. I shot him when he made Mai go to sleep because I thought he was a fae. He needs a healer."

"Nicholas?" Mrs. Lannigan cocked her wolfie head. "Nicholas of Myra?"

"Aye," he said wearily.

"What on earth are you doing in a vampire's home?" Mrs. Lannigan exclaimed.

"Trying to find this little one." Nicholas petted Bella, and she licked his nose.

"Can you sit up a little so we can get your jacket off?" Miko said.

Bella clambered off Nicholas. With Miko's help, he managed to shed his jacket and prop himself against the wall. Red stained the left shoulder of his white thermal undershirt. Miko pulled out a pressure bandage from the med kit and held it over his wound. Sweat rolled down his forehead and dripped into his beard. What little Tiffany could see of his face was pale.

Guilt rolled over her at what she'd done. She turned back to the werewolf. "We need to find him a healer, Mrs. Lannigan."

She nodded and shifted the rest of the way to her human form. "I'll call a friend. Could you please fetch me a robe? I'm sure Kensai and Jamal keep some on hand for guests."

Tiffany dashed off for the laundry room. All the vampires she knew kept extra clothes for their guests. Of course, all the vampires she knew were enforcers for Uncle Caesar, and being an enforcer could be a very, very messy job.

———•———

An hour later, a witch named Benjamin had healed Nicholas's shoulder. The witch looked as old as Nicholas, except he had very little hair on his head, and everyone could see his laugh lines and crow's feet. Tiffany knew looks could be deceiving with the supernatural community. Witches and weres aged much more slowly than regular humans, and the vampires and fae even more so.

While Mr. Benjamin had taken care of Nicholas, Mrs. Lannigan carried Mai back to her bed and arranged the enforcers on Grandpa Kensai's couches so none of them would have kinks in their necks when they woke up.

"How did you know there was a problem here?" Tiffany asked Mrs. Lannigan.

"All of our enforcers in Los Angeles, whether they be witch, were, or vampire, have regular check-ins with each other." She glanced at Tiffany. "Day and night. When no one heard from the enforcers here, I came to scout the situation as beta of the pack."

"Thank you for that," Tiffany murmured.

"You girls should have called your emergency contact as soon as you knew there was a problem," Mrs. Lannigan chided.

"I thought I could handle it." Tiffany's shoulders sagged as she realized how angry Uncle Duncan would be. "I was wrong."

"That's a good start on learning an important lesson." Mrs. Lannigan laid the enforcer she carried on the couch in the family room.

"They will wake up, won't they?" Tiffany stared up at the lady werewolf as she arranged the last enforcer in a comfortable position.

"Not before dawn." Mrs. Lannigan smiled and straightened the fluffy white robe Tiffany had found for her. "Normally, adult humans aren't allowed to see Nicholas."

Tiffany frowned. "Why not? He was scarier to me than you are, even when you're hairy and fangy."

Mrs. Lannigan chuckled. "I suppose his story has been watered down enough you would find the actual thing scary."

"His story?"

"Nicholas is nearly as old as your Master Augustine." Mrs. Lannigan walked back toward Grandpa Kensai's den and the panic room.

The connection gnawed on Tiffany's mind while she followed the lady werewolf until it chewed through the rest of her thoughts. Flying reindeer. Nicholas of Myrna. A man in a red suit.

"He's Santa Claus?" she blurted.

"No, he's the man the story of Santa Claus was built on," Mrs. Lannigan corrected.

Benjamin shook his head as they entered the panic room. "You aren't getting the girl all excited over nothing, are you, Laura?"

This time, she laughed loudly. "Tiffany's a smart one for a Normal. She figured it out on her own"

Miko looked at each of the adults before her gaze met Tiffany's. "You can't be serious?"

"You saw how Bella saved me." Tiffany walked over to Bella and wrapped her arms around the calf's neck. "Nicholas is right. I'd love for you to stay with me, but you need to go home where you'll be safe."

The caribou—no, the baby reindeer bleated and nuzzled the side of Tiffany's head. The calf's words made sense in a weird sort of way.

Tiffany turned to Nicholas. "She really doesn't like the name Frigg. She would prefer it if you call her Bella."

"Oh, all right." Nicholas heaved to his feet with Mr. Benjamin's help. From what Tiffany heard from the adults, a healing was very tiring for both the witch and the patient. "We need to get going. It's very, very late."

Together, they all walked out to the backyard. Nicholas put two fingers to his lips and whistled.

Bells sounded above them, the big brass kind that animals wore. Tiffany stared at the sky. Eight reindeer flew over the house, their legs galloping as if they were running on land. The reindeer were harnessed to a wood and brass sled with shiny runners. The wood was painted red and green. The animals and sled swooped past them before they made a lazy two hundred-seventy degree turn, descending the closer they came, until they landed on the back lawn.

More than anything, Tiffany wished she could take a ride in that sled.

"Oh, man," Miko whispered. "Jamal is going to have a fit when he sees what those runners did to his grass."

The lead reindeer stared at Bella and let out a horrendous bellow that caused both Tiffany and the calf to jump. Tiffany hugged the calf again.

"When you're busted, it's better to suck it up and get the punishment out of the way," she whispered to Bella.

The calf snorted, a sound that meant "Tell me about it." She trotted over to the reindeer who seemed to be her mom and hung her head as she was lectured.

Tiffany looked up at Nicholas, ur, Santa Claus. "I'm really sorry I shot you, sir."

He rested a mittened hand on her shoulder. "All's forgiven, Tiffany." He nodded to the rest. "Ladies. Thank you, sir healer." He strode over to the sled and climbed aboard.

The lead reindeer nudged Bella, and she half-jumped, half-flew into the back of the sled. Santa said something in fae, and the reindeer raced for the other end of the yard. Just when Tiffany was sure they would crash into the stone wall, the team swung around, the sled careening behind them. They ran even faster, and as one, they jumped into the air.

Deep laughter echoed through the sky, followed by a cheery "To all, a good night!"

— ·•· —

Surprisingly, Tiffany found herself waking up at dawn next to Miko. Maybe Santa had another spell, like the glitter spell he used on the enforcers and Mai that made children go to sleep. She nudged her cousin.

"Miko," she whispered. "Wake up."

Her cousin shot into a sitting position. "What am I doing in your room?"

"Really?" Tiffany stared at Miko. "You don't remember?"

"Wow," Miko murmured. "I was hoping it was just a crazy dream."

"Do we tell Grandpa Kensai and Uncle Duncan?"

Miko rolled her eyes. "You know Mrs. Lannigan already reported it to her husband, and he would have told Caesar, who in turn, would tell Grandpa Kensai and Duncan." Miko grinned. "You'd better hope we don't have coal in our stocking after what you did last night."

"Screw you," Tiffany growled. She wasn't exactly sure what it meant, but the epithet made Miko laugh.

Both girls flung back the covers, leapt from the bed and raced down to the Christmas tree. Both girls skidded on hardwood as they tried to brake at the entrance to the family room. Uncle Duncan, Aunt Phillippa, Uncle Alex,

Aunt Anne, and Uncle Caesar all sat around the tree with Grandpa Kensai and Grandpa Jamal.

Phillippa burst out laughing. "Look at those guilty faces. We don't even have to ask for their side of the story."

"It wasn't our fault!" Tiffany trembled. She wanted to hit something so bad, but she remembered what the therapist said.

Oh, dear. What would the therapist say if Tiffany told her she shot Santa Claus?

"No one said it was." Uncle Duncan reached out and pulled her into his arms. "We are simply happy you girls are all right."

His cheek was cool against her forehead, but then, it always was. She relaxed and hugged him back. "So, you aren't angry with me?"

"No." He smiled, a careful smile so he wouldn't show his extra sharp canines. "Why don't you two open your presents? Mai may not be up for a while."

Tiffany launched herself from his lap. She didn't need to be told twice.

She sat next to the pile with the card marked with her name, but it was the stuffed animal the card was propped against that drew her attention. A little reindeer complete with a red harness and shiny brass bells.

Tiffany read the tag attached to the harness.

Thank you for taking care of me. We'll meet again someday.
Bella

ZOMBIE CONFIDENTIAL

Author's Note: This story takes place four weeks after the events of *Zombie Love.*

CHAPTER 1

The sickly-sweet smell gave away the house's secret. Something really bad had happened. The partially open front door would have been the hint to a Normal stumbling on the scene. But no, it had to be me. And it had to be the smell of death.

Shit. I swear this crap never happened to me while I was alive.

Shoving my camera case behind my back, I toed the door open a little further. I so didn't need any more broken equipment from some supernatural jumping out at me.

The Malibu beach house was quiet, except for the drone of voices at the back. A subsonic electrical buzz said the sound came from a device, not people.

For once, nothing creepy leapt out of the shadows at me. Maybe my luck was changing. If a dead woman can have luck, that is.

No lights were on, but it's not like I needed them. I followed my nose to the kitchen. A man sat at the table, not moving, not even breathing. I flipped the wall switch anyway. Sometimes I needed confirmation from something more *real* than my zombie sense of smell.

Under bright fluorescents, Josh Williams, Hollywood's latest "It" boy, sat in a designer chair and slumped over the matching designer table. Or his body did anyway. The tourniquet wrapped around his bicep and the needle sticking out of his outstretched arm told the story.

Damn. Williams definitely wouldn't be accepting the Best Actor award if he won it this weekend. All that work to rebuild his career for nothing.

I crossed to the body, but two fingers confirmed what my olfactory nerves already told me. Closing the half-opened eyes didn't work because rigor had already set in. I shuddered at the blank eyes staring at me. Double damn.

I didn't take any pictures. I couldn't. Before my own death, I wouldn't have thought twice about it. But now?

I pulled out my cell to call for an ambulance and had pressed the first two numbers when I caught the sense of *presence.* Someone else was in the house after all. I followed my undead spidey sense down a hallway. Well, my ESP and the sonorous tones of a program narrator. Inside the game room, a plasma TV blared some History Channel Word War II documentary. A couple of bare feet stuck over the end of the couch.

Translucent feet.

I thought about walking out the front door. But what can I say? My sense of curiosity was morbid before all the shit that happened to me at the end of January.

Circling around the black leather confirmed my suspicion. Josh's ghost sprawled on the cushions and watched the screen.

It wasn't like this was my first experience with a ghost. But the séance to talk to my dead best friend didn't compare to *seeing* a ghost for the first time. Goosebumps rose on my arms.

One of the nice things about my nanites was they made me appear alive, with a heartbeat and a physical reaction to the woo-woo stuff. Right now, I could have done without the woo-woo.

Eyes a few shades less than their normal, alive blue glanced up at me. Anger quickly chased the surprise off the ghost's face. "What the hell? You're in a private residence, Ridgeway." He rose and charged for the bar.

"Wait, Josh, you don't—" I held up my hand.

"This may not be my house, but I can still have you arrested for breaking and entering. The damn tabloids have gone too far." Icy cold swept through me when he passed through my outstretched arm. Josh didn't realize what had happened and kept yelling about what his lawyers would do to me.

Until he reached for the phone perched on the bar and his hand went through the device.

"—understand," I finished lamely. His expression of horror made even my Grinch-like heart thaw a little. "I'm so sorry, Josh." I pressed the final number on my cell. When the 9-1-1 operator came on, my voice faltered at the look on the ghost's face. I watched realization sink into him as he kept trying to pick up the handset. And couldn't.

I cleared my throat. "My name is Samantha Ridgeway. I want to report a death."

A headache grew between my eyes with Detective Jorge Sifuentes and Josh Williams both talking at once. Well, yelling was a better description.

I raised a hand. "Please, guys. I can't understand either of you when both of you are blabbing. One at a time."

Sifuentes's dark eyes glittered in the flashing lights from the black and whites responding to my call. "Tell Williams I need to go first. The sheriff wants an update in a half-hour."

I wasn't sure I liked being tagged in the Los Angeles Sheriff's Office computers, which meant a Family-connected officer was sent to the scene. But as Family, Sifuentes took the whole ghost thing in stride even if he couldn't see Josh. When the ghost clamped his ectoplasmic mouth shut, I nodded to the detective to continue.

Sifuentes clicked his pen. "Did you touch anything, Sam?"

I shook my head. "Just the kitchen light switch and the body's neck to check for a pulse."

"Hey, I'm not a body!"

I held up an index finger to halt Josh's tirade. His mouth opened and closed like a landed fish gasping for its last breath. The techs loading Josh's corpse into the hearse distracted the dead actor.

Sifuentes stifled a threatening grin as he watched my reaction to the ghost. "What were you doing at Elise Manfield's house?"

The look I gave the detective should have melted the badge off his suit jacket.

He shrugged. "You know I have to ask, and I need an answer."

I stared at my Nikes. "My assignment was to catch some photos of Josh Williams and Elise Manfield in compromising positions."

The ghost let off a stream of invectives that made even my potty mouth sound like Annette Funicello.

Sifuentes chuckled. Could he hear ghosts? Some Normals could. Or maybe being married to a werewolf forced the detective to develop an odd sense of humor because I really didn't think his laughter had anything to do with my assignment. I bit my tongue to keep from asking if his kids chewed on his shoes.

He continued to jot notes, then asked, "Did you?"

I shook my head. "Elise was gone and Josh already dead when I arrived."

Sifuentes held out his hand and waggled his fingers. Repressing a sigh, I handed over my digital camera. He flicked through the photos in the viewer, raised eyebrows at a couple of shots from another story, but otherwise said nothing before setting my camera inside his unmarked car.

"Dammit, Jorge."

He shrugged again. "Sorry, but I gotta take it in and make sure you didn't erase anything from the memory card."

I clenched my fists to keep from reaching for my equipment. Sifuentes was just doing his job. I knew he was, but it didn't make confiscation of my camera easier to take. "I swear if you damage it—"

"You'll what?" He shot a mocking grin in my direction. "Have your boyfriend suck my blood?"

"It's not like you have any brains for me to eat."

All humor vanished from Sifuentes's face. "Are you threatening an officer of the law?"

"No. I—" I threw up my hands in frustration. Pissing off the man wasn't going to get my camera back. "Look, I did the right thing and called 9-1-1, and now you're punishing me for it."

A sympathetic look appeared in his eyes. "So why didn't you call St. James?"

I folded my arms over my chest. Duncan St. James was the vampires' equivalent of a police chief and the guy I happened to be dating.

Go ahead. Get all the zombie-dating-a-vampire jokes out of your system.

Actually, calling him had been the last thing on my mind. Not that Duncan wouldn't help, but I didn't need another one of his lectures about my penchant for attracting trouble.

I glared at Sifuentes. "Give me a little credit. A Normal death is not his jurisdiction." I tried to ignore Josh. His attention flicked between the detective and me, total confusion on his pretty face.

A third shrug lifted Sifuentes' shoulders. "Don't sweat it. Give us a week. Once the medical examiner performs the tox screen, it'll be written off as another celebrity OD, and I can get your camera back to you."

"I did not OD!" Josh's fury fluttered the pages of the detective's notepad.

Sifuentes shot me a quizzical look since the Los Angeles night was perfectly still otherwise. "I take it Mr. Williams has a statement."

I turned to Josh. "Do you want me to tell him what you told me?"

The ghost nodded emphatically.

I faced Sifuentes again, who surprised me by turning to a new page on his notepad. "Josh says he's been clean since he got out of rehab two years ago."

The detective tapped his pen against the pad. "Then how does he explain the speedball?"

"I've never done junk!" All around us dogs started to howl at the ghost's shout. Even my psychic eardrums hurt at the high-pitched screech.

I raised my hands. "Calm down, Josh." One of the Normal uniformed deputies spotted me talking to empty air. A frown creased his face. I suppressed a wince. This night was getting better and better.

I repeated Josh's statement to Sifuentes. "And he says he was asleep on the couch in the game room. He never heard Elise leave, and he doesn't know how the bod—" I amended my words at Josh's dirty look. "How he ended up in the kitchen." I waited for the detective to finish writing before I added, "Jorge, what if Williams is telling the truth that he didn't shoot up? What if someone slipped him something to knock him out before they injected the heroin?"

The detective's face showed nothing. "If someone did, then the M.E.'s office will let us know. Who'd want him dead?"

Josh looked like a lost little boy. "I don't know." I repeated his statement.

Sifuentes jotted the info on his pad and snapped it shut. "I'll check out your stories and Elise Manfield's." He gave me a wolfish grin. "And if Williams's brains are missing, I know who to arrest."

I kept my mouth shut at his lame insult. It wasn't like I didn't hear the same crap from my future sister-in-law on a daily basis.

Humor didn't reach the detective's eyes though. He shook his head. The flashing lights made the circles under his eyes even darker. Sifuentes had the courtesy of addressing the correct spot even if he couldn't see the ghost. "I'm sorry, Josh. Without something more, there's nothing I can do."

While I was semi-pleased Sifuentes took my story at face value, something that could only be raw rage filled the ghost's features. A pebble rose from the limestone that edged the driveway and shot straight for Sifuentes' head. It connected with the detective's skull with a soft *thunk*.

"Shit!" Sifuentes raised his hand to the tiny cut.

"Stop it, Josh," I hissed as I dug into my bag for a tissue. "You're not helping."

The detective glared in the ghost's general direction. "If I were you, Ridgeway, I'd talk to a witch about exorcising Williams's ass before he does something stupid."

A cherry red convertible pulled into the driveway. We watched Elise Manfield climb out and race for the front door, only to be grabbed by a uniformed policeman. Her anguished scream set the neighborhood dogs into another frenzy. For once, I didn't make matters worse by saying Josh had already done something monumentally stupid.

CHAPTER 2

I stayed silent as Dr. Bebe Zachary circled Josh in the darkened conservatory in her significant other's mansion. If my boyfriend was the vampires' police chief, hers was the king.

What can I say? We both had a thing for hunky bloodsuckers.

Because we both shifted our normal waking hours for our boyfriends, Bebe was still up when I banged on the front door at three a.m.

Gold tendrils of energy extended from her, waving and dancing around my new pet ghost. Part of me was glad she could see spirits of the dead, too. It made my weird situation a little more bearable.

Josh gave me a skeptical eye. "Who is this chick again?"

"She's my witch doctor." I ignored the irritated look Bebe shot in my direction. "Shut up and let her work."

The tendrils retracted to the golden aura that surrounded the only witch I personally knew. She strode across the room and flicked the lights back on. The illumination reduced Josh to a hazy blur.

Bebe shoved a hand through the mass of dark curls that threatened to blind her. "He's not under any spell or compulsion."

"Hey, I'm standing right here," the blur protested in Josh's voice.

A beatific smile lit Bebe's face. "You're right, Josh. I'm sorry." The smile faded. "I think you have to face the possibility that you—"

"I did not fucking OD! I didn't take any drugs!"

This time Bebe winced along with me at the pain ringing through our heads at Josh's anger.

I crossed my arms and stared at the haze. "Then the only other possibility is someone murdered you."

Josh was silent for a long time. "That doesn't make sense. Who? And why?"

My stomach chose that moment to growl.

Bebe cocked an eyebrow. "Your appetite still hasn't tapered off?"

"No." My response was a little sharper than I intended. It had been too long since my last meal. A whole whopping four hours and fifteen minutes. I was testy without adequate food before I died. Now . . .

"No cravings for blood? Raw meat?"

I shook my head at each of her questions.

"Brains?"

"Don't push it, Bebe."

She gave me an innocent smile before heading for the door. "Then don't call me a witch doctor."

"But you are."

The hazy presence trailed after me as I followed Bebe through the huge, airy Mediterranean-style mansion. For a vampire, her boyfriend Caesar had a thing for windows.

When we reached the kitchen, Josh tapped me on the shoulder. Or rather, he tried to. It felt more like a Gatorade bath in sub-zero weather. "Uh, Sam?"

"Yeah, Josh?"

If it was possible for a ghost to feel nervous, Josh Williams sure sounded anxious. "Why does everyone bring up the subject of eating brains around you?"

I exhaled. It had to come up some time. "Because I'm a zombie."

"Excuse me?"

"I died a little over a month ago and got turned into a zombie." I opened the fridge. Luckily, the daytime guards took pity on me. They'd been over-ordering take-out and leaving it for me to eat during my morning check-ups with Bebe for the last couple of weeks. I reached for the extra-large pizza box and cracked open the lid. Everything, extra cheese, no anchovies, only two pieces missing. *Thank you, Tiffany.*

"But you're, um, rather, um . . ."

"Fresh?" I grabbed the two-liter bottle of Coke as well and nudged the door shut with my knee.

Bebe set her tea mug on the counter harder than necessary. "Sam . . ."

I eyed her as I chugged the first half of the Coke. Taking a seat on a stool, I grabbed the first slice. "Who's he going to tell?"

She glared at me. "Do you have any idea how big the ghost population of Los Angeles is? Or how many non-Silver Bear witches pass through the city on a given day?"

"You think Josh will blab to someone who doesn't already know?" I mumbled around a mouthful of pizza. I swallowed a Coke chaser. "Half the supernatural world attended the fiasco at Mallory Labs. Anyone not there got the e-mail by now." The same fiasco where Caesar's twin sister announced the use of nanites as a cure for everything, including vampirism.

She lied. Big time. I was proof.

A wave of cold sent my teeth chattering.

"Look, Sam, help me find who killed me and I'll keep my mouth shut," Josh said.

"You weren't murdered," I muttered. Why the hell had I even brought up that theory to Sifuentes? Josh clung to that story. An addict's self-delusion, right? "*You* couldn't even think of someone with a motive to do it."

The haze moved closer. Frost formed around the plastic soda bottle and on the edges of my leftover pizza. "Oxycontin and alcohol were my vices, not heroin. And if you don't help me find whoever set me up, I'll haunt your ass until it falls off your body. *Capice?*"

Bebe watched me over her mug, a smug grin on her face. "People have been driven insane by hauntings before."

"Yeah, but everyone thought I was nuts before I died." I chewed as I considered Josh's words. He made sense as much as I hated to admit it. Why do a speedball when he could have gotten any prescription pharmaceutical he desired in this city? Unless he couldn't handle the strain of all the recent publicity with his award nomination and decided he needed a bigger thrill.

I swallowed my half-frozen pizza and looked at the haze. "Here's the deal, Josh. I'll check things out."

"Thank—"

"But no matter what I find, even if I find out you *did* accidentally kill yourself, you will walk quietly into the light, or tunnel, or whatever it is. *Capice?*"

"Deal."

"And don't even *think* about possessing me."

"What?"

Bebe laughed. "Somehow, I doubt if you could possess Sam if you tried." She sobered immediately. "And, Josh, you even try to possess someone without their permission, that's grounds for an automatic exorcism and containment."

I could feel Josh's attention turn from the witch to me in confusion. "Containment?"

"No trial. Eternity in prison. No possibility for parole," I said.

"Ouch. Okay, no possession, no annoying hauntings, and in return, you'll investigate my murder." An amorphous blob extended from the haze.

"Death," I corrected. I looked down at the pseudo-hand. "Josh, you're a ghost. I'm a zombie. We can't shake hands."

"Then how do I know if you'll keep your word?"

I turned to Bebe.

She shook her head. "Don't look at me. A Blood Seal doesn't work on a ghost, and you'd heal before I completed the ritual."

I turned back to the haze hovering beside me. "If you trust me enough to ask, Josh, then you're going to have to trust me to keep my word. And I'll have to do the same with you."

"Okay," he muttered.

I took another bite of pizza. This situation was not okay, but if someone had murdered Josh, then he or she was not getting away with it.

CHAPTER 3

The sun was peeking over the horizon when I pulled into the parking lot of *The National Scoop*. Josh crossed his translucent arms. "Seriously? You're starting here?"

I glared at my passenger. "Got a better idea, ghost boy?"

"Stop calling me 'ghost boy'. Besides, even your friend Bebe said the reason I might be still here is because I was murdered."

"Then if you can't give me a list of suspects, I need someone who can. You heard Sifuentes. We need hard evidence." I opened the door on my Honda and slid out before Josh could launch another fit. He simply melted through the passenger door and followed me.

For the first time in a month, my luck wasn't total shit. Agnes Durley was returning from taking Emerson for his morning constitutional and met us at the building's front door.

I handed her the caramel macchiato bribe. "Agnes, I need a favor."

She shot me a half-amused look as I held the door open for them. "You always need a favor. What is it this time—"

Emerson planted all four feet and yanked her to a halt. The leash was merely for show since it's extremely difficult to explain to most LAPD officers that the huge English bulldog was really a weredog trapped in his canine form. Emerson stared at Josh and emitted a low growl.

"It's okay, Emerson. I know him." I jerked a thumb at the ghost for emphasis.

Emerson cocked his head. The look on his slobbery mug could only be translated into *Are you nuts?*

Agnes quickly sobered. "What's with you, Sam?"

I lowered my voice, mainly because the security guard at the reception desk was giving us all a funky look.

"Can we talk about this upstairs?" I whispered. "Please."

For a split-second, I thought she'd freak on me. I didn't know the whole story, but sometime in the past, Agnes had been abused by supernaturals. It said something about her internal strength that she could work at the *Scoop* since our editor Ralph was one of Emerson's littermates and a vampire conglomerate owned the magazine.

Concern was written all over her face, but she nodded. Together, the four of us headed for the elevator.

Once the doors closed, she took a sip of the hot coffee. "Whose ghost is with you?"

O-k-a-a-a-y. I knew she believed in some weird shit, like UFOs and government conspiracies. "You can see him?"

She shrugged. "Only if I don't look at him directly, and even then, he's a little fuzzy. Like a picture out of focus."

"It's Josh Williams. He died last night."

"Oh!" She looked directly at the corner where Josh stood. "I'm so sorry! I was rooting for you to win on Sunday. I adored *Cowboys in Love!*"

Ghosts couldn't blush, but Josh looked properly abashed. "Uh, thanks." I relayed his answer.

The elevator doors wheezed open. Despite the earliness of the hour, activity hummed in the bullpen.

"Hey, you!"

We all whirled to our left. Ralph O'Malley, editor-in-chief of *The National Scoop* barreled toward us. He raised his fist and shook it. "This is private property! No trespassing!"

I should have known. If Emerson could see Josh, it made sense that Ralph could as well.

I stepped between my editor and my unwanted ghost. "Ralph, I need to talk to you about my assignment." I inclined my head toward Josh.

Ralph stopped and blinked his watery eyes. "It's true?"

I gave him a tight smile. "Can we talk in your office?"

He shot another curious look at Josh, then nodded. Under his breath, he said, "You cause one single problem with my magazine, Williams, and I'll have a witch exorcise your ass before you can say 'Oscar.'"

A wave of frigid air flowed across my shoulder. "He can see me, too?"

"Yes," I hissed. "Now shut up until we're in his office."

As soon as we were inside, Agnes and I claimed the visitor's chairs. Emerson sat on his extra-large doggie bed. Josh hovered behind me and sent cold air across my neck. I undid my ponytail for a little insulation.

Ralph plunked down in his chair and lit a cigarette. "The word is someone died at Elise Manfield's, but the sheriff's office is tight-lipped. Claim they need to notify the family." He glared at me. "I thought you'd be here with pics long before now."

I shrugged. "I found the body, so LASO confiscated my camera."

"Who?" Ralph's voice was practically a growl.

"Sifuentes," I said. Ralph knew the detective was by-the-book, and he rolled his eyes. "And I didn't take any. Rigor had already set in. That's gross even by my standards."

Ralph made a "come on" gesture. "Talk to me."

I repeated everything: the suspected speedball, Josh's claims, and Bebe's examination. Bebe's boyfriend Caesar owned controlling interest in the *Scoop*, so I didn't have to worry about Ralph or Agnes blabbing to the wrong people.

"Murder, huh?" Ralph stubbed out the butt and leaned back in his chair, his eyes on the ghost behind me. "You sure, Williams?"

"I'm clean," Josh repeated for the umpteenth time in the last eight hours.

Agnes nodded emphatically. "The only way the *Cowboys* producers could get insurance was if Josh submitted to weekly drug testing. Same thing for *Joker's Wild*, the movie he just wrapped."

"Don't remind me," Josh mumbled.

I turned in my seat and grinned at him. "Look at it this way—you'll never have to pee in a cup again."

"Ha. Ha. Ha."

Wow, his sarcasm was thicker than mine.

Ralph leaned forward again. "The story's yours, Ridgeway. Agnes, give her any support she needs."

I stood and turned to Agnes. "Conference room?"

She nodded as she rose. "Let me grab my laptop."

I crossed my fingers she wouldn't also bring her tin foil hat.

—•—

An hour later, I stared at my notepad. Our shortlist of suspects gave me the willies. While the culprit may be one of the two women arrested for stalking Josh, the rest consisted of family. Agnes insisted I flag a couple of business associates, including his manager, Wendall Cummings, and Elise Manfield. I stuck them under my "Maybe" list. The motive for the alleged sane ones? Greed, pure and simple. Josh was pushing the Will Smith $20 million-a-picture barrier.

I looked at Agnes. "See what you can find by following the money trail. I'll check on the autopsy and our obsessed fans."

Josh made the ghostly equivalent of a cough. "Would you mind if I stay here with Agnes?"

I shrugged. "If it's okay with Agnes." I cocked an eyebrow. "Though I'd like to know why."

"If you're going to the county morgue, I really don't want to see my body."

That was something I could definitely understand.

— • —

By nine a.m., I strode down the hallway of a particular condo building. I could have gone to Duncan. As chief enforcer of the Augustine Coven, he had access to all sorts of information. He also made the uptight Sifuentes look like a '60's free spirit.

Luckily, there was one enforcer who'd help me without narcing on me to his boss.

I banged on the door.

Alex Stanton opened it, dressed only in jeans and a grin. A big toothy one that showed off his extra-pointy canines. "Well, if it's not my favorite yellow journalist. To what do I owe the pleasure this morning?"

If that Texas drawl of his wasn't enough to melt my panties, his body would. If I wasn't totally hung up on his boss, that was.

Alex blinked. "That does not help a man's ego to learn he comes in second place for a lady's affections."

Crap. I was accidentally transmitting again. So I resorted to my usual defense—snarky sarcasm. "Oh, please. Like I'd come in first on your list. Or are you saying you are no longer enamored with a certain demigoddess?"

His normal cheerfulness disappeared. "What do you want, Sam?"

Oops. Maybe I'd pushed the wrong *Alex* button. "A possible murder investigation, and I need help." I shoved past him and entered the living room. His home was an odd mix. Remington paintings on the wall. Medical textbooks were scattered across a coffee table made of petrified wood. The latest in AV equipment. The paused picture on the big screen held the biggest shock of all.

I pivoted and stared at him. "*Bridget Jones's Diary*? Seriously?"

He crossed his arms over that fabulous, if slightly too pale, chest. "And why didn't you go to Duncan?"

"Because, technically—" I spread my fingers. "—it's Normal jurisdiction."

Alex cocked a disbelieving eyebrow.

"Detective Sifuentes is writing this off as an OD, and I've got the ghost swearing up and down he didn't inject himself with heroin."

"Is the ghost here right now?"

I shook my head.

A frown tilted Alex's lips. "Sifuentes can be an asshole, but his instincts are usually on the money."

It killed me to admit Alex was right. "I know." I wiped both hands down my face. "But the ghost is haunting me, and Sifuentes can't do anything without a solid lead."

Alex's grin was back. "If he's haunting you, why isn't he here?"

I grinned as well. "Because I said I was going to sneak into the morgue. Who wants to look at their own corpse?"

Alex shook his head and laughed. "What do you need?"

"A run-down on the whereabouts of two women convicted of stalking, and entrance to the L.A. County morgue. Can you swing that?"

Alex placed a hand on his chest in mock dismay. "You doubt my abilities?"

"Never, cowboy."

—•—

Neither stalker had panned out. One had been committed to the state facility by her family after she tried to stab her brother over some M&M's. She was definitely locked up in the high-risk ward. The other woman was doing time in New York after breaking into Ashley Anderson's Manhattan apartment.

Ashley Anderson. Josh's ex-girlfriend. The mother of Josh's son. Another person on the shortlist Agnes and I put together.

Alex had dressed and insisted that he drive to the morgue. So an hour later, I was headed for downtown Los Angeles in a Texas vampire's pick-up with UV-lined windows.

"There's no enclosed parking at the morgue. How are you not going to be a crispy critter?"

He glanced at the sun. "The unloading bay's in deep enough shadow. I'll be fine."

I pulled my hair into a ponytail to distract myself from the image of deep-fried vampire. Duncan wouldn't blame me for Alex's stupidity, would he?

— • —

Alex strode into the morgue like he owned the place. At the reception window, he asked for a Dr. Xavier and flashed an ID.

A second later, the receptionist buzzed us through the locked door. She simpered and said, "I can call him for you, officer."

Alex gave her one of his charming grins. "Thank you anyway, ma'am, but I know the way."

All this meant Alex used a little vampire mojo to make the poor receptionist think he was a Normal policeman.

"You'll get the hang of it someday, Sam."

Crap. I was transmitting again. It annoyed me nearly as much as it irritated most of the supernaturals around me. Thankfully, Alex kept his mouth shut.

I race-walked to keep up with his long-legged stride down a hallway. "Who's this Dr. Xavier?"

"A friend."

"Let me guess. Bald. In a wheel-chair. Can read my mind without me transmitting."

Alex shot a dirty look at me. "A man died. Does everything have to be a joke with you?"

"This? From the king of practical jokers?"

Another annoyed glance. "Not when we're talking murder, darlin'."

He stopped in front of a door stenciled with "Dr. Ramon Xavier" in black and rapped on it. A muffled "Come in" penetrated the wood and glass. When Alex twisted the knob and opened the door, the distinctive scent of sandalwood drifted on the air.

He entered the room, me on his tail. "*Que pasa?*"

The man, or I should say vampire, looked up from his paperwork. I swear vampires must have their own version of *America's Next Top Model* for their selection process. When the other vamp stood, he came in a hair under Alex's six-two. Black, wavy hair was brushed back from a high forehead and hung an inch past the collar of his lab coat. Wide, full lips set off his aquiline nose. Even the freakin' lab coat and his blue plaid shirt didn't hide the lines of muscle along his shoulders, arms and chest.

The only weird thing was the thick black frames perched on his nose. I'd never seen a vampire wear glasses before.

Dr. Xavier smiled, but not enough to show his fangs. "Stanton! How's it going?"

Alex pulled the door shut. "Not bad, Ray, but I've got some Family business."

Xavier's eyes widened at Alex's proclamation, then his nostrils flared as he got a good whiff of my scent. My body odor usually freaks out a new were or vampire because I smell more like a steak knife than a steak. Surprisingly, though, he held out his hand to me. "You must be Sam Ridgeway. I'm Ray Xavier."

Like I pointed out to Bebe, everyone in the supernatural community had heard about my creation and the Los Angeles vampire coven taking me under their wing.

The assistant M.E.'s skin had the same cool feel I was becoming accustomed to as I shook his hand. "Nice to meet you, Ray."

He gestured at the chairs filled with files. "Just set those on the floor." He flopped back into his seat. "What's up?"

Alex flicked a look at me and moved the piles before we sat.

I swallowed hard before I started. "This is about someone brought in this morning. Josh Williams."

A black eyebrow rose above the rim of Ray's glasses, and a sly smile spread his lips. "Sifuentes commented that someone might stir up some trouble." He glanced at Alex. "Is this official?"

Alex shook his head.

Ray looked back at me. "Is Williams here?"

"You mean his ghost?" At Ray's nod, I continued, "No. He didn't think he could handle seeing his body again."

Ray took his glasses off and rubbed his eyes. "They usually can't. A lot of times, seeing their corpse sends the ghost over the edge." He stared at me. "If this isn't an official coven investigation and I see any information I give you published in your gossip rag before the M.E.'s official report is released, I'll tear your throat out myself. Got me, little girl?"

I nodded. I already had *that* godawful experience a month ago. I really, *really* didn't want a repeat.

"Williams did die from an overdose of heroin." Ray held up his hand when I opened my mouth. "I just sent the samples over to the lab. It'll be a day or two before I get the tox screening back to confirm what was in his blood. But Sifuentes may be right that the speedball was administered after he was unconscious." I bristled at the detective taking credit for my theory, but kept my mouth shut when Ray added, "I smelled another drug in his blood besides heroin."

I leaned forward. This was the first possible lead confirming Josh was telling the truth. "Any ideas what it was?"

Ray shook his head. "Just slightly bitter and very faint. It could be any number of things, from Phenomyl Nite to a half of a Valium, which is why I'm waiting for the tox report." He rested his elbows on his cluttered desk. "Why is this so important if it's just a ghost? It's not a vampire matter." His gaze swung from me to Alex and back.

"The guy was getting his life back together. None of this makes sense, and he asked me for help. If he was murdered, I'm going to find out who because it isn't right that his son will grow up without a father." I rose to my feet. "Thanks for the info, Ray."

"*De nada.*" He stood as well and took my proffered hand. "Good luck."

I turned to leave when Ray said, "Wait."

I looked back.

He held out a business card. "In case, you and your ghost come up with anything else."

I smiled. It was nice to have a vampire take me seriously for a change. I took the card with a nod. "Thanks."

As Alex and I walked back down the corridor, I glanced at him. "You're being awfully quiet."

"Has it occurred to you that maybe the man's delusional?" Alex stopped and fixed me with a pointed look. "Most folks in his situation don't want to admit they can't handle their life. Sometimes, an accidental overdose isn't quite so accidental."

I crossed my arms and stared back. "You think Josh is playing me."

A sad expression crossed his face, and he wiped a hand across his mouth. "Maybe not intentionally, but it's something to consider."

"What about the second drug in his system?"

"Mixing the wrong things together is not unheard of, Sam."

"And here I thought you would help me." I pivoted and stomped down the hallway.

Alex caught my arm. Damn vampire speed. "Sam, in an investigation, you've got to look at all the possibilities."

I met his gaze. "Right now, I think I'm the only one who is." And something about this whole situation smelled worse than the rotten meat odor of a dead vampire.

Chapter 4

It was close to noon by the time I returned to the *Scoop*'s offices, so I came bearing a salad for Agnes, a roast beef on rye for Emerson and a dozen ham and cheese sandwiches for me. The package of brownies we shared while we reviewed Agnes's notes.

Bill Morton, my office nemesis, poked his head into the conference room just as I handed Emerson his half of the last brownie. "Jesus Christ, Ridgeway! You can't give a dog chocolate!"

The asshole had gotten the assistant editor's job only because I died. At least, that's what I kept telling myself.

I also couldn't say anything about weres, even canine weres, being perfectly able to metabolize God's real gift to the human race. Luckily, Emerson said everything by trotting up to Bill and growling.

I just smiled. "Sorry, Bill. I won't do it again."

Bill ignored Emerson. "I need the conference room. You two, clear out."

Emerson growled even louder.

There hadn't been anything on the schedule posted on the wall outside the door. "For what?" I said.

Red suffused Bill's cheeks. "None of your damn business."

Emerson stepped closer to Bill and lifted his right hind leg.

"Emerson. No." Agnes glared at the were.

He tilted his head and glared back at her.

"She's right, Emerson." I narrowed my eyes as I stared at Bill. "He's not worth it."

Bill shot me an ugly look. "One of these days, Ridgeway, I'll fire you."

Reality smacked me hard. I still hadn't decided whether to tell my parents about my death, and I had only thirty-two days left in my grace period. If I couldn't tell Mom and Dad, I'd have to enter the vampires' equivalent of the Witness Protection Program. If that happened, the whole issue of getting fired was a moot point.

I rolled my eyes because I couldn't give in to Bill that easily despite my personal issues. "Look, Mr. Moron, you know the rules. If your name ain't on the sign-up sheet, it's first-come, first-served."

"That's it. I'm writing you up for insubordination."

If I had any Coke left in my cup, I would have thrown it in his face. Emerson trotted up to me and laid his head on my knee. I got his message and followed my own advice. Bill wasn't worth wasting our time.

"Chill. You can have the conference room."

"Make sure you clean it up first." Bill favored me with one last sneer before he stalked out.

Emerson looked up at me and barked.

"Yeah, I know he's an asshole, but it was *your* brother's idea to make him second in command."

The were snorted.

"By the way, where's Josh?"

Agnes used her index finger to shove her reading glasses back in place. "I put him in Mr. Augustine's office."

I shivered. Caesar had always been nice to me, but even I had the sense not to piss off a 2,000-plus-year-old vampire. "Why did you put him in there, Agnes?" I asked with as much patience as I could muster.

"So he could watch E! He was very bored down here."

I just buried my face in my hands.

— • —

I jogged up the stairs and knocked on Caesar's office door. No answer, so I opened it.

Josh Williams sat on the plush purple sofa, staring at the TV. On the flatscreen, a helicopter showed an aerial view of Elyse Manfield's Malibu mansion. The picture flipped to a shot of a reporter who stood in front of the gates. He recited Josh's résumé, including his nomination for this year's best actor award. Along the bottom of the screen, a banner ran. *Actor Josh Williams, Dead at age 28 from suspected overdose.*

It was the look on Josh's translucent face that made me want to kill Agnes. Normally, she was as weird as hell, but she meant well. Of course, the story had reached the rest of the media. Actually, I was surprised it had taken this long. I'd found his body nearly sixteen hours ago.

I reached for the remote and turned off the TV. "Josh, we need to talk."

He turned toward me. The expression on his face went beyond depressed. It was hollow, desolate. "I'll never hold my son again."

My chest hurt. There wasn't a damn thing I could do. I couldn't hug him or joke or anything that would alleviate his despair. Even though I was technically dead, I could still touch my family. It wasn't fair.

I crossed to the couch and sat down beside him. "Where is Reid?"

"With my parents." He turned back to the dark screen. "Ashley and I thought it would be best for him to spend some time with his grandparents with all the ceremonies and parties going on this week." His voice was dull, flat.

"Josh, I need to ask you some questions about yesterday."

Silence. Could a ghost have an emotional breakdown? He almost acted catatonic.

"Did you take anything, any over-the-counter medicine before you took your nap?"

His head whipped to face me again. "I've lost everything, and you're questioning me about a fucking aspirin!" Through him, I could see some expensive *objet d'art* shimmy. It rattled and bumped on its pedestal.

I couldn't let him intimidate me. I don't think he even realized his effect on inanimate objects. Besides, if he did something to hurt me, the nanites would repair the damage almost instantaneously.

I matched his glare. "*You* claim you didn't OD. *You* asked for my help. If you don't want it, leave." I stood and headed for the door. I wasn't a total soulless bitch. I just couldn't handle his pain on top of my own confusion and uncertainty about my status.

"Sam, wait."

I paused with my fingers wrapped around the door lever. "Why?"

"I—" His Adam's apple bobbed, but it was only his memory of swallowing that formed the action. "I'm sorry. I'm not dealing well with this whole dead thing."

A bitter laugh tore through my throat. "I know it's hard to believe, but I know exactly where you're coming from."

He stared at the floor. "You said you had some questions."

I crossed my arms over my A-Team t-shirt. "Why didn't you have a new will made after Reid was born?"

He looked up and blinked. "What are you talking about?"

"Your parents filed a will this morning. It's dated ten years ago and it names them as the sole beneficiaries of your estate."

Josh slowly shook his head. "That's the one I had drafted after I got paid for *Shining Armor*." His first big hit. "I had one done when Ashley and I were together, then we both re-did our wills after we split. Everything's supposed to go into a trust for Reid."

"Why would your parents try to file an old will?"

"They didn't know about the last one." He grimaced. "And they weren't happy I named Ashley the beneficiary of the second will. They never liked the fact that Ashley refused to marry me."

It was my turn to blink. "She's the one who said no?"

Josh leaned back against the sofa and started to drift through the cushions before he caught himself. "You gotta understand. Her parents split when she was three and their divorce was pretty ugly. She was afraid if we got married the same thing would happen to us."

"But you split up anyway," I pointed out.

"Yeah." He ran his hands over his face. "Tell me about it."

"What's really going on between you and Elise?"

"Nothing!" He glared at me, and the funky art piece behind him started dancing on its pedestal again.

"Josh." I stepped forward. Icy air was rapidly filling the room. "I'm trying to eliminate suspects here. You getting pissy about it is not helping."

"Sorry," he muttered. "Nothing's going on between me and Elise. I swear. She—" His nostrils flared and the piece of art stilled. "She's a friend. She's been supportive. You know what her sister went through when they were teens."

The child stars had their own predicaments with fame from the time they were babies. Except for Elise's twin sister, the problem hadn't been drugs. Her addiction had been dangerous, kinky sex, particularly asphyxiophilia. The D.A. gave up after two juries deadlocked when he tried her boyfriend for manslaughter. And the stupid-ass "special assembly" in high school taught by teachers too embarrassed to say the word "orgasm" when the news hit? Oh, yeah. I remembered.

"Was anybody else at Elise's house while you were there?"

He started to shake his head, but paused. "If you're making a list of suspects, you'd have to include the rep from Folbes & Benini, the chairman of Elise's foundation, my manager and my parents."

I toyed with my ponytail. "Well, I think we can rule out Folbes & Benini since they needed you alive to wear their rags on the red carpet. Are you donating anything to Elise's charity?"

"No." He shook his head for emphasis. "And she's never asked me."

His parents were on my shortlist of suspects. Their filing of an outdated will spurred them to the top. But with his anxiety, it was probably best to change the subject.

"You mentioned taking an aspirin yesterday." I held up my hand as the *objet d'art* shivered on its pedestal. "Josh, I really need you to calm down and listen. I talked to the assistant M.E. He smelled something else in your blood besides heroin."

The face he made would have been comical if the situation wasn't so serious. "Smelled? What do you mean he smelled my blood? The guy that did my autopsy was sniffing my blood? Who the hell did my autopsy? Dracula?"

Enough was enough. I stood and walked over to the bizarre sculpture thing and laid it on the plush carpet. I barely could afford to feed my insane appetite on two salaries. Josh Williams was *not* making me replace Caesar's expensive piece of shit.

Pressure grew behind my eyeballs. Sucking in a deep breath didn't help. I faced Josh, who was now standing, even if it was in the middle of the couch. "No. You're in the Prince of Darkness's office. One of his minions performed the autopsy."

"A vampire performs autopsies?"

"Yes." The black ball appeared in my vision.

"Did he drink my—"

"Answer my question!" I couldn't hold the energy. It aimed straight at the target of my ire.

He staggered at the psychic blow and lifted his hands to his ectoplasmic ears. "That . . . hurt."

"Serves you right. Now answer my question." Bill Gates couldn't pay me enough to tell him that my weird little part-telepathic, part-telekinetic stunt left a dull ache between my eyeballs as well.

"I had a headache from the stress of this week's press junkets, and I took two Phenomyl before I lay down on the couch to nap."

The picture clicked in my brain. Chicago. The pain reliever scare back in the '80's that triggered anti-tampering packages for over-the-counter meds.

But all the factory protections in the world can't stop someone with access to the drugs inside the house. "Regular Phenomyl?"

He nodded. "The Rapid Release capsules if you're picky."

Fuck. "You're sure it was just Phenomyl and not Phenomyl Nite?"

Josh frowned. "I'm sure. The sleep aid makes me incoherent, and I had the ceremony rehearsal today..."

I'd already pulled out my cell phone and Ray's card from the front pocket of my jeans. I prayed I was wrong. Ray picked up on the second ring.

"What did you find in the stomach contents of Josh Williams?"

The assistant M.E. chuckled. "And *buenas tardes* to you, Sam."

"This is serious, Ray. Did you find gelatin capsules?"

"Yes." His tone sobered. "What's going on?"

"Are you having the stomach contents tested for heroin?"

"Of course—"

"What about diphenhydromine?"

There was silence on Ray's end for a second before he said, "Sam, I'm having the lab test for a list of sedatives based on the scent I picked up."

As much as I wanted to make a snarky comment about his patronizing tone, now wasn't the time. "Do me a favor. Call Sifuentes and tell him the needle and tourniquet were just for show. Have him meet me at Elise Manfield's house." Deep down I knew the detective would listen to Ray as both a vampire and a medical examiner before he'd listen to a zombie tabloid reporter. I thumbed the "End Call" button.

I was already heading for the door, and I glanced over my shoulder at Josh. "You're coming with me."

He stood stock-still in the middle of the couch. "Why are we heading for Elise's?"

"To stop anyone else from becoming an accidental heroin overdose victim."

CHAPTER 5

I whipped around another city bus, only to slam on my brakes as a Mercedes cut me off from the left. Fucking rush hour.

"Sam, if Elise takes one of those pills . . ."

"We'll get there in time." I didn't have the heart to tell him I wanted to make sure she didn't dispose of the evidence. *Think, dammit!* I didn't have a siren or lights. What I did have was super speed, strength and reflexes.

I pulled into the valet parking of a shopping center and paid the attendant.

Josh melted through the body of my Honda as the valet drove off. "This is no fucking time to shop, Ridgeway!"

I ignored the pain in my head from his shout and tried to act nonchalant as I strode into a beauty salon. Luckily, the receptionist was busy with three people, all yelling about being double-booked the day before the big movie awards ceremony.

The icy spot on my neck meant Josh was following me.

I hit the back door and jumped the ten-foot wooden fence.

Josh, on the other hand, simply passed through the boards. "What? How did you—?"

"Shut up and keep up, Williams." I took off for Elise's as fast as my feet would go.

Only a homeless guy and a couple of maids with questionable green cards spotted me as I zipped down alleys and through yards.

Then I hit my one problem.

Reporters camped on the street and the beach. It would take too long to circle around and approach Elise's place from the north. That meant cutting through *his* yard.

He'd smashed my camera at a red carpet. He'd had my car towed more than once. The bastard even tried to get the Sabretooths to rescind my dad's half-court season tickets next to his out of spite.

Swallowing my misgivings, I jumped the stone wall.

Of course, Jack was laying on a pool lounge canoodling with his latest baby mama.

He glanced up as I ran past. His double-take would have been funny if the situation hadn't been dire. "Ridgeway?"

I grinned and waved as I leapt the wall on the other side of his yard.

Then I was on Elise's property and running full tilt for the main house. I didn't bother trying the front door and raced for the rear of the building. Like I suspected the patio door was unlocked.

I slid the glass door open and stepped inside. After the brilliant sunshine, it took even my zombie vision a second to adjust to the dark. My undead spidey sense pointed the way.

I walked into the kitchen as Ashley Anderson handed Elise a large bottle of Phenomyl.

Chapter 6

"Put the bottle down, Elise."

Both women jumped at my voice. The plastic bottle hit the floor with a loud rattle.

Elise's surprise didn't last long. Anger twisted those perfectly plucked brows. "What the hell are you doing here?"

"Are those the capsules you took, Josh?" I was breaking a zillion rules by addressing a ghost directly in front of Normals, but at this point, I didn't really care. I needed to figure out who was trying to kill who.

Ashley's flawless skin paled, but Elise looked downright pissed. "How dare you—"

"Shut up," I ordered. The look on my face must have been nasty. She clamped her jaw shut.

He crouched next to the island where they stood and looked at the label. "Yeah."

"Where did you buy them?" My question was for my ghost, but I kept my eyes on the ladies. Elise was a natural transmitter, and she'd already let me know her plan.

He looked up at me. "I didn't. Elise has everything delivered."

The actress in question eased away from me.

I frowned at her. "Don't bother reaching for the taser, Elise. The sheriff's department is already on the way. I told them about the doctored Phenomyl." A lie, but they didn't need to know that. I trusted Ray's loyalty to Caesar as his vampire master meant he took me seriously and called Sifuentes.

Elise's mouth dropped open.

Ashley turned an even lighter shade of white. "Wh-what are you talking about?"

I knew better than to say anything. The women stared at me. I stared back.

The loud banging on the front door interrupted the silent tableau.

A millimeter of relief trailed up my spine. "You'd better answer that. It's Detective Sifuentes."

Elise's gaze flicked from me to Ashley and back. She was scared to leave her friend alone with me.

Then I spotted the two capsules next to the can of Red Bull on the counter next to Anderson. "Those pills are more of a danger to Ashley than me." I gestured at the possible murder weapons. More banging from the front of the house. "You'd better answer that before Jorge decides to break it down."

Elise stalked from the kitchen, but she was back seconds later with Sifuentes and a couple of uniformed deputies.

Sifuentes scowled as he looked from Elise to me to Ashley and back. "What the fuck is going on, Sam? I got a message from the M.E.'s office to meet you here."

"Your murder weapon's on the floor."

Before I could stop him, Sifuentes donned a latex glove and reached through Josh. He jerked his hand back before he touched the plastic.

"Shit! That's cold."

"Serves you right."

Sifuentes closed his eyes. Exasperation rolled off him. The scent reminded me of barbequed pork, which in turn triggered a series of stomach growls.

"He's . . ."

"Yeah," I answered and tilted my head.

Josh got the message, rose and floated through the island.

Sifuentes waited for my nod before he picked up the bottle. "Did you touch it, Sam?"

"No. So now you're taking me seriously?" I crossed my arms.

He stood, an ugly smile on his face. "The needle and the spoon came back negative for heroin." He shook the bottle. "Williams's medical records and the producers from his last two movies confirmed your story from last night."

Josh rolled his translucent eyeballs and muttered a suggestion for Sifuentes that was anatomically impossible.

I pointed to the two capsules on the counter. "Don't forget those as well."

Sifuentes sobered, his intense gaze flicking between the two actresses. "Did either of you ingest any pills from this bottle?"

They both shook their heads.

"I was about to," Ashley volunteered. "I had a headache, and I can't take ibuprofen or aspirin."

Suspicion tattooed Sifuentes's face. "Why?"

All earnestness and big eyes, Ashley said, "It interferes with my blood pressure meds."

"Aren't you a little young?" he shot back.

She shrugged. "It's the business."

The detective tilted his head toward the living room. "A word with you, Ridgeway." He handed the bottle to one of the uniformed deputies, who had also donned gloves. "Bag this and the two pills on the counter for evidence."

I followed him out of the kitchen. From the frigid air on the back of my neck, Josh was tagging along.

Sifuentes turned to face me once we were out of Normal earshot. "Can Williams confirm Anderson's story about her blood pressure?"

I looked at Josh, who nodded. "Yes."

The detective stared at his polished wingtips. In my four years at the *Scoop*, I've never seen him hesitant.

"I hear through the grapevine you've got telepathy like the vamps."

As I told Bebe, gossip spreads twice as fast in the supernatural community. "Where are you going with this, Jorge?"

He met my gaze. "What did you pick up from them?" He waved in the direction of the kitchen.

Josh gave me a look of utter disbelief. "You can read minds?"

"Do you have any idea how creepy this is?" I said.

Sifuentes's expression was totally serious. "Yes. Either you do it or I have to haul them both in. We both know the chaos that'll ensue. Not to mention the effect having his mother arrested will have on Williams's kid."

I stared at him in amazement. Sifuentes could be a rule-following ass, but this? "That's hitting below the belt."

"I know." Those sharp, dark eyes bore into mine. "But I'm betting there's more tampered pills in that bottle. Or do you want Williams's murderer to walk?"

"Mind-reading isn't admissible."

"Tell me anyway. You're the one who pushed the murder theory," Sifuentes said.

I shrugged. "I mostly got surprise and confusion from both of them when we showed up. Elise was pissed I was in her house again. Ashley freaked out when I spoke to Josh."

"Anything else?"

"Elise has a stun gun in the island drawer closest to the refrigerator."

"Good girl." Sifuentes gave me his wolf grin.

"Fuck you, Detective."

He chuckled. "Need to talk to my mate about that one."

——•——

An hour and a half later, I stood outside in the deepening twilight. Like last night, Sifuentes and Josh were both talking at the same time. Except tonight, my headache was even worse. Losing my temper and accidentally throwing a psybolt at Josh had been bad enough. The pain worsened when I had concentrated on picking up the two actresses thoughts and not transmitting while the detective questioned them further.

As a result, my forehead throbbed, and Ashley's grief clung to me like a shroud.

Damn, she'd really been in love with Josh.

And Elise knew. Had been working her ass off to get her two best friends back together.

The whole situation made me sick. And Sifuentes and I were back to square one in our respective investigations.

"Guys, please shut up." I held my cup of Coke to my forehead. At least my stomach had calmed down after three double cheeseburgers and a twenty-piece box of chicken nuggets.

After I explained to the good detective I needed to eat if he wanted to keep the Normals intact, Sifuentes sent one of the uniforms to a local burger joint for me.

Neither the ghost nor the detective stopped yelling at each other. Well, technically, yelling at me since I was the translator.

"My parents wouldn't kill me! That's insane!" Josh waved his arms.

The neighborhood dogs howled their distress at the ghostly shrieking, but the frigid breeze felt good on my aching head.

Meanwhile, Sifuentes repeated for the umpteenth time, "Which hotel is Williams's parents staying at?"

I hit the proverbial last straw, mainly because I didn't have that many left after I'd died. "I said shut up!"

Both men backed away two steps.

"Holy shit," Josh whispered.

"Sam, do I need to call someone from Augustine Coven," Sifuentes added.

"No." At this point, I didn't care if I'd sprouted fangs or my eyes glowed. I lowered the cup. "I just need you two to stop talking over each other for two seconds. I've got a headache, and unlike the rest of you, I can't take anything."

Josh made a snorting noise. "I wouldn't advise swallowing anything for a headache right now. Look what happened to me."

For a moment, I wondered what the heroin-laced pills would do to my nanite-altered physiology. God knew no other drug affected me. Bebe and I had been experimenting.

I looked at the ghost. "Josh, your parents filed the first will this morning."

"They made a mistake." The stubborn set of his jaw told me I wouldn't get any farther.

Sifuentes cleared his throat. "Who all knew about the third will, Josh?" I tried not to notice that the detective stayed a couple of paces away from me.

"Besides the estate attorney and his staff? Ashley and my manager, Wendall Cummings."

Sifuentes and I stared at each other after I relayed Josh's answer. I could see my own thoughts mirrored on the detective's eyes.

I turned back to the ghost. "Josh, does Cummings have any control over the estate in the third will?"

"Yeah, he's the . . . he's the . . ." Comprehension dawned on Josh's face. "The executor and the trustee for Reid."

My eyes met Sifuentes. "Cummings is a lawyer. If he's the executor and the trustee for Reid, he's got fifteen years to siphon off the funds, and he'll know all the tricks to keep anyone from questioning him."

Disgust filled the detective's face. He stomped across the lawn and spoke quietly with one of the uniforms. A Normal standing where I was wouldn't have heard his order to pick up Cummings for questioning.

I focused on the ghost. "Josh, where are your parents and Reid?"

"Sam, they wouldn't—"

"Listen to me. Someone wanted your money bad enough to kill you and set it up so it looked like you OD'd. Even if your parents are innocent, they have your son, which makes them a target. Got me?"

What I said must have sunk through the thick ectoplasm passing for his skull because he finally muttered, "The Malibu Grand Hotel."

When Sifuentes rejoined us, I repeated the info.

"Let's go," he said and circled his car.

Since I didn't want to be left out, I climbed in the passenger seat. Josh slid through the chassis to take a place on the back bench.

I waited until we were cruising down the Pacific Coast Highway before I asked, "Why didn't you call for backup?"

Sifuentes didn't look at me. "A cruiser will meet us there. If I'm walking into a bad situation, I prefer to have a super at my back. But pack will jump into the fracas first. I need someone who'll look out for the kid."

His faith in me was touching until he added, "Just don't eat the boy's brains."

"You want an easier way to test the Williams?"

He flicked a glance in my direction. "What do you mean?"

I smiled to myself. "Stop at the next pharmacy."

CHAPTER 7

Sifuentes banged on the hotel door. "L.A. County Sheriff's Office. Open up."

His fist on the wood made a solid *thunk*. No fake veneer here. The Malibu Grand was built in the '30's, a glorious art deco hotel. Despite the passing decades, she'd retained her charm.

When the door opened, an older gentleman stood before us. I got a very good indication how well Josh would have aged if he had the chance. A full head of silvery hair. Sharp, blue eyes. A spine that was still ramrod straight. "Yes?"

"Dad," Josh whispered behind me. I didn't look at the ghost. Couldn't. Not because I worried about what his father thought. I just couldn't imagine never hugging my own dad again. If I looked at Josh, the waterworks would start.

Sifuentes held up his identification. "May we come in and speak to you for a moment, Mr. Williams?"

Joshua Williams, Sr., carefully examined the detective's I.D. before turning to me. "Where's yours, missy?"

"Ms. Ridgeway isn't with the sheriff's department, sir." Sifuentes's voice was commanding and sympathetic at the same time. "She's a friend of your son's."

Not quite a lie based on the last twenty-four hours.

Williams's eyes narrowed. "The only Ridgeway Josh ever mentioned was a tabloid reporter."

I tried to follow Sifuentes's example and project confidence and compassion. "I do work for an entertainment magazine, Mr. Williams, but I was the one who found Josh."

Red flared in Williams's face. "My son didn't OD!"

"I don't think he did either." I tried a small, wry smile. "Detective Sifuentes will be the first to tell you I've been harassing him for the last twenty-four hours to turn Josh's death into a murder investigation."

Williams blinked. "Murder?"

The detective gave me an inquiring look. I made a subtle shake of my head. Josh's dad definitely wasn't involved.

Sifuentes waved toward the suite. "That's why I want to talk to you and your wife, sir. May we please come in?"

Williams stepped back and gestured for us to enter.

As soon as we did, a high-pitched shriek split the suite's living room. "Daddy!"

The toddler raced for us. Dark hair. Big blue eyes. Just like his father.

Out of reflex I'm sure, Josh dropped to hug his son. "Hey, squirt."

Reid leapt for his dad's arms and passed right through him. He ended up crashing into me, banging his head on my knee.

Fuck. The kid could see ghosts.

"Daddy?" He rubbed his little forehead. Confusion filled his face as he tried to hug his father again. "You're all cold," he said in a bewildered voice.

The anguish in Josh's expression made my own heart break. This so wasn't fair. I had to give Josh credit. He schooled his expression.

The new one was supposed to be a reassuring smile. "I'm sorry, squirt. It'll be okay."

No, it wasn't. And I hated that lie. And I got the impression Josh hated himself for telling it.

Mr. Williams's attention flicked from Reid to the empty space he addressed.

Before I could figure out how to handle Reid's revelation, Mrs. Williams walked in from the open balcony. "What's going on?" Suspicion filled her eyes as she took in Sifuentes and me.

I didn't wait for Sifuentes to go through his official schtick again. I pulled the large bottle of Phenomyl I'd bought on the way to the hotel out of my purse. "This was found in your son's bathroom at Elise Manfield's house."

"And?" she said.

I had to concentrate since she was a little harder to read than her husband. I signaled negative to Sifuentes.

Reid toddled over to Mrs. Williams and held up his arms. "Grandma?" Automatically, she picked him up, but kept her attention on the detective and me.

Josh took a step closer to them, his expression ragged because he couldn't comfort his son.

Sifuentes began his spiel. "Ma'am, I'm sorry to disturb you—"

Presence. Outside the room. I nudged the detective with my elbow. "There's someone else on the balcony."

Mrs. Williams took a step back, angling her body to shield Reid from us. "Our guests are none of your business." Frost coated her words.

Another man walked into the suite. One I recognized from his website publicity photo. Wendall Cummings.

It didn't take any mind-reading to see the change in his expression when he spotted the bottle of pills in my hand.

"Jorge!" My warning was too late.

Cummings wrenched Reid from his grandmother and shoved her into Sifuentes and Mr. Williams. Somehow, in the same motion, he pulled a handgun out of his suit pocket. "I'll kill the brat. So help me, I will."

"Daddy!"

Josh started forward at his son's plaintive wail. Then he looked at me, desperation in his translucent eyes. "Sam, I can't touch him."

"I've already got deputies at every exit, Cummings. It's over." Sifuentes voice sounded calm, cool, but I could see his muscles tighten. The ashy scent of fear permeated the room.

Cummings backed toward the open balcony doors, hauling the squirming toddler with him.

Even my super-speed couldn't stop a point-blank bullet. I'd found that out the hard way back in January. And while I'd heal in minutes, none of the Normals would be that lucky, especially little Reid. No one, but . . .

Josh, can you hear me?

"Yeah."

I need you to possess Cummings.

The ghost stared at me like I'd lost my last marble. Maybe I had if I thought this crazy plan would work.

"Your friend Bebe said possessing someone was a bad thing."

I just need you to do it for a second. Long enough for me to get Reid away from him.

Uncertainty flickered in his eyes. "Okay, I'll try."

No trying. If you can't do this, Reid and your parents are dead.

Determination set his expression. "Let's do it. One. Two . . ."

On three, we both rushed forward. Josh flowed into Cummings. The lawyer was a big man, but when the fight was totally spiritual, things were a little more equal. The Normals, except for Sifuentes, probably thought Cummings was having some kind of epileptic attack.

Cummings tried to whip Reid over the railing before Josh was totally inside him. I snagged the kid, but Cummings crashed into my back as he fought Josh's control.

I overbalanced.

All the super powers in the world can't stop the laws of physics.

For one horrifying instant, Reid and I were in mid-air, five stories above the hotel's colorful flowerbeds and a couple of decorative trees. I grabbed for the railing.

And missed.

Chapter 8

Somehow, I pulled Reid to my chest and curled around him.

My side cracked the fourth story balcony. The impact also broke a rib. The familiar pain of a punctured lung fried my nerves.

Can't let go. Can't let go.

Fortunately, the hit bounced Reid and me into the foliage of a tree. Branches tore my skin and clothes.

Despite everything, I remembered my stuntman ex-fiancé's advice to roll at impact to shed momentum. Grass rushed up, I twisted through the agony and kept tumbling.

We came to a stop next to a concrete birdbath with me on my back and Reid huddled on my torso. I couldn't breathe. Everything in my body hurt like hell.

Big, blue eyes peered into mine. "That was fun! Can we do it again?"

Duncan's intense green eyes stared into mine. Not quite glowing vampire neon, but on the verge. He leaned forward in the hospital visitor's chair and grasped my hand. "Next time, please phone me first."

I grinned at my boyfriend. "Who says there'll be a next time?" The nanites had done their job once Bebe had maneuvered the broken rib out of the area it shouldn't have been. Even though I was technically healed, she still wanted me kept another night.

He raised a black eyebrow. "We are discussing Samantha Ridgeway. There *will* be a next time." He leaned a little further. Cool lips brushed mine in a delectable kiss.

"Sam? Oh! Sorry."

Duncan and I reluctantly broke our contact.

"Come on in, Josh," I called.

The ghost passed back through the closed hospital room door. "Sorry, I would have knocked." He gave a self-deprecating shrug.

"It's okay." I made introductions even though Duncan couldn't see or hear the dead actor.

Josh ran a hand over his head. "I just stopped by to say thanks. For everything. Especially saving Reid's life."

"No worries. How is he?"

"Just some scratches and bruises. Otherwise, he's fine." He chuckled. "One good thing about my death is my parents are talking to Ashley. They're working out a visitation schedule."

I smiled. "That's good."

The door swung open. Sifuentes charged into my room. "Hey, Ridgeway—" He plunged right through Josh. "Shit! Don't tell me he's still here?" He pivoted to face the cold spot. "Walk into the light for chrissakes!"

"Be nice," I chided.

Duncan raised both eyebrows. I glared back at him before I returned my attention to the detective. "Josh was just letting me know Reid is all right."

Sifuentes shoved his hands in his pockets. "If it helps, we got a full confession from Cummings. Apparently, he'd been embezzling from Williams for sometime. He was afraid Williams would discover what was going on since he'd been sober for a while. He stole the original bottle, emptied the capsules, mixed Phenomyl Nite with heroin—"

"Refilled the capsules and swapped bottles when he was there yesterday. So he knew Josh would be dead soon because he saw him take the doctored pills." I leaned back against the rock hard hospital pillow and closed my eyes. "I knew it was about the money."

"Yeah, you were right."

I opened my eyes, surprised at the detective's admission.

Sifuentes wiped a hand over his face. "He'd already made a copy of Josh's keys. Let himself in after Elise went to meet Ashley. Set the body up in the kitchen and locked up long before you got there."

He eyed me. "Which brings me to another problem. How'd you get into the house without forcing the lock?"

I blinked. "I didn't. Like I told you before, the front door was partly open when I arrived."

Sifuentes shook his head. "I guess it's not an issue since the prosecutor has more than enough to convict the bastard for life."

I glared at him. "I'm telling you the truth, Jorge."

"Anyway..." Sifuentes smiled his wolf smile. "If you decide to quit the gossip rags and get into law enforcement, let me know."

Duncan's eyes shifted to neon. "She will not."

I glared at him. "Excuse me. That's not your decision." I recognized Sifuentes comment for the compliment it was. Turning back to the detective, I said, "My best to your wife and the pack."

He nodded and turned to leave, but paused. "Tell me where Williams is."

Josh rolled his eyes and stepped closer to the bathroom.

I giggled. "The path's clear." Sifuentes charged out the door.

Williams gave me a rueful grin. "I owe you, too. Thanks for believing me."

I wasn't about to tell him I didn't at first. "What are you going to do?"

"I promised to spend a little time with Reid."

Crap, I totally forgot the kid could see his dad. "How's he handling...this?"

"Better than I am. Your Dr. Zachary thinks either Ashley or I have an ancestor who's a witch. That's why Reid can see me. I made him promise to keep it a secret. He's only three. He doesn't really understand."

He looked at the floor for a moment before continuing. "What Sifuentes didn't tell you was that the D.A. put a rush on my lab tests after Cummings confessed. They released my body. There'll be a graveside service on Tuesday." He gave me the time and place.

Josh raised his head. "I'd appreciate if you'd come to the service with me."

"Sure. I'll come."

Relief relaxed his translucent face. "Thanks." He floated through the door.

Duncan squeezed my hand. "What was that about?"

I repeated Josh's side of the conversation. The whole situation left me . . .

Sad wasn't the right word. Neither was depressed. For a woman who made her living by the written word, I was stuck.

"Are you all right, Samantha?" Duncan squeezed my hand again.

"Yeah." I tried to force a smile. I was sure it looked pretty pathetic.

"I seem to recall we have enjoyed hospital beds in the past." He waggled his black eyebrows like some lecherous villain.

Something was seriously wrong in the universe if Duncan was cracking jokes.

"Would you please just hold me?" I scooched over on the mattress.

He kicked off his boots. Somehow, he maneuvered his six-four frame into the hospital bed with me. We lay there, me curled up in his arms as we watched the motion picture awards ceremony on TV.

I managed not to cry until Josh Williams was proclaimed the winner of this year's best actor award.

CHAPTER 9

On Tuesday afternoon, the sky was sunny with white puffy clouds. Josh and I stood under a tree, well away from the other mourners.

Reid had waved to his dad when he hopped out of the limo behind the hearse. I hoped everyone would think he was waving at me. Bebe had made arrangements with Ashley for Reid's "therapy." I had enough problems dealing with my undead status as a twenty-six-year-old woman. I couldn't begin to imagine what little Reid's life would be like with his talent.

I noticed the stranger under another nearby tree while the pastor was reading the Twenty-Third Psalm. He was dressed a little casual for a funeral, in jeans and a white t-shirt. He kept his head bowed while the pastor spoke. His long, dark hair hid his face.

"Josh—" Then I realized he was staring in the direction of the mystery man.

"Can you see it, Sam? It's so beautiful." Wistful longing filled his face.

"See what?" I glanced around the cemetery. There was nothing here but the mourners, the two guys who would fill the grave, Josh and the mystery man.

"The light." He started walking, well, floating toward the stranger.

The pastor finished speaking, and everyone, including the cemetery workers, said, "Amen."

The stranger raised his head. His eyes were so freaking blue they were nearly white. He smiled at Josh, his arms held out to hug him.

And damn, if he did just that.

With his arm around Josh, they started to walk away.

Josh!

They both turned to look at me. Josh raised a hand in farewell. The stranger . . .

First, confusion, then curiosity flickered across his handsome features. He wanted to check me out, but Josh was obviously his first priority.

My weird little undead instinct said I shouldn't be able to see him at all.

Both men turned away. And then . . .

I blinked. No way. The most gorgeous white plumage expanded from the stranger's back. The huge wings wrapped around Josh.

A flash of brilliant white light.

When I could see again, both men were gone.

A small hand tugged mine. I looked down to find Reid, solemn blue eyes staring up at me.

"Was that an angel who took Daddy away?"

I glanced around. Several yards away, Ashley stood, patiently watching me and her son.

I crouched down next to Reid. "I think so."

A serious nod. "Then Daddy's in heaven."

Not a question. An affirmation.

"Yeah, but that's something we need to keep between you and me and Dr. Zachary, okay?"

He smiled, then whispered, "I'm real good at keeping secrets."

He wrapped his pudgy arms around my neck and squeezed. "Bye, Sam." His little legs chugged as he raced back to his mother.

I stood and brushed off the knees of my dress slacks. The next issue of the *Scoop* would be a tribute issue to Josh Williams. My story about the murder investigation wouldn't be the focus, just an addendum, not the cover. I didn't mind for once.

Out of curiosity, I strode over to where the stranger had been. There was nothing I could see. No unusual sound. Just the faint scent of baby powder in the air.

A little niggle of jealousy and worry whispered in my brain. Why hadn't an angel come for me when I died?

LOVE, WAR & A BULLDOG

Author's note: This story takes place three weeks after the events in *Blood Sacrifice*.

Emerson O'Malley trotted beside Agnes Durley as they headed for the park. Contrary to popular belief, it was not his favorite place. Pissing on a tree wasn't what a civilized man did.

He'd sue his brother for ADA violations if he could. Trapped in bulldog form surely counted as a disability. If Ralph could put a damn stepstool in their bathroom at home, then surely he could put one in the john at work.

But noooo. That may raise suspicions. Jesus Christ, it wasn't like either of them could change shapes. Ralph was just as trapped as Emerson, only in human form.

Emerson sighed. He'd give just about anything to trade places with his brother.

"What's wrong?" Agnes asked.

A heaping bowl of self-pity. Especially when it came to the tabloid's staff writer. Even though Agnes wore a lot of frumpy crap, she had on a pastel cotton skirt today. The woman had a set of gams that were made for . . .

"Emerson!"

Unfortunately, she was also an empath.

He looked up and let his tongue loll out of the side of his mouth.

Pink shone on her cheeks, and she poked at the nosepiece of her glasses. "That's not funny. Sometimes, I think you do that on purpose."

He snorted, and they continued down the sidewalk.

She muttered, "Typical man." A little humor lay in her tone though.

Except he wasn't a man. And he was right back in his original funk. Sure he and Agnes could flirt a little, but nothing was going to happen. He was fifty-three and doomed to die a virgin because he walked on four legs instead of two.

Dusk had settled in when they reached the entrance of the park. Agnes left the concrete path for soft grass. She took a careful look around before she leaned over and unclipped the leash. "I'll wait for you here."

Thank god for small favors. The rest of the staff felt they needed to watch when he took a dump. But then, the rest of the staff didn't know he was a fucked-up werebulldog.

He was covering his hole when he heard the shriek. That wasn't Agnes. He charged toward the sound.

Three nymphs cowered next to an oak tree. Facing them was an enraged, impossibly beautiful woman. Golden hair hung in ringlets down to her waist. She wore a pink toga-thing with gold-encrusted sandals. Jewelry dripped from her. Power crackled at her fingertips. Everything about her said, "Goddess."

"I smell him on you!" the gorgeous blonde screamed.

"We haven't touched him!" the brunette nymph shouted back.

With a start, he recognized her. Melissa. One of Ralph's old girlfriends. The one who made a hell of a baklava.

Emerson rushed forward and planted himself between the pissed-off goddess and Melissa and her friends. He bared his teeth and growled.

A range of emotions flashed across the goddess's face. She settled on pissy amusement. "Do you have any idea who I am?"

He barked twice.

"Such a brave little were. Too bad you need to die for threatening me." She raised a hand.

Agnes and her incredible legs stepped in front of him. "Don't even think about it, bitch." Ashy fear rolled off her. Her outstretched hand holding the can of mace shook. Despite her terror, despite the torture she suffered years ago at the hands of a supernatural mob, she stood up for him and the frightened nymphs. It took a hell of a woman to step into potential death when she was scared shitless.

Yep, he definitely had it bad for Agnes.

"How dare you?" the goddess screeched. "I'll kill you all."

Agnes pressed the button, and the goddess's rage turned into a howl of pain.

Seeing his opportunity, Emerson scrambled around the writer and clamped his jaws on the goddess's delicate ankle.

"Get him off," she shrieked.

From the corner of his eye, he saw the nymphs melt into the surrounding foliage. Unfortunately, fear had Agnes in its grip. She stood there, muscles quivering and the mace still aimed at the goddess.

A sharp kick sent him flying through the air. He slammed into the same oak the nymphs had been huddled under. His landing drove the air from his lungs. Three or four angry blond goddesses danced in his vision.

"Don't you hurt him," Agnes wailed, but before she could spray more mace, the goddess's backhanded blow sent the writer sprawling on the manicured grass.

Emerson growled low in his throat, but the best he could manage was to crawl to Agnes. He licked her face.

"I'm okay," she whispered. But she wasn't. The blow had opened a nasty cut on her cheek, her glasses were bent nearly in half, and one of her lenses was shattered.

"Oh. Oh, this is too rich." Tears poured from the goddess's red, swollen eyes as she laughed. "The crippled were is in love with the mortal."

He growled and tried to rise, but dizziness swept through him.

"And she loves him, too." More laughter poured from the goddess. When it ceased abruptly, Emerson knew they were in deep shit. Maliciousness lit her bloodshot eyes. "As one of the poets said, 'Tis better to have loved and lost.' One night together is all you shall have." She flicked her hand and white light exploded.

"No!" Agnes threw her body over his.

He tried to wiggle out from under her, but she kept her arms locked around his neck.

It was too late. Agony raked through him, as if his very bones and muscles were being ripped apart. *So help me, if she hurts Agnes . . .*

Then the pain was gone. He opened his eyes. Agnes's arms still clung to his neck. The lamp by the path flickered on. The goddess was nowhere to be seen. "Are you all right?"

Her eyes met his, and they widened.

"Agnes, are you all right?"

"Emerson?"

"Who else do you think—" Holy crap! He was speaking English. Very carefully, he lifted his front left paw.

A hand. A human hand. He tried wiggling his toes and the fingers moved.

His attention returned to Agnes. "What do I look like?"

She released him and leaned back. "You look like Ralph, except . . ." Her gaze drifted down his body, and red bloomed on her cheeks. Of course, he was naked.

He reached up and felt the collar. The leather was a lot looser now that he had a human-sized neck. He looked down at his body again. At least, he didn't have Ralph's pot belly. But then, he didn't eat junk food, drink beer and smoke like his brother did either.

"Oh, yes, he definitely looks like Ralph."

He looked up to find Melissa standing over him.

"Dreamy," added the second nymph.

"Doable," said the third.

"We've got to cover you and get back to the office." Leave it to Agnes to throw cold water on the situation.

"No, don't do that." The second nymph gave him a not-so-demure smile.

And his brand-new human body responded to the attention.

"Lydia, get him a blanket," Melissa ordered.

"Why do you two get to watch?" Despite her pout, Lydia disappeared into the oak. She emerged a moment later with a large piece of green cloth that looked more like a lady's scarf than a blanket.

"Can you stand?" Agnes's words matched her deadly serious expression. Maybe he should just be thankful he wasn't dead.

"Yeah." But even with Agnes and Melissa's assistance, the ground seemed to wobble under his two feet. His two human feet.

Agnes bit her lip. "Maybe I should go get my car."

He flashed her a grin. "I'll be fine. I've never walked on fewer than four feet before." Besides, he was a little afraid of being alone with the nymphs. The walls between his and Ralph's bedrooms weren't that thick. Coupled with canine hearing, he knew a lot more about Ralph and Melissa's sex life than he cared to admit.

"Let me put this on you." Lydia the nymph had a wicked expression on her face.

"Oh, no, you don't." Agnes held out her hand.

Lydia pouted some more but handed over the scarf/blanket. Agnes wound it around his waist and tied it. At least, the material was sufficiently thick that he wouldn't get arrested for indecent exposure.

"Stay here," Melissa ordered the other two nymphs.

As they exited the park, Agnes leaned over to look at Melissa. "Who was that threatening you?"

The nymph blinked, as if the question didn't make sense. "Aphrodite."

"Who was she accusing you three of being with?"

"Ares, but we weren't *with* him. We work in his daughter's antique store, and he came in to visit with her and see what she does in the mortal realm."

Emerson's stomach churned. A goddess on the warpath was never a good thing. And he'd already pissed her off.

With the ladies' assistance, he managed the three blocks back to the magazine's office building. Roberto, the night guard, peered at him, then his face split in a grin. "Hey, Waldo! I didn't know you were in town."

Emerson swallowed the smart-ass retort fighting to come out. It actually made sense that he'd be mistaken for his other brother.

"He's been mugged. Call Ralph and tell him to meet me in Mr. Augustine's office." Leave it to Agnes to save the situation. Thankfully, Roberto didn't ask Alice about the dog she'd left with.

"Can you get him upstairs?" Melissa whispered. "It's best if Ralph and I don't—"

Agnes nodded. "Thanks for your help."

The nymph pivoted and headed for the door.

"Hey, Melissa," Emerson called.

She turned back.

"Thanks, and it's good to see you again."

A sultry smile appeared on the nymph's face. "And it was very good to see you." She sauntered out the door, the sway of her hips definitely distracting Roberto from asking any more questions.

— · —

Emerson wanted to punch Ralph. It was bad enough his brother had to feed him and bathe him for years at home, but helping him dress now was the last straw. "You couldn't find something without buttons?"

"I had a zombie employee who went through my entire stock of t-shirts, so quit your bitching," Ralph snarled.

Emerson shoved his brother away and tucked the shirttail into the borrowed jeans. Last thing he needed was a sibling's mitts near his equipment.

"Tell me about this Aphrodite thing again," Ralph said as they exited Mr. Augustine's executive bathroom. Thankfully, the magazine's publisher was rarely in the office.

Emerson repeated the entire encounter.

Ralph grunted. "A goddess of love on the rampage would explain some of the weirdness happening today."

"What are you talking about?"

"Incidents of domestic violence are up a thousand percent." Agnes sat behind Mr. Augustine's desk. Lights flickered across her spare glasses as she browsed the internet. "Unusual divorce filings. Stars who hate each other caught smooching and—" Agnes's face flamed red, and she coughed.

Emerson stifled a chuckle. "We get the picture."

"I've got every reporter out covering the chaos. I've called Mr. Augustine more than once, but I'm not getting an answer from any of his people."

Agnes looked up from the computer screen. "Oh, dear. If the Normals are reacting badly to Aphrodite's influence, the supernaturals' state could be much worse. Do you know where Ares is staying in town?"

Ralph's expression turned even more sour. "If I knew that, we wouldn't be having this conversation."

"But we know where his daughter Phillippa lives and works," Emerson said.

"She's not answering her phones either. I suppose I could have Bill Morton run over to her shop and her condo."

Emerson rolled his eyes. "Bill's a Normal. You can't send him out. Not to mention, he'd make things worse, then Los Angeles will have the joy of two pissed off gods causing trouble."

Ralph stroked his drooping jowls. "I don't like sending you two out."

Emerson snorted. "Agnes is right. Aphrodite is probably affecting the supernaturals as much as the Normals or worse, which is why Augustine or anyone in the vampire coven hasn't returned your calls."

Agnes stood and circled the desk. "Then we need to go and warn them."

"You just want to show me off." Emerson grinned. It nice to be able to do that without his tongue hanging out.

Lucky for him, Agnes didn't have Superman's heat vision. Otherwise, he'd be a puddle of melted goo.

———•———

Seven Wonders Antiques was closed for the evening, and no one answered Phillippa's condo door. In neither case could Emerson hear anyone moving around inside.

He shrugged as they stood in the condo building's hallway. "That doesn't mean I'm right. I've noticed my hearing isn't as sharp as it is when I'm in bull-dog form."

Agnes pursed her lips. "Let me try something" She fished in her purse and pulled out her phone. She hit an icon and nibbled on her lower lip while she waited for whoever she was calling to pick up.

"Hi, Sam. I'm trying to reach Phillippa, and she's not answering her home or cell phone and her store's closed for the evening." A pause. "Thank you." Agnes sighed. "Yes, this pays one of your debts to me." She thumbed the "End Call" icon and started punching in another number.

"Does Sam know why Phil's not picking up?"

Agnes glanced at him. "Her old phone was ruined in Uku Pacha. Phil didn't want to take any chances, so she got a new number when she got a new phone."

"What the hell is Uku Pacha?"

Agnes smiled. "Hell. Or one of them. Ms. Mann?"

Emerson heard odd noises coming through the receiver, then "Who the Hades is this?"

Agnes identified herself and added, "We're at your home, looking for your father."

"Are you insane?"

"Please, Ms. Mann. It's about the problems in Los Angeles tonight."

"You think he's behind this?" More sounds of fighting.

"No, but he may know how to stop it."

"Try a bar." There was a muffled *whoomp* and the line went dead.

Agnes frowned and placed her phone back in her purse. "Would he go to just any bar?"

"I doubt it." Emerson scratched behind his ear, then realized what he was doing and dropped his hand. "There's one supernatural bar in the city. Let's go there first." He stared at her. "Maybe I should take you home before I check it out."

"And how will you get there? You don't know how to drive."

She wasn't nasty about it, just concerned. And she was right.

"Okay, but you do exactly what I tell you."

She nodded and shoved her spare glasses back up the bridge of her nose.

———•———

Supernaturals packed Reno's. Vampires. Members of the Los Angeles werewolf pack. A group of witches on an obvious bachelorette night from the veil on one girl's head. Even a couple of fae drinking quietly in the corner.

All of them gave wide berth to the man in black slouched at the bar. He showed his back to the rest of the patrons because he had a death wish, or he was the predator to beat all predators.

Emerson bet on the latter.

He leaned over to Agnes. "Maybe you should wait in the car,"

"No." She glanced around nervously. Too many of these assholes were taking too much interest in the only Normal in the joint. "Someone needs to watch your back."

He couldn't spend the time fighting with her. "Stay close to me."

Emerson approached the bar. He aimed for confident deference. "Lord Ares."

The god faced him. His eyes were as black as his hair and clothing. He smirked. "I was wondering when someone with balls would walk in." He tossed back his shot, ouzo from the licorice odor, and slammed the glass down.

"Think you can take me down, little were." Ares stood.

Emerson blinked. The god was easily a foot taller than him. "I didn't come to fight."

"Sure you did. That's what weres do. They've got to prove who's alpha." He leaned over and eyed Agnes. "You even brought a wager, though she's a little old for my taste."

Emerson shove down his anger at the insult and stepped into the god's line of view. "I came to warn you. Aphrodite's tearing up the city, looking for you."

Ares roared with laughter. He slumped back in his chair and motioned for the bartender, who set another bottle of ouzo on the bar. The god took his time pouring a shot and slamming it back. "What makes you think I care?"

"The sooner she sees you, the sooner she'll be satisfied and leave everyone in the city alone."

"Oh, little were, you are sadly mistaken." Ares waggled his index finger under Emerson's nose. "Aphrodite is never satisfied."

"She cursed me into human form earlier tonight."

"And you're searching the city for me instead of taking your woman home and fucking her brains out while you can?" Ares howled with laughter again and slapped the scarred surface of the bar. "Oh, you mortals are too much!"

Agnes circled in front of Emerson before he could stop her. "She's been threatening Phillippa's employees, and we're afraid she'll go after Phillippa next. I was talking to her on the phone tonight when the signal went dead."

The god abruptly sobered. His face turned dark red, nearly purple. He jumped to his feet and shouted, "Aphrodite!"

Every supernatural in the bar slapped their hands over their ears at the horrendous noise. The walls shivered, and the one window set in the door cracked. Emerson shoved Agnes behind him again.

A flash of white light, and Aphrodite stood in the middle of the room. Instead of the pink toga-thing, she wore jeans and a pink t-shirt.

Very tight jeans and an equally tight pink t-shirt.

Ares strode over and grabbed her upper arms. "Why are you harassing this city? Threatening my daughter's employees?"

Surprise melted into lust on her face. "I was looking for you. You haven't come to visit me in so long."

"And instead of looking for me, you run around cursing Phillippa's friends?"

"I—I—"

Emerson couldn't resist grinning when the goddess looked around and spotted him and Agnes. "Hi there. Remember us?"

"I cured the stupid were of his affliction," she sneered.

"For one night," Ares ground out.

She stared up at him. "I used his love to help him. It's not my fault he's wasting it."

"You mean like how you used love to set up the rest of my daughters to die?"

"I don't know what you're talking about." But there was a glimmer of fear in her eyes.

"Well, I may not be the genius Athena is, but I know your handiwork when I see it." He stepped closer to Aphrodite. "Hippolyta and Heracles. Antiope and Theseus. Melanippe and Telamon. Penthesilea and Achilles." With each set of names, he invaded her space, and she retreated until her back was against a dartboard. He placed his huge hands on either side of her head. "Only you would twist love until someone dies."

No one moved in Reno's. Not a soul stirred. Hell, Emerson was pretty sure a few had stopped breathing.

But underneath, he could feel the tension. Everyone hovered on the verge of running. The only question was how many would make it out alive when the two deities started slinging power.

"You left me." Huge, crystal tears formed in Aphrodite's eyes.

"I didn't *leave* you. You didn't care enough to come looking for me when I was in trouble. When the Old Ones' demons abducted me. Phillippa did, and so help me, if you go near my daughter or her friends, much less touch them again, I will gut you like the sow you are." Ares stepped away.

She reached out to him, but thought better of it. In a flash, she disappeared.

Everyone in the bar released a collective sigh of relief.

Emerson squelched his own apprehension and held Agnes behind him when Ares strode over to them.

A wry smile twisted the god's mouth. "She won't be any more bother to your city. I'm sorry, but I cannot undo the curse she laid on you."

"It's . . . okay." Except it wasn't. A few hours of being human was all he would ever have.

Ares clasped his shoulder. His touch sent a trickle of energy through Emerson. "Go home. Make love to your woman. You still have a few hours before dawn."

Agnes eased from behind him. "Thank you for your help, sir." But the god was already immersed in his bottle of liquor.

———•——

Emerson pulled Agnes tight against him. He tried to memorize everything. The softness of her breast. The slickness of sweat on bare skin. The soft little moans she made when he was inside her.

Outside, the sky gradually brightened. Neither of them said anything. The words seemed so damn inadequate.

He knew the moment the sun crossed the horizon. Almost like a bell ringing. The pain wasn't as bad this time. An odd sensation like gas passing. *Figures, I finally lose my virginity, and I fart in her bed.*

Honestly, he would have been happier if it were gas. Color faded. Agnes's sweet scent grew sharper. He wanted to say, "I love you," one last time, but all that came out was a whine. He laid a paw on her hand.

"Oh, Emerson." She hugged him tight.

He cuddled against her and licked the tears from her cheeks as she wept.

———•——

Emerson rolled onto his back and wriggled against the couch cushion. With stubby limbs again, he couldn't reach the itchy spot in the middle of his spine anymore.

Ralph had been reticent about him moving in with Agnes, but in the end, he agreed. He even brought over the step stool so Emerson could use a toilet properly.

Keys jingled, and the deadbolt slid back. He jumped off the couch and raced for the door.

Agnes's face lit up when she saw him. "Hi, baby!" She crouched down and kissed his forehead.

The most incredible smell came from one of the shopping bags she held, and he shoved his head inside.

"Emerson, that's our dinner!" She smacked him on the ass.

He jumped, pulled his head out of the canvas, and growled. He should be the one slapping her on the ass, but that was never going to happen.

She opened her mouth, but she changed her mind about whatever teasing thing she was going to say. "I'm sorry. You have every right to be grumpy."

He head-butted her calf. Dammit, they were not going to feel bad about this. They had one incredible night together, and they should be grateful.

"Yes, you're right."

He wanted to take away her sad smile, get her mind on something else. He pawed the bag.

"I thought we should celebrate us living together. I hope you like filet mignon. The clerk recommended a nice red to go with them."

A T-bone and a couple of beers would have been better, but he didn't want to upset her more than she was. He barked twice and wagged his tail.

"Good. Why don't you watch TV while I cook?"

Actually, he'd prefer watching her cook naked, but no sense torturing himself.

The odor of the broiling steaks made his mouth water, which created a giant wet spot under his head. *Damn saliva.* He rolled onto his back once more.

Maybe moving in with Agnes hadn't been such a good idea. Living with him was like living with an elderly Normal. Except he had the added luxury of shedding.

Agnes came in and spread a tablecloth on the floor. When he cocked his head, she smiled. "So we can eat together."

He definitely didn't deserve her. What the hell had he been thinking? She deserves a real lover, not a mutated were who drooled all over her furniture.

Agnes lit some candles and started some sweet jazz tunes on the stereo. All this girly, romance-y stuff was making his pelt itch. She brought in the wine, hers in a goblet, his in a bowl, then their plates. He hopped down from the couch to join her, and they ate quietly.

Well, she did. For the first time, he realized how loud his chewing was as a dog.

She set down her goblet. "Emerson, stop it with the self-pity. I wouldn't have agreed to this if I didn't want you."

He stared at her, but her form seemed to waver in his vision. He shook his head, but that only made him dizzier. His legs didn't work right, and he collapsed on his side.

Distantly, he heard a bell ring. The sun had sunk below the horizon.

"Emerson!"

The impression of passing gas came over him. That's all it had to be. He shouldn't have eaten that cereal for breakfast. He knew what it did to his digestive system, but Agnes had been out of eggs.

"Emerson!" She was holding his face, but her voice came from very far away.

"What?"

Her hands covered her mouth and her eyes glittered. He tried to roll to his feet, but his legs were too long to tuck under his body.

He stared at his front paws to find hands once again. Flexing his fingers brought reality to the situation. "How?"

"Ares," Agnes whispered. "It must have been Ares. He said he couldn't remove Aphrodite's curse, so he must have altered it."

"To be human for one night." Emerson carefully climbed to his feet. It wasn't as hard as it had been last night. "Bulldog during the day. Human by night." He held his hand down to Agnes. "Can you live with that?"

Her shy, sweet smile was all the answer he needed as he drew her to her feet. He swung her into his arms and headed for the bedroom.

"Emerson! What do you think you're doing?"

He grinned. "I've got fifty-three years of catching up to do. And I'm starting with you."

REALITY BITES

Author's Note: This story takes place approximately a year after *Sacrificed.*

Chapter 1

Mai Osaka stood next to the limousine and waited for the small private jet to taxi closer to the Augustine hangar.

St. James hangar, she told herself sternly. She wasn't the only one who'd slipped over appropriate names and conduct the last two weeks. But as the head of security for the Las Vegas branch of the Western United States Vampire Coven, she was expected to set the example.

Even if she was a Normal.

Sharp-edged sunshine bounced off the tarmac and penetrated her standard black pantsuit and boots. Her extra dark sunglasses barely held back the rays. The only color marring her standard uniform was the blue and gold watch with the obnoxious cartoon duck on it. It wasn't her taste, but when the new boss's wife gives you a gift, you don't argue.

Especially since said wife was a brand-spanking new goddess of death who wasn't entirely in control of her powers at times.

The enforcer standing next to Mai pulled a white handkerchief from his back pocket and wiped the sweat from his face and neck.

"I don't know how you can stand this heat, Ms. Osaka," Thad Wolford said.

"It's a dry heat." Her standard reply. Personally, she couldn't wait to climb back inside the limo. It was a wonder her sidearm and watch didn't rust with the amount of sweat overwhelming her antiperspirant and trickling down her torso and arms.

Thad grunted in response. Given that his wife was a werecoyote, noncommittal sounds probably kept the peace at home. The former small-town sheriff didn't feel the need to make constant small talk, which was why she brought him instead of one of the were or witch enforcers.

The men standing by the fuel tanker didn't say much either as they waited, too. But maybe that was more due to the hearing protection they wore.

Engines whined as Miko Osaka guided the coven jet into an "L" turn and a stop at a safe distance. She waved off the tow vehicle and cut the power. Crap. That meant her little sister couldn't even stay for dinner.

The jet's door swung down, creating the staircase to disembark, while the workers set about refueling the plane. Mai's heart did a little pitter-pat when Stan Gryffudd ducked his six-six frame through the opening. Brown and green canvas bags were slung over both broad shoulders. A tight scarlet t-shirt covered his torso. Equally tight jeans covered his lower half. His white-blond crewcut literally glowed under the afternoon sun. His long-legged stride made a beeline for the limo.

Thad popped the trunk, met Stan, and offered to carry the bags. The new general manager of the Karnak Hotel and Casino flashed a genial smile and politely refused the offer of assistance.

Unsure of what to do, Thad shot a confused look at Mai. She shrugged, and he backed off. When Duncan St. James had been Normal, he was nobility. Before him, Selene and Ptolemy Antonius had been literal royalty. They all expected a certain amount of deference from the people who served them in Vegas beyond the usual vampire hierarchy bullshit.

Between those three, Grandfather Kensai had been in charge of the coven's interests here for two and a half very short years. But even his Normal status as a military man had carried through with how he expected the staff to behave. Frankly, all the vampires, employees, and Family in Las Vegas were looking at a huge adjustment.

A vampire would have been a better choice, but with a potential cure for the virus on the horizon, there wasn't anyone Duncan totally trusted. By the same token, he couldn't appoint a Normal Family member. The other vampire masters would consider such a move a sign of weakness.

Which meant he needed someone with supernatural abilities. Someone who could protect themselves, like Stan.

"Getting maudlin in your old age, sis?" A devilish grin lit Miko's face as she approached the limo.

"No."

"Right." She wrapped her arms around Mai. "I don't need telepathy to tell when you're thinking about Grandfather," she whispered.

Mai returned her baby sister's hug. "What happened? Vegas was supposed to be your last stop today," she said softly.

Miko released Mai and scowled. "Alex happened. I swear he's getting more paranoid than Duncan ever was as chief enforcer. He scrambled travel plans because he thinks someone leaked the originals." She held up her hands. "So don't ask me where I'm going next. I'm not allowed to tell you."

There was more to the story, but Mai wouldn't press right now. Alex Stanton didn't panic over nothing, and she was fairly certain Stan would tell her later.

"In the meantime, I get to babysit new pilots." She gestured toward the cockpit. A vaguely familiar face looked back at them. The man behind the windshield smiled and waved enthusiastically.

Mai saluted him before turning to her sister. "Who is that?"

"Tom Wellington."

"Who?"

"One of the Billings, Montana, vamps." Miko rolled her eyes. "He's been a bush pilot for a century but I've got to get him up to snuff on jets."

The name finally clicked in Mai's head. "Wait a minute. Doesn't he write romance novels?"

"Yep, with his wife." Miko grimaced. "They're branching out to same sex romance."

"And he's using our need for additional pilots to do a little research?" Mai tamped down on her irritation on her sister's behalf. Even though they'd been raised by their bisexual grandfather and his male partner, Miko still got weird bout being out of the closet herself.

A shadow loomed over them. "You don't have to say anything about your personal life to Tom, Miko." Stan's voice rumbled with his displeasure.

"It's not him. It's me." Miko fidgeted, which wasn't like her at all. Finally, she said, "Brittany and I broke up last night."

Mai cupped her sister's cheeks with both hands. "Why didn't you call me?"

"Because it was a long time coming." Miko sighed. "With the demon craziness the last couple of years, coven matters have taken precedence in my life." She drew Mai's hands from her face and held them. "We'll have a sister night soon. I promise. And I'll tell you everything, but right now, I have a schedule to keep before a certain vampire has a cow."

"All right, but I expect a call in the next two days."

They hugged again before Miko jogged back to the little jet and climbed inside. The fuel truck had already departed. She waved at Mai before she closed the door. A minute later, the engines roared to life, and the plane headed for the line of aircraft awaiting clearance for take-off.

"Mai, would you ride in the back with me?" Stan said.

"Yes, sir." She tried not to shiver at his voice. It wasn't his fault he was part fae. Half the time, she didn't think he even realized the affect he had on her.

Thad opened the rear door for them and stiffly held it.

And despite protocol, Stan insisted she climb in first. Mai bit her tongue to keep from chewing him out and wasting even more time. Duncan had to adjust his normal responses when Caesar appointed him the city master of Las Vegas. Her experience with Stan indicated it would take twice as much time to retrain him.

Once they were settled in the back seat, she looked at Stan. "Did something happen?"

He rubbed his temple. "Yeah. A car bombing in Seattle two days ago. We're pretty sure the target was Donna Whitefeather."

Thad climbed into the driver's seat. "Is she okay?" Something else bothered the other enforcer than the attempt on Donna's life. His slight accent became noticeable only when it was personal.

Stan reached into the satchel he still carried. "Shrapnel cuts and mild burns. Nothing the V-virus couldn't handle, but one of her Normal nieces and the girl's were boyfriend were killed. Pissed doesn't begin to cover Donna's mood."

"Suspects?" Mai thumbed through the reports. As she suspected, the additional attacks weren't limited to Seattle, or even the western U.S.

"The Vampire Liberation Front is claiming responsibility." Stan shook his head wearily. "Despite Caesar's fears of an all-out civil war, they're the only real problem. And the incidents with them have been limited to guerilla tactics."

A particular name sent a trill of worry down Mai's back. Her eyes met Stan's. "Dare Coven?"

"What about Dare Coven?" Thad asked as he guided the limo down the service road around the airport.

"An explosives-filled van rammed into Virginia's main house in Maryland at twelve-oh-five in the afternoon last week," Mai answered as she read. "Three daytime enforcers died. Virginia and her inner circle weren't there at the time, and the surviving staff were able to get the two vampires in residence to safety. That doesn't make sense. Virginia's on their side when it comes to the cure."

"So far she hasn't accused Aug—" Stan sighed. So Mai wasn't the only one slipping. "She hasn't accused St. James of sponsoring the VLF, but Duncan's concerned that was the terrorists' intent. The DNA of the driver matched one of Caesar's grand-nephews who remained loyal during Selene's rebellion."

"It says here his wife reported him missing two weeks ago," Mai said.

"Yeah, he was supposed to pick up his kids from school and never showed." Tension bled off Stan.

"They could have threatened to kill his kids when they nabbed him," Thad offered.

His suggestion sent a chill through Mai. Was that the real reason Miko and her girlfriend had broken up? The possibility of harm coming to the woman she loved might have driven her baby sister to do something stupid.

Mai frowned as she looked at Stan. "Those kind of stunts will attract too much Normal attention."

"Alex thinks that's their plan," he replied.

"Why out themselves if they want to stay vampires?" Thad said. "That makes no gahddamn sense." He flipped the turn signal and pulled into the second left turn lane to exit the airport.

Mai sighed. "There's more than a few sadists who enjoy spreading fear on both sides. If they get enough people afraid, no one will take the cure or the vaccine. They can increase their numbers and make a play for world domination."

"And how do we know this Vampire Liberation Front are actually vampires?" Thad asked.

"What are you suggesting?" Stan asked.

"The ones with the most to gain from the collapse of the Vampire Nation are the fairies," Thad bit out as he drove down the Strip.

"Wolford," she snapped.

"I'm just saying what none of you will," he growled back.

"And I will not tolerate racial slurs from any of my staff. Is that understood?" Mai said. Good. Now, she knew where things stood with him and could take steps.

After a long moment, Thad said. "Yes, ma'am."

"Do you have a particular problem with me or just sidhe in general?" Stan asked.

"I had a bunch of Unseelie murdering people in my jurisdiction." Thad glared at them in the rearview mirror.

"Ah. You're the former sheriff from Ohio." Stan shifted to look at Mai as well. "Wanna explain to me what's going on?"

There wasn't any tickle in her mind indicating Stan read it, but then, he never needed to resort to those tactics. She shrugged. "I wanted to see how Mr. Wolford would react given his previous encounters."

Thad didn't say anything more until he pulled in front of the Karnak's private entrance and stopped the limo. He turned to glare at her over the driver's seat. "You expected me to shoot the new boss?"

"Given Anne's report of what happened in Millersburg, it was a concern of mine." She returned his glare. "Considering your use of inappropriate language, it seems my concerns were warranted."

Thad sucked on his teeth for a moment before he turned to Stan. "I apologize, Mr. Gryffudd. It won't happen again."

"Good." Stan scowled at the Normal. "I'd hate to start my tenure here by turning you into a mushroom for insubordination."

Mai made a sound low in her throat. She didn't need Stan making his first day here a total disaster.

He shot her a look. "I'm just teasing him."

"I wouldn't go there if I were you, Mr. Gryffudd." Thad smirked. "You need Mai. She's the only one I've met who can keep Sam Ridgeway in line."

"Really?" Stan's left eyebrow quirked upward. "This could be an interesting assignment."

"You have a series of meetings tonight, sir," she reminded him. "You might want to get settled and cleaned up before then."

Thad climbed out of the driver's seat and circled the limo to the right side. "Slave driver," Stan whispered in her ear.

A shiver ran through her body that she managed to quell before Thad opened the passenger door. She climbed out on unsteady legs. Thankfully, Stan's attention was on his luggage after he followed her out of the vehicle. Maybe she should have Kunal deal with their new boss. Her judgment was too . . . compromised when it came to Stan.

It wasn't exactly either of their faults really. Maybe her cousin Tiffany was right that Murphy was the one true god. Mai swallowed a sigh. Anything that could go wrong had gone wrong in her life.

When Thad drove off to return the limo to the coven's vehicle pool, she led Stan to the private elevator for the penthouse. Sanjay, one of Kunal's Normal cousins, guarded the alcove. He pulled a pin made of Olympian bronze from his lapel.

She held out her hand, and he poked her little finger. Bright red blood welled on her skin, and Sanjay handed her an antiseptic wipe. While she cleaned off the excess blood, he repeated the procedure with Stan.

The enforcer inclined his head. "Thank you for your cooperation, Mr. Gryffudd."

"I'm happy you're not poking me with an iron pin," he said dryly.

A wry smile tilted Sanjay's mouth. "As Ms. Ridgeway says, it takes something a little more to detect the dino demons."

Mai headed for the elevator door.

"Have you had any more incidents here?" Stan asked, his long legs keeping pace.

"Not since Master St. James and his wife moved back to Los Angeles."

"So six months, then?"

She didn't want to talk about what had happened. The demon who had gotten into the kitchen still gave her nightmares. "Your biometrics are already encoded for access. Place your hand on the plate." She indicated the black plastic panel on the wall. "And say your name."

She turned to leave when he grabbed her arm. "Who else has access to the penthouse?"

His inquiry only reminded her of her limitations as a Normal. Something she had never questioned until the dinosaur demons had started their campaign against Sam. "Unfortunately, I haven't devised a way to keep out all deities."

He flashed his bright, charming smile. "I meant staff? Security?"

"Only myself, Kunal Saravati, and your executive assistant Staci Warner. One of us has to authorize access for anyone from another department such as housekeeping or room service. The enforcer on duty checks everyone who goes upstairs, but he or she can't control the elevator." At his odd expression, she added. "St. James is the only coven looking for dinosaur demons. They're not bothering anyone else."

"I'm aware. But maybe you should come up?" Another grin. "To make sure I understand all the security measures. I'd hate to set off a false alarm by brushing my teeth."

Her back stiffened. "I adhere to the standards set by our chief enforcer."

Stan glanced around and lowered his voice. "C'mon, Mai. No one's going to suspect anything by you showing me around."

She could feel her resolve melt. They'd never been assigned to the same city, so things between them had slipped under everyone's radar for years. But Stan Gryffudd had become her private addiction, and she didn't know how she'd deal with their new status.

And if she asked for a transfer, Duncan would want to know why since she was the highest-ranked enforcer within the Las Vegas branch of the coven. Hell, she had five years of seniority on Kunal, who'd been perfectly content with his string of drycleaners in Houston until Selene's rebellion.

"Please?" Stan's pale blue eyes didn't glow like a vamp's, but they held a different kind of intensity. One that dissolved the rest of her control into a massive puddle.

She mutely nodded.

He slapped his palm on the panel and said his name. With a *ding*, the doors parted, and they stepped inside the car. He pressed the "PH" button and glanced upward, no doubt noticing the security cameras.

"Guess I'm not sneaking a woman up here without you knowing."

She didn't take his bait. "There's a facility outside of the city that caters to supernatural clientele." She couldn't suppress her grimace. "It's my understanding Selene made frequent use of their services."

"Are you equating me with that bitch?"

Mai suppressed a smile at his aggrieved tone. "Of course not, sir."

He frowned at the panel. "Is 'L3' the old safehouse vault?"

"Yes."

"Maybe we should clear it out. We may need it if we catch one of these VLF bastards."

She chuckled. "Unfortunately, we cannot at this time."

"Why not?"

"Sam's storing some . . . courtship presents from previous suitors that she cannot exactly return. We don't have any other adequate facility to put them."

Stan groaned. "Should I ask?"

"The worst is a rosebush Ares gave her. It drinks blood, and has a tendency to wander around if it's not locked up."

"And she didn't take it with her to L.A. because . . . ?"

Mai looked up at Stan. "Do you really have to ask that?"

He rubbed his forehead. "Forget I said that. No interfering in other people's marriages. I blame jetlag."

The elevator doors slid open. Mai was pleased Staci had followed her suggestions. Greenery filled the penthouse living room. Compared to Duncan's minimalist tastes, it almost felt crowded with the multitude and variety of potted plants.

His gaze swept the area. "Did you do this?"

"Not in my job description, but since you couldn't bring your greenhouse with you—"

Stan dropped his bags, grabbed her and pressed her against the wall. His warm mouth covered hers. And she willingly gave in to him.

She was breathless when his attention turned to her neck.

"Morrigan, help me," he murmured against her skin. "You have no idea how much I've missed you."

She chuckled. "I can guess." It didn't help that his huge hands cupped her ass, and her legs were now wrapped around his waist.

"A quickie is not what I had in mind for the next time I saw you—"

Mai's walkie-talkie crackled to life. "Ms. Osaka, we need you in holding." Mike Warner's voice. Despite the werecoyote's youth, he didn't call her unless it was a real problem. Hell, he'd been the one to realize the new busboy wasn't remotely humanoid.

Her forehead fell to Stan's shoulder. "And we're not even going to get that."

He lowered her back to the floor, making a point of sliding her body down his length. Like she wasn't frustrated enough already.

She unclipped her radio from her belt. "What's the issue, Mike?"

"We have a player from Marley's roulette table who was a little too lucky. She smelled ozone."

Mai groaned. Last thing they needed was a cheating witch in the middle of all the Karnak's other problems. But Marley had been running roulette eighty years ago when she'd been Normal, and she had an eye for the scammers.

"I'll go down with you," Stan said. "A witch won't randomly fling spells if I'm there."

Mai pressed the response button. "We're on our way." She released the button before she said, "And they'll be fucking lucky if I don't stick them in the vault with the blood-sucking rose plant."

Chapter 2

Stan was all for Mai's idea of sticking the cheating player in the vault. It'd been nearly a year since he'd seen her. Phone calls, texts, and video conferencing weren't enough, but he respected her wishes when it came to keeping their relationship quiet.

Though he had a strong suspicion Sam knew, especially after she threatened to castrate him if Mai got hurt just before he left Los Angeles for his flight to Vegas. From the goddess's brimstone and decay scent, it wasn't Mai's personal safety she was concerned about. Sam still held a grudge that both the Summer and Winter Queens had a price on her head when she'd first been created.

Mai led him to the hotel's equivalent of a little jail. A vampire and a werecoyote waited for them in the office area. She quickly made official introductions though he and Kunal had met before.

The werecoyote was the more interesting of the two. 'Coyotes rarely mixed with other weres, much less any of the supernatural races.

Mai took charge. "Where's Marley?"

"Waiting for her table replacement," Mike said. "The pit boss said the back-up was running late because traffic lights on the Strip were out from north of the airport."

Stan exchanged a look with Mai. It wouldn't take much to hex a city's traffic control system, but were the events connected?

"Where's the witch?" he asked.

"Witch?" Mike couldn't suppress his grin. "Dude, the guy in Room Two is one of your people."

"My people?" A sinking feeling in his gut killed whatever pleasure remained in Stan at seeing Mai again.

"Did you test him?" Mai asked.

Mike nodded. "Definitely not a dino demon."

"From the honeysweet smell, he's definitely fae," Kunal affirmed.

"But to warn you, his form shimmered when I stabbed him with the needle. Some kind of glamor on him." Mike frowned. "And . . . he's Summer folk."

Even Kunal gave the werecoyote an odd look. "How can you tell the difference between Seelie and Unseelie?"

The young were shrugged. "That's like saying all vampires smell the same. You don't smell like Marley."

Kunal gave Mai a look that could only be worded as "Please let me drain him."

Duncan was correct that the werecoyote made an excellent addition to the Karnak's security. Stan steeled himself. However, it was time to act like the head of the Karnak. "Has he given a statement?"

Kunal shook his head. "He only said he was perfectly happy to wait until our boss got here."

"Then let's explain the Karnak's policies to him." Mai's icy tone said whoever was here would be lucky to leave the casino intact.

Stan knew better than to touch her when she was in this mood. "How about when we go inside, I do the talking?"

Her eyes narrowed to dark slits. "What's that supposed to mean?"

He matched her glare. "First of all, we're not blowing the vampire-fae treaty out of the water to satisfy our egos. Second, if he is fae, that means he is up to something, but ripping off the casino isn't his primary objective."

After a moment, her body relaxed a fraction. Stan wondered if the other two men could even discern the difference.

Mai's chin lifted. "Questioning a suspect is your prerogative, sir."

"Thank you." He inclined his head.

He strode toward the interrogation room marked with a large number "2" on the door. But when he yanked it open, nothing could have prepared him for the person waiting inside.

"Riley?"

She deliberately flipped her deep red hair back and gave him a sultry once over. "Hi, big boy. How's things hanging?"

Chapter 3

Mai's attention swiveled from the prisoner to Stan's startled expression back to the prisoner. Grandfather had arranged for the spells Selene's eclectic witch had placed on the Karnak to be removed years ago. The bastard had been corrupted by the Old Ones, ancient gods that the dinosaurs had worshipped long before humans appeared on the planet. Except no one had a clue at the time of Selene's rebellion what the witch had really been up to. Grandfather simply didn't trust anyone affiliated with the traitor bitch.

Grandfather also hadn't bothered to ask a witch he trusted to replace any detection spells. He felt a vampire presence, and their keen sense of smell, was sufficient for security purposes, and he didn't want their previous master, Caesar Augustine, to suspect more hinky business was going on behind his back.

Maybe she needed to rethink Grandfather's policy, and have a talk with Quinn, the chief enforcer for the Las Vegas witch coven. He would be willing to cut her a deal in exchange for special grade ammunition.

Not to mention, any fae would think twice before walking into Quinn's casino, the Scheherazade, and casting a spell. Mixing witch and fae magic often had explosively fatal results.

"Stan, tell your pet to quit growling under her breath." Riley flashed Mai a sly smile. "It's unbecoming in a bitch."

She wanted to laugh at the fae's piss-poor attempt to get a rise out of her, but she promised she'd let Stan handle this. But if the fae had cast a glamour to appear male, that may have been the spell Marley and Mike detected.

Stan crossed his arms and scowled at the woman. "Why are you here, Riley?"

"I can't visit an old friend?" She pouted. "After all the fun we've had over the centuries?"

"I seem to recall you leaving me in the Tower of London, chained with iron and awaiting the headsman. Not to mention, I only arrived in Las Vegas a little over an hour ago. How'd you find out I was coming here?"

Mai examined the woman more closely. Maybe Alex's fears about a leak were well-founded after all. However, their suspect may have simply been here to accost whoever Duncan assigned to Las Vegas.

The half-fae's expression transformed from a pout to a smirk. "Really? You think I can't perform a little divination spell?"

"Why are you here?" Stan repeated.

The woman shrugged. "I needed the money."

Enough was enough. Mai didn't wait for his permission. She circled the table, hauled the woman upright, and slammed her torso down on the table. No doubt Kunal and Mike had searched the bitch, but they could have missed something if this Riley's glamour covered the scent.

An elbow on a pressure point on the woman's neck dissuaded her from struggling. Mai swept her Donald Duck watch over the fae. The device beeped when Mai's wrist passed over the woman's brassiere band. She repeated the movement to double-check. Another *beep*.

Thank goodness for Sam and her power practice sessions, though her taste in accessories left something to be desired. One would think there was enough death goddess essence around the Karnak to warn off supernatural stupidity. But the magick detection ability of the charmed watch Sam had given Mai made up for some of the craziness of having a deity in residence.

The fae hissed in alarm. "What are you doing to me?"

Mai pulled out her switchblade and flicked it open. "Not a thing if you hold still. And this is steel. In case you were wondering."

"I have rights," the woman muttered.

Mai flipped up the woman's black gauzy shirt with the tip of her blade. "You not only cast a glamour, you carried an additional spell into a gambling facility. Who would you like us to call first? The state gaming board or your queen?"

"Neither," the woman breathed.

So she was half-fae as Mai suspected. With the negotiated truce between the fae and the vampires, a full-blooded fae would be screaming bloody murder for her queen about now. The Nevada Gaming Board wouldn't be so lenient with any magickal shenanigans in a state casino, regardless of the race of the entity pulling such shit.

Mai ran a finger lightly over the eyelet tape. Something small, maybe button-sized, had been sewn inside. She carefully sliced the fabric. Whatever the little disk was, it sizzled when her blade brushed it.

She looked up at Stan. "Sir, would you please tell Kunal I need a glass bowl and a pair of bronze tweezers?"

Whatever Stan was thinking was well-hidden in the depths of his eyes. He simply nodded and exited the room.

"You're just a passing fancy to him, dear," the woman sneered.

Mai leaned closer to the fae's ear. "If I were sleeping with him, do you think it is wise to taunt me while I'm holding iron at your back?"

The woman kept quiet until Stan returned, Kunal behind him with the requested items. The vampire rounded the table. He plucked the disk from its hiding place with the tweezers and dropped it in the bowl.

"Check her," Mai ordered.

Kunal handed the bowl and tweezers to Stan before the vampire checked the woman's odor. "She's clean as far as I can tell."

Mai snapped the switchblade closed. "Now, you're going to answer Master Gryffudd's questions fully and completely." She released the pressure point and slammed the half-fae back down on the hard plastic chair to emphasize her point.

"I didn't know you were into the receiving end of the rough stuff, Stanley," the woman purred. "We could do a threesome."

"Why are you here, Riley?" Stan said for the third time. "You could have hit any other casino." He glanced at the small object in the bowl he held before he set it on the table out of her reach. "And this is definitely not a luck charm."

The woman's attention settled on Mai. "What are you? You smell like death."

Mai regarded her prisoner. Was the half-fae smelling her charmed watch? Or had she spent so much time with Sam that she'd been affected by the goddess? Had the supernatural staff noticed the change in her scent and not told her?

On the other hand, the prisoner had given her something to use.

She let a slow smile stretch her mouth. "You should smell death through this entire city. Or don't you know whose territory you're in?"

The woman's gaze flicked to Mai's wrist and back. Good. The bitch wasn't entirely stupid.

With one hand on the back of the chair and the other on the table, Mai leaned closer. "Don't even think about stealing my watch. Or destroying it. *She*'ll know." She took a step back. "Now, answer Master Gryffudd's question. Unless you really want to enjoy our coven facilities in Los Angeles. Maybe *she*'ll even let you gamble for your life."

All hints of femme fatale fled from their prisoner. A sheen of sweat shone on the half-fae's forehead, and her alabaster skin turned pasty gray. Good. If she wasn't aware of the deal between Sam and Morrigan to keep their respective people in check, she was still smart enough to not want the attention of a death goddess.

The woman turned back to Stan. "I was sent here to plant that charm inside the Karnak."

"Who sent you?" he said.

"Your father," she whispered.

Any color left in Stan's face drained away. "That's impossible. He's dead."

The prisoner shrugged. "That's what I heard, too, but I swear on Lugh's sword your father and one of his men approached me with the job."

Mai kept her own face impassive. Stan never talked about his parents. No one outside of his cousin Harry, except perhaps Caesar and Duncan, even knew which of his parents was fae. That this woman knew sent a little trill of jealousy through Mai, which she quickly tamped down. She and Stan may be lovers, but there had been no declaration between them. Not even a request for exclusivity though she hadn't looked at another male since their affair started five years ago.

"Why are you doing this?" Stan asked.

The prisoner shrugged again. "They offered me a lot of money, and they said they'd kill me if I didn't agree."

"What does the talisman you snuck in do?"

"I don't know."

Mai flicked her wrist, grabbed the half-fae's hair, and rested the edge of her blade against the bitch's neck. The woman hissed in pain. Her skin turned red, and a faint burning smell filled the room.

"Want to try again, Riley?" Stan asked.

The woman involuntarily shivered beneath Mai's grip. "I swear by Lugh's sword. I don't know what it is."

Stan's frown turned into a scowl. "Where did they tell you to put it?"

The woman's throat bobbed. "I was supposed to place it on a door in the Karnak's basement."

"Which door?" Kunal growled.

The woman flicked a glance at him. Mai pressed her knife to remind the half-fae of the real danger. Her skin blistered around the edge of the blade.

"Th-the door to your second vault. Th-the old vampire safe room."

Several words flitted through Mai's mind, none of them fit for polite company. This wasn't a simple robbery. Whoever extorted Stan's former associate planned to unleash Sam's things they kept locked up. From the expressions on Stan and Kunal's faces, the two men had come to the same conclusion.

"What is it they want from the vault?" Mai said.

"I don't know."

Mai pressed the tip of her knife to the half-fae's skin. A droplet of blood sizzled and steamed. "What are they planning to do with the contents of the vault?"

"I don't know!" Riley wailed.

"Ma'am, she's telling the truth," Kunal murmured.

Mai withdrew the blade and deliberately made a show of wiping off the blood on the half-fae's blouse. Beyond Stan and the handful of half-fae who'd sought sanctuary with Augustine Coven, she didn't trust any of the fairy folk. Not after what the Seelie did to Duncan. And especially not after they sided with the necromancer who killed Grandfather and Jamal.

Maybe she was just as biased as Thad was.

"We have everything we'll get out of her," Stan said. "Kunal, you want to escort her to the front door—"

"No!" Riley shrieked. "You can't let me go!"

Mai didn't need supernatural senses to detect why the woman panicked. "They'll kill you for failing."

"Stanley, I beg you!" Tears trickled down Riley's face. "For our past, if not our future, grant me sanctuary."

He gave her a bemused look. "Tower of London," he enunciated slowly and clearly.

"I'm sorry. I'm really and truly sorry for abandoning you." When he didn't respond to her apology, she turned to Kunal. "Don't let him do this. Let me talk to your master. I'll pledge my allegiance to him!"

Mai couldn't stop her abrupt bark of laughter. It was better than the fury boiling under the surface of her skin. "A fae begging a vampire? Now I've seen everything."

"May I speak to you outside, Ms. Osaka?" Stan said. His scowl was back, this time aimed at her.

She fixed a neutral expression on her face and tried to still the anger writhing underneath her skin. But her tone wasn't properly deferential when she replied, "Yes, sir."

Mai stalked around the table. She didn't need extra-sensory powers to see Riley's slight smirk from her peripheral vision. Stan motioned for Kunal to join them in the hallway. The vampire grabbed the bowl with the talisman as he exited.

Once the interrogation room door was closed, Mai whirled to face Stan.

"With all due respect, Master Gryffudd, you may not be thinking clearly in this matter."

"Do you really hate fae that much?" His blue eyes stared into hers.

Shit. She hadn't realized how far she stuck her foot down her throat. "This isn't about you. Or me. But you have to admit the queens have been causing trouble for Aug—" She swallowed her frustration. "—us for years."

"Am I really part of 'us'?" The hurt was evident in his expression. "Sam had every reason to be suspicious of me. She's right. I could have used her to buy my way into the good graces of the Winter Queen. But I'm not stupid enough to believe turning Sam over to my father's people would have actually bought me anything than enemies. The fae dislike halflings more than the humans do. I'm not stupid enough to turn my back on the people who've watched out for me when no one else would."

Stan was right. Mai crossed her arms and stared at the floor for a long moment. Her bluntness was the reason she'd had so few romantic relationships. But this wasn't just her lack of tact. This was about competition. Another trait she took too far, as Grandfather had often reminded her.

"I'm sorry," she whispered. "My concerns aren't about you or Harry." Admitting her jealous streak in front of Kunal would be a damn stupid move. She looked up at Stan. "However, I still don't believe you're thinking clearly when it comes to an ex-girlfriend who betrayed you."

"This isn't about my past either." He sucked in a deep breath and raked his hands over his crewcut. "Okay, this isn't about my past with Riley. I'm more concerned about who or what approached her to plant that thing, whatever it is."

Kunal cleared his throat to remind them he was still there. His eyes glowed a dim gold even under the hall's fluorescent lighting. "Forgive me for asking the obvious, Master Gryffudd. While your acquaintance may have told the truth concerning who she believed approached her, why do you believe your father is dead?"

Mai held her breath, waiting for Stan's answer. If his father was Normal, he would have died centuries ago.

Stan's jaw muscles twitched before he finally said, "Actually, it depends on whether you believe Anne, Colin and Sam. My father is, or was, Duke Hoaran-cill. The Winter Queen's assassin."

CHAPTER 4

Stan waited, expecting condemnation to follow the shock on Mai and Kunal's faces. Or worse, Mai to break up with him. He hadn't realized how deep her prejudice went. Maybe he'd been fooling himself, given her loyalty to Sam.

"Oh, Kali-ma." Kunal groaned and wiped a hand down his face. "Please tell me you're kidding."

"Believe me, I wish I wasn't," Stan muttered.

Instead of anger, Mai turned thoughtful. "I don't doubt anyone's word concerning the events in Ohio and the attempts on Anne and Sam's lives." She cocked her head and focused on him. "Let's assume Colin indeed killed your father. Then we have three possibilities. Someone constructed a glamour good enough to fool another fae. There's a family member with enough of a resemblance to pass as your father. Or we have a dino demon masquerading as your father."

Kunal snorted. "Passing for a sidhe noble is a lot harder than passing as a busboy."

Mike poked his head around the corner. "Ms. Osaka? Marley's here."

Stan headed toward the set of cubicles Mai and her people used as offices. She could have used the original security chief's private office. Instead, she'd turned it into a changing room for her staff. According to her official request, she claimed it would provide a more congenial atmosphere. After the revolving door the Las Vegas positions had become over the last decade, the coven needed all the congeniality it could achieve in the city.

According to her bio, Marley Wyckoff had worked for Bugsy Siegel's casino when he moved into what was then a dusty, little town. Her boyfriend at the time had been stupid enough to skim from the gangster. The gangster assumed Marley was in on the plan with her boyfriend, and the pair of lovers had been taken out into the desert and shot. She survived long enough to be found by members of the coven and was the next to last person to formally petition Caesar Augustine, the coven's former master, to be Turned in the twentieth century.

Marley grinned when she spotted Stan. The vampire had chopped off the waist-length blond locks she'd worn the last time he'd seen her. Now, her hair was nearly as short and spiky as his.

"It's been a while Marley. I miss your old style."

"That was in the '70's, Mr. Gryffudd," she said. "You might want to consider blending in a little bit yourself."

He returned her smile, ran a hand over his hair, and shrugged. "I just wait a couple of decades for my style to swing around again."

Marley shook her head. "We can reminisce later. This is about the red-headed broad who came back disguised as a man, right?"

"Came back?" Stan glanced at Mai who frowned.

Marley shrugged. "That's the other reason I reported her. Besides the smell of active magick, of course."

"Wait a minute." Mike actually appeared offended. "How could you tell he was a she? He, ur, she definitely smelled male."

"Shampoo." Marley grinned. "She remembered to use men's grooming products everywhere but her hair. Not too many men use Strawberry Spring shampoo *and* conditioner."

"I'll give Quinn a call and have him check out the talisman—" Mai started.

"Excuse me?" Stan wasn't sure whether to be offended or amused at her presumption. Nor did he miss the slight inhale of Marley and the other two enforcers. Damn, he hadn't been in Vegas two hours, and here he was, undermining his girlfriend's authority. Centuries ago, he'd been the outsider the vampires didn't trust. Not to mention, Duncan wouldn't trust any enforcer that didn't meet his exacting standards, much less the head of his personal security team.

Mai blushed. "My apologies, sir. Master St. James gave me far more latitude in these matters."

Stan grinned to take the sting from his accidental insult. "It's not Duncan's judgment I'm questioning. It's my own ego getting in the way. I've been edged out of the coven picture as the go-to person for magickal questions long before Quinn."

"Yes, sir." Mai had a curious expression on her face. He'd be hearing about this later.

"Please call him. It wouldn't hurt to have a backup in case Riley's employer booby-trapped the talisman." Stan frowned as he stared at the little object in the bowl. The idea of his father still alive and running around concerned him more than the possibility of a dino demon attack.

Because if the Unseelie who approached Riley was his father, he'd be gunning for revenge.

Chapter 5

After giving the chief enforcer of Golden Eagle, the Las Vegas witch coven, a call, Mai pressed the number for Thad's house.

"Wolford."

"Thad, we need you to come to Master Gryffudd's office—"

"If this is about what I said when we picked him up at the airport—"

"It's not," she snapped. She took a deep breath. "I'm sorry, Thad. This is about your encounter with the Unseelie in Ohio. Could you bring Leslie with you?"

The other end of the receiver was quiet other than the jabbering of small children before the enforcer muttered, "Shit. This isn't good, is it?"

"No. It's not."

"Doug will be at the house to pick up the grandpups in about ten minutes. We'll come straight there."

"Thank you, Thad." Mai hung up, her faith in him reassured. Whatever his personal feelings, when the chips were down, he was all about duty.

—•—

Mai stood with Mike by the seated and cuffed Riley in the darkened room. Stan's office smelled like a thunderstorm rolling off the mountains and into the city while he and Quinn used their respective abilities to inspect the button-sized object in the glass bowl.

Thad and his wife slipped inside and quietly shut the door behind them. Leslie gave a quick smile to her youngest, but was smart enough not to give him a hug while he was on duty. For as crochety as the werecoyote was, she could be pretty damn maternal when it came to anyone she decided she liked.

Which meant Mai was the recipient of her hug. She awkwardly patted the older woman on the back.

Leslie released her, leaned over Riley, and sniffed. "What's a Summer fae doing here?"

"That's what the new boss is trying to find out, honey," Thad murmured.

Finally, Quinn whistled while Stan hit the switch to open the vertical blinds. The setting sun flared red and orange over the mountains.

"Well, the spells on the talisman only activate when they're at a very specific set of geographic coordinates and altitude." Quinn folded his hands together and rested them on top of his tight black curls as he eyed Mai. "Someone with specific knowledge of your casino helped with the planning of this little escapade."

"Spells?" she asked.

"Yeah." Stan crossed his arms over his chest. "There's the one that melts the secondary vault door. A second opens a passage to Otherwhere. The third calls the Wild Hunt."

Thad grunted. "Thought only the queens' consorts could do that."

Suspicion flared on Stan's face, but Mai interrupted before the two men started sniping at each other again. "There's a difference between the ability to call a hunt and the authority to do it. Technically, any of the high fae or sidhe could call the lesser fae to a hunt. But the queens claim it as their royal prerogative. The consorts are only supposed to do it with the queens' permission."

"So there's nothing really stopping any sidhe from doing it, right?" Thad insisted.

"Mr. Wolford!" she snapped. The last thing she wanted was to dismiss a capable enforcer, but if Thad kept up, she'd have to. They couldn't afford dissension in the ranks.

Thad scowled at the group. "Would you please hear me out before you start labeling me as a racist redneck asshole?"

Stan blew out a deep breath. "Go ahead, Mr. Wolford."

"Here's how I see it. The last Summer Queen tried to use that basketball player to kill Sam, but one of the dukes staged a coup and cut a deal to keep Sam from killing 'em all. Rather than learn a damn thing from that little trick, the Winter Queen sent her assassin who used that Indian spirit—"

"Native American," the entire group, except Leslie and Riley, said, though the female half-fae snickered.

"Jesus Christ!" Thad yelled. "Can I finish without the PC commentary?"

Stan waved his hand. "Please continue."

"—to try and kill Sam. But Sam and Morrigan cut a deal that the vampires and fae stay outta each other's way. Well, there was a group of sidhe with Hoarancill that we exiled from Holmes County," Thad continued. "They were Hoarancill's people. Wouldn't they want revenge? Or would the Winter Queen stop them?"

Mai looked at Stan along with everyone else in the room, but it was Riley who answered.

"The Winter Queen is even less tolerant of failure than the Summer Queen's predecessor, especially since Hoarancill and his band were thwarted by a group of Normals. Best case scenario was their immediate execution."

Thad glared at the woman. "And in what scenario would they remain alive?"

"Shit," Stan muttered. "She would have banished them to Otherwhere."

Thad scratched his chin. "Well, the last time any of St. James Coven saw Marcus Giovanni and the red-headed daughter of the last full-blooded dino demon was in California when she cut a path into Otherwhere and they both went through. From what Anne said, it took a lot of Tuatha to fix the rip in reality."

Too many ugly thoughts wound through Mai's brain. "I know they wouldn't have given you names, but did you—"

"I brought copies of all my files from that case, and yeah, I got pictures." Thad grinned. "As pissed as Hoarancill's ninja squad was that a bunch of Normals busted 'em, thought it'd be a good idea." He eyed Stan. "Mind if I use your computer, Mr. Gryffudd?"

Stan stepped aside and waved Thad to his desk. The expression on his face disturbed Mai. Whatever was going on, he knew more than he was saying.

Which meant they needed to have a very long talk once they were alone. She couldn't do her job effectively if he had more skeletons in his closet than the ex-girlfriend showing up at their roulette tables.

Thad punched the button that turned on the monitor which nearly covered one wall. "Anne and John Robbins, Dare Coven's chief enforcer, could only identify a couple of the deceased."

Crime scene photos popped up on the large screen. "First one's Hoarancill himself. John said the lady was the duke's only daughter. The first guy was her husband. The rest he didn't know."

"Aren't you going to tell them who the rest of those bodies are, Stanley?" Riley taunted.

"Well," Leslie drawled. "At least he ain't their omega, little girl."

Riley opened her mouth, and Mai stepped between the two women. They needed the Summer halfling alive. For now.

"I'd take a closer look at those pictures before you say anything more, Riley," Mai said. "The corpses with weapon marks are the deaths caused by a vampire and a Normal. Make sure you count them. Who do you think was responsible for the rest of the deaths?"

The halfling audibly gulped. Good. Maybe it was sinking through her brain just how deep in shit she was, and what Leslie could do to her.

"Thad, let me see the pictures of the survivors," Stan said quietly.

Ten more photos appeared on the screen, the faces of all in various stages of anger. "One of my deputies Jimmy Birkheimer made sure to take a photo of each one before he'd let 'em off the stock truck at the county line." Thad chuckled. "He's got 'em in a mugshot book in case they break their word and come back to Holmes County."

"They can't," Stan murmured as he stared at the photos. He must have felt Thad's attention. "From how Colin worded things to extract their promise, they literally cannot put a foot in your old stomping grounds until something happens that dissolves Holmes County as a legal entity."

"Well, damn," Thad said. "I should have extended it to the whole of the United States."

"That would have caused other problems," Stan said absently as he resumed staring at the photos.

Mai stepped forward staring at the screen herself. The resemblance among most of the Unseelie squad to the dead duke was too great to be chance. She turned to examine Stan's face. Thin the bone structure a bit. Narrow the lips. Lengthen his hair. Add pointed ears.

Her heart skipped a beat. If it weren't for his human genes, Stan and one of the exiled sidhe could pass as twins.

His blue eyes met hers. There was so much anger and sorrow in their depths. She wanted to hug him, comfort him. But she couldn't. Not in front of witnesses.

And what she knew of Unseelie culture chilled her to the bone.

"He's not going to stop until we're dead, or he's dead," she said.

"I know," Stan murmured.

"Who?" Thad looked from Mai to Stan and back again.

"Jarunmisanrill," Riley said. "Stanley's big brother."

Chapter 6

Stan tried to quell the race of emotions in his heart. Everyone here at the Karnak was in danger because of him. When Caesar had told him his father was dead, why had he foolishly believed the insanity of his father's family was over?

Thad glanced between the monitor and Stan. "Ah, shit," he muttered. "Hoarancill's second in command. He's your brother?"

"Half-brother, and it's not like we were raised together. He's at least a millennium older than me."

"That explains how he was able to fool Riley." Mai waved a hand at Stan's ex, who pouted in her chair.

"I wasn't fooled," she protested. "Both Hoarancill and Jarunmisanrill came to me."

"That's impossible," Thad declared. "We turned the duke's body along with the others over to the Dare Coven to return to the Unseelie."

"We're not questioning your or John's actions." Mai shook her head. "Jarunmisanrill probably recruited another family member to masquerade as his father. Someone willing to defy the Winter Queen to satisfy their clan honor. However, it doesn't explain why Jarunmisanrill plotted to set that talisman here in the hotel. He had to have started this scheme long before Master St. James named Stan to head the Karnak."

"Master Gryffudd arriving here today was simply convenience." Kunal spoke for the first time. "Jarunmisanrill can't touch Anne or Colin without bringing the full wrath of the courts down on his head for breaking the truce. Sam's essentially invulnerable to his power. He definitely cannot harm those still in Ohio, who were responsible for his defeat, because of his oath. Thad, Leslie, and their family were probably Jarunmisanrill's original targets."

"Wait here just a damn minute." Leslie's fingers twitched toward her purse and stopped. The need for nicotine must be driving her insane. Thankfully, she didn't pull out a cigarette. Stan didn't want to start his working relationship with the were over her habit. The lingering smoke on her body and clothes was barely tolerable as it was.

"Why go through all this bullshit?" Leslie continued. "Why not hit us at the house during Sunday dinner?"

Leslie was right. There was something they were missing. Stan stared at the screen again. His half-brother was nothing if not economical. He'd want to kill the maximum number of people with the least effort.

He turned to Riley. "How would your employer know you followed his orders?"

She shrugged. "Why wouldn't I do what I agreed to?"

Stan chuckled. He should've known. "You haven't been paid yet."

Quinn snapped his fingers. "Of course! The geo-location spell would tell them when it was activated."

"And when they have neither the confirmation or Riley appearing for her payment, they'll know something's wrong," Mai added. "Is there any way to replicate just the geo-location spell alone? Or to deactivate the other two spells on the talisman?"

Stan rubbed his lower jaw as he considered her words. "We can't deactivate the other spells. All of them are too intertwined. However, I can replicate the geolocation spell." He looked at Riley. "What do you plan to do with her?"

Mai's smile was pure viciousness. "She's going to collect her payment."

———•———

An hour later, Stan had his geolocation spell prepped to the same frequency as the one on the talisman. If he hadn't been working with the witches in San Francisco and Los Angeles the last few years, he wouldn't have been able to recreate the delicate spell to pull off Mai's plan.

He still didn't like the idea of Mai accompanying Riley to the rendezvous. And his feelings had nothing to do with the ugly looks the two women had been shooting each other all evening when they thought no one was looking. Sending any supernatural would have tipped off his half-brother.

He set the bit of deer bone in the carpet at the base of the door and muttered a word in Old Gaelic. An inaudible hum filled his head. He rose and stretched before he said, "Ms. Osaka, I'd like to speak with you privately for a moment."

She followed him as he walked far enough down the hall not even Kunal or the werecoyotes could hear him. When he turned to face her, her hands were clasped behind her back and her feet positioned as if she were at parade rest.

"Yes, sir?" She blinked innocently, but he wasn't fooled for a moment.

"You don't have anything to prove to me. And you definitely don't have anything to prove to Riley."

"I don't know what you're referring to, sir." But the twitch along her jawline said she did.

He crossed his arms and scowled down at her. "What do I have to do to convince you things have been over between me and Riley for a very, very long time?"

"Let me kill her."

He blinked a couple of times as he tried to process her words, not sure if she were joking. She did have a dry sense of humor, but he'd seen Mai at her deadliest. He'd also seen her drunk and terrified in the aftermath of the zombie attack that killed half her family and left her sister in the critical care unit of the hospital. He knew damn well he was one of the few people she let see her softer side. But this jealousy thing?

"You can't do your job if you let your emotions get in the way." He uncrossed his arms, wanting to grab and shake her, but he caught Kunal from the corner of his eye, giving them an odd look. "And right now, you are getting too worked up over Riley."

"I am, or you are?" The look she gave him couldn't be called a glare. More like . . . disappointment. "Because I'm not the one acting like an idiot since she let herself be caught."

"Let herself be caught?"

"Let herself," Mai repeated. "She made a point of coming in twice and sitting at a vampire's roulette table both times. Riley could have been in and out the first time with none of us the wiser, but she didn't. She made a point of waiting until you arrived before she brought in the talisman. She made a point of getting herself caught in order to confront you. And if you don't know why, and you won't let me kill her, then it's my job to discover what she's really up to."

Mai pivoted on her boot heel and stalked back down the hallway. And for the first time in centuries, Stan felt thoroughly confused by a Normal woman.

CHAPTER 7

Mai grabbed Riley's arm and hauled her out to the hotel's vehicle pool. Thad marched behind them, whistling an old Disney tune. This was one situation were the enforcer's wariness of the fae would be useful.

One of the Fryer girls sat in the booth. She grinned when they walked up. "What'll it be tonight, Ms. Osaka?"

"Five-oh-one." Mai couldn't tell the twins apart to save her life. If anyone asked, she'd lie and say she didn't want to reveal the werecoyote's name to a hostile fae.

Thad stepped up to the counter. "How's your mom doing?"

"A little stir-crazy being on half-time." The girl handed the keys to him before she gave Mai a pleading look. "I know Mr. and Mrs. St. James wanted to make sure Mom was fully recovered, but could you put in a word with the new boss about Mom coming back full time?"

Mai understood Duncan and Sam's guilt. The dino demon had gutted Natalie Fryer when it rampaged through the hotel kitchen. Even with her were-coyote toughness and Golden Eagle Coven's healer, Natalie almost didn't make it. A couple of the busboys and one of their sous chefs hadn't.

"We'll talk to him," Thad said. When Mai glared at him, he shrugged. "We need everyone on deck if we're going to keep getting unwanted visitors." He shot a pointed look at Riley, who pretended to examine the nails on her free hand.

Mai jerked her in the direction of the armored and weaponized SUV she'd selected. Riley had to jog on her heels to keep up, which had been Mai's intention.

"They're going to know something's up if you walk into the restaurant with me," she huffed.

"Let me worry about what your employer thinks."

Thad chuckled as he pressed the fob. The *beep* of the vehicle unlocking echoed against the low concrete ceiling.

"What's so funny?" Riley snapped.

"Scammers are all the same no matter the species," Thad replied.

Riley sneered at the enforcer. "Says the stupid mortal mated with a 'coyote."

"Sweetheart, your people's shenanigans are the reason the Millersburg pack split in two. And the gals that moved out here with their kids to give 'em a better life like fae 'bout as much as I do." Thad delivered his speech in a matter-of-fact voice, but a hard glint shone in his eyes as he opened the rear passenger door.

Mai suppressed a grin, but it wasn't due to Thad playing the race card. It had been apparent Leslie never pictured herself as an alpha. But when it came to old friends trying to make a living with their mates imprisoned or dead and getting their pups away from the heroin epidemic that had replaced meth back home, the werecoyote couldn't turn them away. And Thad and his daughter had been part of the exodus, although for very different reasons.

Ironically, Sam had brought Leslie and her pups to Las Vegas five years ago because she feared the Unseelie Queen would find a way to retaliate against the family for assisting Anne in rescuing Sam from Hoarancill.

Mai sighed. Unfortunately, the fae's memories were as long as their lives, and they were very patient. The odds were Sam's initial concerns had merit. Why else would someone enlist Stan's ex-girlfriend?

Once she and Stan's ex-bitch were seated in the rear bench seat, Thad climbed into the driver's seat. He started the vehicle and guided it out of the private garage. The subtle vibration of the electric motor beneath the soles of Mai's boots were the only indication the SUV moved on its own power.

Her watch beeped, and the acrid odor of ozone filled the cabin a split-second before Riley yelped.

Mai eyed the half-fae. "Feeling suicidal?"

Riley pressed herself against the opposite door. "I wasn't even trying to—"

"Slap a glamour on us?" Thad growled from the front seat. "Yeah, you were." He mumbled a few other impolite terms, though they questioned her hygiene and intelligence, not her parentage.

Good. He'd taken Mai's lesson earlier today to heart.

"Just because we aren't witches doesn't mean you aren't going to suffer magickal backlash. And I'm fairly certain a goddess trumps a half-fae." Mai watched the other woman. "And I've already seen what happens to a full sidhe stupid enough to sling spells at a mere necromancer."

She left out the nightmares still plaguing her years after the Seelie Queen's betrayal of David Head. Of what he'd done to the fae who'd been ordered to kill him.

For now.

"I heard . . . about that," Riley muttered.

Mai cocked her head. "So why don't you believe St. James Coven would protect itself? Even Morrigan admitted your people had been picking a fight where none previously existed."

"They're not my people," Riley spat.

"Then why work for them?"

The half-fae stared at the neon-lit night sky of the Strip before she turned back to Mai. "Like I said, they threatened to kill me if I didn't do what they wanted."

"So why not simply use a Blood Seal if they wanted to guarantee your co-operation?" Thad asked.

Riley jumped. "How do you know about a Blood Seal?"

The enforcer snorted. "Sweetheart, I may have been born at night, but it wasn't last night."

Something wasn't right. No fae Mai had ever met was that naïve about Normals. It was an act. It had to be. Maybe Riley had counted too much on renewing her relationship with Stan. Was that what attracted him to her all those centuries ago? The pretense of innocence?

And it had to be centuries because the Tower of London hadn't been used for executions in ages.

Damn, she really should have taken the time to question Stan more thoroughly about his relationship with Riley. Not because she really wanted to know.

Of course not. She needed to know her opponents better because her gut said Riley was in this mess deeper than even the half-fae realized.

———•—•———

Mai examined the dark windows of the little strip mall. The place Riley claimed for her rendezvous site certainly wasn't reassuring.

"Gahddamn, this screams, 'Set up,'" Thad drawled.

"As the coven master's wife would say, 'No shit, Sherlock,'" Mai replied. "Were you really expecting anything different? I'd have to get closer to detect any illusions though."

Thad snorted. "I'd ask Sam for an upgrade to that watch if I were you."

"You're not going to ask me if there's a glamour on the building?"

Mai and Thad looked at her and then each other before returning their attention to the hulking mass of glass and steel. Did their little sneak really think they'd believe anything she said?

Mai watched for movement, unusual shadows, anything that could indicate who or what may be inside. Nothing about this smelled right. She would have preferred more planning, but as Kunal pointed out, they wouldn't know the purpose of the trap until it was sprung. Personally, she would just kill Riley if she were their opponent. Her usefulness was done at this point. "If we're not back in ten—"

"I know the drill." Except Thad sounded worried, not defensive.

Mai didn't blame him, but she refused to place any of the enforcers under her command in a situation she was not willing to face herself. "Let's go."

She and Riley climbed out of the SUV. At least, the half-fae wasn't foolish enough to try to run. Which meant she expected Jarunmisanrill and whoever had disguised himself as Hoarancill to hunt her down.

Or she planned to trade Mai for additional money. If Mai gambled, she'd place a year's salary that it was the latter.

She followed Riley a pace behind and to the right. Hopefully, it was enough of an appearance of a bodyguard to throw off whoever, or whatever, the half-fae was meeting.

Riley yanked on the glass door of a defunct Mexican restaurant from the faded signage. The tickle of dust in Mai's nostrils as they entered felt too real. Riley sneezed before she called out, "Hello?"

"Are you that afraid of us, little halfing?" A shadow separated itself from the rest. Moonlight glinted in his silver-white hair. The midnight black chain-mail he wore absorbed the rest of the ambient glow from the streetlights. "You brought a champion?"

Mai recognized the Unseelie from Thad's photo of Stan's half-brother. She shrugged. "The lady hired me."

Jarunmisanrill cocked his head, amused contempt smeared over his pretty face. "Really, Riley? A mortal?"

"I wouldn't talk if I were you," Mai said. She matched his expression. "Your kind can die just as easily as mine."

He stepped closer. "Is that a challenge, little champion?"

Riley inserted herself between Jarunmisanrill and Mai. "No, she wasn't challenging you. I needed someone to watch my back while I did the job. Pay me for the work your father hired me to do, and we'll be out of each other's hair."

Mai squelched the urge to yank Riley out of the way. Why would the bitch try to protect her? Unless she was more afraid of Stan than she was his big brother.

Which definitely did not make sense.

Unless Riley still loved Stan.

"You really shouldn't have brought someone with you, child." The sibilant voice came from their left. Something crept out of the shadows, but Mai's eyes refused to focus on whatever it was. The creature was cloaked in black, its back hunched over as if it were an old human.

Mai drew her handgun. "No one told my boss about extra guests at the party. Riley get behind me."

Surprisingly, the half-fae obeyed her.

Bad move, bitch. Still, Mai needed to play her part a bit longer. "We're going to back out slowly, and no one has to get hurt," she said.

Jarunmisanrill chuckled. "Ah, little mortal. Someone always has to get hurt."

Of course, it was a set up. Mai dropped and spun in one smooth motion. Her leg shot out to sweep Riley's out from under her. The length of pipe the half-fae tried to brain her with hit the floor with a *clang*. Nor was Stan's ex much of a fighter. She landed hard, stunned. Mai suppressed a smile. Good to know her instincts were on track.

The spinning sweep turned into a roll. The dust she stirred up burned Mai's eyes and clogged her throat, but she put a couple of booths between herself and the Unseelie. She reached into her pocket and yanked out one of the charms Quinn had given her. Neither he nor Stan could detect magick within the field generated by her watch. Given that Jarunmisanrill hadn't so much as flinched when she entered the defunct restaurant, full-blood sidhe couldn't detect magick on her person either.

Mai peeked over the laminated table edge and flung the wooden disk at the Unseelie noble. If Quinn's research was right, the charm would activate as soon as it left the watch's influence. They hadn't had a chance for more than a quick practice with simple spells at the Karnak.

The wooden disk glowed neon pink when it passed the first booth. A third voice cried out, and two figures darted toward Jarunmisanrill. One dragged him down. The other flung a hand in the direction of the bright pink disk.

Oh, fuck.

Mai dived under the table and covered her head.

Soundless noise drove a spike through her mind, and the world turned upside down.

CHAPTER 8

The flash of light and soundless thunder blew out the windows of the restaurant. Thad hung onto the wheel of the SUV for dear life as the vehicle skidded sideways, and debris *ping*ed off the body. He'd been at his mother's condo in Florida once when a hurricane rolled in, and the wind noise had been incredible. This eerie silence amid the violence scared him more than the Category Two storm had.

And the effect was exactly what Mai described when fae and witch magicks hit head on, which meant she had been desperate enough to use one of Quinn's charms.

He turned the key, but nothing happened, not even the click of the starter trying to engage. *Shit.* The SUVs shielding should have protected it from the EMP. Damn modern vehicles and their onboard computers. There must have been enough of a residual charge pulled from the batteries to fry a circuit or two.

Thad reached down and grabbed the air horn from under the passenger seat. He popped the SUV's door and let off three short blasts. Mike claimed weres weren't affected by magick backlash like fae and witches were. Thad prayed it was true because he had no fucking clue of how many people Jarun-whatever had brought with him.

Even with the horn's obnoxious sounds, nothing moved inside the store. Maybe the blast disabled everyone. No, Mai had said the backlash didn't do a damn thing to Normals. Meaning it shouldn't have affected her.

Which meant the damn fairies must have done something to her before the blast. If they'd rifled her pockets while she was out cold or dead—

No. He couldn't think that way. But if Mai hadn't come out, she was in a load of trouble. He slid out of the driver's seat and drew his sidearm.

Claws on concrete stopped him from exposing himself. Mike crept up to him, another lighter-colored werecoyote behind him. Steve. The enforcer must have grabbed his brother from the restaurant before the backup troops left the Karnak.

"Were Stan and the witches out of the blast zone?"

Mike nodded, then inclined his head toward the storefront.

"No movement inside, and Ms. Osaka hasn't come out."

Mike growled low in his throat and started for the storefront.

Thad laid a hand on the 'coyote's back. "Wait."

The kid nipped at him, though his teeth didn't touch Thad's skin.

"Get yer hackles down, Michael Luke Warner." Thad gestured at the silent, demolished storefront. "The fae already know I'm out here. They'll still be half-blinded from the blast. You two slip around the back, and make sure they don't sneak out. Howl if they come your way."

Mike dipped his head, and the boys trotted around the edge of the parking lot, avoiding the couple of street lights that still worked.

Thad inhaled deeply. The air had the tang of a thunderstorm. If the scent of magick were strong enough for him to smell it, he wasn't sure how the boys would manage to pick up Mai's scent through the ozone. He rounded the SUV and headed for the destroyed doors of the restaurant.

Glass on the broken pavement crunched beneath the soles of his boots. He reached for his flashlight and flipped the switch. The beam penetrated the gloom, showing overturned equipment and broken booths. Everything was dusted with powdered drywall.

"Osaka?" No sense remaining quiet. Even if the fae were spellblind and couldn't see the flashlight, they damn sure could hear his footsteps and breathing. Hell, maybe they could even hear his heartbeat like the vamps.

A body lay near the door, but scarlet tresses glinted under the beam. He knelt and checked her pulse. The fairy bitch was still alive.

Thad rose and swept the flashlight across the area. A neon pink object beneath a table caught his attention. He crossed the room.

The previous dust beneath the lucite had been disturbed, and someone or something had been dragged out from under the table. Four pink wooden disks lay in the bare spot on the floor. Mai had five with her.

Huge, shaggy shadows approached from the back of the store. "Either of you find a sign of other fae or Ms. Osaka?"

Both werecoyotes shook their heads.

"Shit," Thad muttered. The urge to spit tugged at him, but he and Leslie made a deal to give up their respective tobacco vices when the grandpups came along. He glanced at the unconscious half-fae. "We'll take her back with us. She'd better know something worthwhile or there's going to be hell to pay."

Stan tried to shunt his emotions aside while Wolford and Warner gave their reports on the meeting that had gone horribly wrong. Mai was alive. It would be the only reason Jarunmisanrill would have taken her. His half-brother had no need for a dead hostage.

But why take Mai and not Riley?

He didn't realize he'd spoken aloud until Wolford snorted.

"My guess?" the enforcer said. "She's no longer of use to him, or she's here to fuck with your head some more while he interrogates Ms. Osaka."

Stan could no longer hold back the tide. Rage surged through him at the mention of Mai in his half-brother's hands. Jarunmisanrill had wanted their father's approval so badly, he'd excelled in the art of torture. Fuck, both Stan and his cousin Harry carried the scars to prove it. Ice crackled as it coated the closest walls.

Wolford held up his hands, and his breath came out in puffs of steam. "Calm down, son."

"Son?" Stan glared at the very Normal enforcer. Even Mike backed away a couple of steps, and a sheen of fur appeared on his face and hands.

"Sorry, Mr. Gryffudd." Wolford didn't look the least bit sorry though. "When you look like one of my daughter's high school boyfriends, it's a little hard to take in your real age. But going off half-cocked isn't going to get Ms. Osaka back either."

"You don't understand—"

"The Unseelie?" The enforcer grinned. "You're forgetting I've already had a run-in with your daddy's people. This brother of yours in particular." He sobered. "And by the way, your daddy, brother, and their buddies murdered a bunch of Normals in mah old jurisdiction in Ohio just on the off-chance they could lure Sam out of Augustine territory and kill her. They'll keep your girlfriend alive until they get what they want. But mah guess? Considering their previous stunts, maybe what they really want isn't in the Karnak vault."

Stan folded his arms. He'd underestimated Wolford. "All right. I'm listening."

Wolford scratched the stubble on his chin. "After your dad died, and Fitz negotiated the Unseelie out of Holmes County, what happened with your brother?"

Damn. He'd *really* underestimated Wolford. Not to mention, the enforcer danced around the fact Colin Fitzgerald had beheaded Stan's father with a farming implement while still a Normal. For any fae, that would be embarrassing as hell.

"Jarunmisanrill and his assault team were exiled for two reasons: their failure to kill Sam and their defeat at the hands of one Normal lawyer and a bunch of pacifist, Normal farmers."

Wolford nodded. "So how would they get back in their queen's good graces?"

"Kill Sam, of course." A frisson of fear wormed its way up Stan's spine. "Shit. If the Winter Queen never had any intention of honoring the peace accord with the vampires, she would use the exiles' desire for revenge and need to reclaim their honor to her own ends. They would give her plausible deniability."

Wolford shrugged. "That's what I thought. Ms. Osaka doesn't let Sam intimidate her, which is why they're such good friends. And why yer brother grabbed her. If he can hurt you in the process, all's the better."

Chapter 9

Mai wanted to throttle the idiot banging a gong inside her head. Or kill Sam. That damn watch had to be the reason the magick backlash from the fae and witch spells interacting affected her. Surprisingly, Jarunmisanrill hadn't removed the watch from her wrist.

Maybe he sensed Sam's power in the device. Or more likely, he worried its removal would let Sam know something was wrong.

Which was true.

Mai tugged at the chain binding her wrists above her head again. Whatever the metal was, it couldn't be steel or iron. The fae wouldn't take a chance with something so poisonous to them.

The chain was looped over a set of copper pipes a yard over her head. Weak sunlight penetrated the high, dusty windows, showing concrete block walls. The concrete slab floor gently sloped into a drain a few feet from her boots. A huge ancient sink sat in the corner closest to the single wooden door, its faucets fed by the pipes above her. Nothing else was in the room so she couldn't begin to guess its purpose.

How long had she been out from the backlash? The fae could have taken her anywhere, but the air was fairly dry. She needed to get out before someone came back to check on her.

Mai leaned her head back and examined the pipes. Support brackets were nailed into the wooden beams roughly every yard or so. The only joins in the copper she could see were the curves down to the faucets. The other end of the pipes appeared to go through a hole in the top concrete block from the amount of sealant smeared around the pipe and wall.

She slid the chain toward the door until the links hit a bracket. Now, if she could accomplish her plan without breaking her wrists or dislocating them . . .

Mai raised up on her toes and gripped the chain as firmly as she could with both hands. She dropped, putting her full weight on the pipes. With a rattle and a bit of a screech, the nails loosened. Thank goodness, some contractor took shortcuts. If they'd used screws for the brackets, she would have been screwed as well.

And if Sam were here, she'd be laughing hysterically at the really bad joke.

With another hop and drop, the bracket tore loose from the beam and clattered across the concrete floor. Mai slid to the next bracket and repeated the process. Her wrists ached and the links bit into her skin, but it would be a minor discomfort compared to the tender mercies of the exiled Unseelie if she didn't get the hell out of here.

The second bracket clattered to the floor. The pipes groaned and rattled. Mai slid her chain down to the next bracket.

Once again, she grabbed the chain and jumped. The third bracket popped out on the first try. Even better, water hissed from the pipe joint above the sink.

Mai slid the chain to the last ceiling bracket. She clenched the chain and jumped. Like the bracket's predecessor, it shot from the beam. However, this bracket hit the door.

She held her breath and waited. No one came into the room. Of course, they didn't have a guard on her, not a mere Normal.

Mai slid the chain down to the sink. The links loosened without her body weight keeping them taut. After stripping off the chain, she clenched her fists and rolled her wrists to test the joints and bones. Painful, but everything still moved correctly.

Her gun, wallet, and phone were gone, so Jarunmisanrill wasn't a complete idiot. She still needed weapons. She retrieved the brackets and all the nails. Good, old-fashioned steel. Yep, that would definitely work. She stuffed her makeshift weapons into her jacket pockets.

Now, her issue was how to get out of this damn room.

The door had no latch or knob on this side. No hinges. She ran her wrist along the seam of the doorframe. Her watch beeped steadily along the entire perimeter.

Some sort of magickal seal or possibly a booby trap. Setting it off might be a good way to commit suicide.

Mai took a few steps back and examined the windows. Plain basic glass from the looks of them. The problem was they were eight feet from the floor. The only thing she had to climb on was the sink.

Water still sprayed from the loose joint. It would make her perch slippery at best on the ancient painted cast iron. She was a little surprised the fae had left it here, but maybe moving it was more of a danger to them.

Once she broke the window, she wouldn't have much time to get out. And that was assuming the fae hadn't warded the window like they had the door. Her boot seemed to be the best option.

She yanked off her right boot and carefully climbed onto the edge of the sink. Looking through the window didn't offer any indication of where she was. There was another building across what appeared to be an alley. And she was located in the basement of her building.

Mai held her left wrist to the window. No beeps issued from the device. She placed the heel of her boot over her right fist. She cocked her arm and punched the window.

Glass shattered into huge jagged pieces. It took a few precious seconds to clear the frame and brush the fragments from the edge. She tossed her boot through the opening before she hoisted herself up and wiggled through the frame.

Unfortunately, she couldn't avoid all the sharp pieces. A few nicked her hands. Another ripped her pants and scored a gash along her shin. But for the most part she was intact.

Mai leaned against the building, stripped off her soaked sock, and pulled her right boot back on her foot. Sweat already beaded along her forehead. The heat meant they hadn't taken her far, and traffic sounds echoed off the concrete and brick surrounding her. This was a delivery drive, not an alley. She only needed to find her way out of the complex and some place with a phone.

She'd taken two steps when two Unseelie appeared in front of her. Neither of them looked real happy to see her either. She whirled and ran in the opposite direction.

Chapter 10

Trying not to display his worry and fear, Stan stood with Kunal in another room and watched the monitor. Staci Warner sat across from a secured Riley. The enforcers had checked to make sure she wasn't a dino demon before they brought her in. He didn't feel a damn bit sorry Duncan's, well, his, team had used steel handcuffs on her.

The magick backlash at pointblank range had knocked out Riley for a good ten hours, but she was finally awake. And for the first time, she actually looked scared, though she also tried to hide it.

"Where's Stanley?" she demanded.

Staci shrugged. "Off doing important boss stuff."

"Why am I here and cuffed?" Riley's eyes narrowed. "I did what he told me to."

"Really?" Staci crossed her arms and leaned back in her chair. "Is that what you call stabbing the boss in the back? Why else did your buddies leave you behind?"

"I want to talk to him." Panic seeped into Riley's voice.

"You're beneath him." Staci's smile deliberately showed her canines. "I'm the one who handles the boss's shit jobs."

The door into the interrogation room opened. Thad rolled a stainless-steel cart from dining services inside. Leslie trotted beside her husband in her coyote form.

Riley jerked at the sight of the implements on a white cloth on top of the cart. Thad had borrowed an assortment of utensils from his stepson Steve, who was currently the assistant manager of the Amun-Re, the casino's five-star restaurant. Stan recognized several types of knives, a wine bottle corkscrew, and what looked like an oyster shucker. The rest he was clueless about. The only thing the utensils had in common was their steel composition.

Leslie walked over to Riley and circled the half-fae. The werecoyote sat beside their prisoner and gave her a big toothy canine grin.

"Anything?" Thad asked.

"Last chance to play nice," Staci said to Riley. "You've pissed off your only ally in this place. The rest of us are 'coyotes, vamps, and Norms. And we hold grudges for what we've been put through because of your people's shit."

"Stan's little bitch was stupid!" Riley spat. "She's the one who started flinging spells in that restaurant. I tried to save her life!"

"Ms. Osaka wouldn't have drawn any weapon, a spell or otherwise, unless someone made the wrong move." Thad's mouth worked like he was chewing something. "Who twitched first?"

Riley sagged in her chair and winced as the cuffs irritated a fresh patch of her skin. "Jarunmisanrill had a ghoul with him."

Beside Stan, Kunal made a derisive sound.

Stan turned to the enforcer. "I thought the ghouls had been wiped out six hundred or so years ago."

"They were," Kunal protested. "You can't possibly believe her."

Inside the interrogation room, Thad and the Warner ladies played things well. "So what did the ghoul do to rile Ms. Osaka?"

"He was there, and I was supposed to meet Jarunmisanrill alone." Riley shrugged. "She told me to get behind her, and she pulled her gun."

"What happened next?" Staci said.

"Hoarancill was behind me." Riley swallowed hard. "He shoved me into a booth, then he-he became me."

"A glamor?" Thad asked.

Riley shook her head. "N-no. His body melted and shifted. F-for an instant, his-his face looked like a lizard's with very sharp teeth."

Stan's breath froze in his lungs. Of course, it wasn't his father. Deep down, he knew it couldn't be true. But why would Jarunmisanrill take the imposter at face value? Did he know the entity really wasn't their father? Or had the dino demon promised him revenge like it had to Caesar's nephew Marcus?

Inside the interrogation room, Thad cursed up a storm while Staci merely shook her head. Leslie, on the other hand, laid back her ears and growled at Riley.

"Leslie, lay off," Thad muttered. "Someone that stupid ain't worth getting stuck in your teeth. Gahd only knows what tricks the dino demon may have planted on her."

"Wait a minute!" Riley looked wildly at each of the people in the interrogation room. "What are you talking about? What's a dino demon?"

Staci stood up and stalked out of the room. Thad and Leslie followed. A minute later, they entered the monitor room for the security wing.

"What do you want us to do with her?" Thad asked.

"Do you have a place to lock her up?" Stan clenched his fists to keep from charging into the interrogation room and throttling Riley himself. She was always looking for an angle, but she was usually smarter than this. Or maybe she'd cut a deal with the dino demon herself.

"Yeah, but it's steel," Thad drawled.

"Put her there for now." Stan rubbed his chin. "This puts a new spin on the attempted break-in of our vault."

"What do you mean?" Staci cocked her head, a puzzled expression on her pretty face.

"The dino demon wants something of Sam's." Stan rubbed the back of his neck while he watched Riley on the monitor. She scowled when she realized they'd stripped her of all her lock pick paraphernalia.

"What?" Thad asked. "Everything in the vault is dangerous to everyone but Sam."

"A gift from one god to another god has inherent magickal power." Stan grinned despite the circumstances. "Haven't you ever wondered why a badass vamp like Alex Stanton has a tiny fluff-mop Maltese?"

Thad shrugged. "I just figured he was secure enough in his manhood he didn't need a huge dog to prove anything."

"That's part of it," Stan said. "According to legend, the Maltese breed was created as a wedding gift to one of the Assyrian goddesses. The descendants of the original pair have inherent abilities." He turned back to the monitor. "The question is how deep is Riley in, or if she's just another pawn."

Thad snorted. "My vote is for playing us some more."

Leslie shifted back to human form. "No, I don't think so. She was genuinely surprised about the dino demon."

"Yeah, but she also wouldn't mind gettin' Ms. Osaka out of the way now Mr. Gryffudd is moving up in the world," Thad said.

"Like Riley would ever become chief of security," Kunal muttered.

Stan never would have imagined a Normal outthinking a vampire. "Kunal, would you and Leslie take Riley to that cell and keep an eye on her for a bit. Staci, get Quinn on the phone and see if he'd be willing to do me another favor. Thad, come with me. I want another look at the old vault."

Once they were alone in the elevator, Thad murmured, "I apologize for blurting out about you and Ms. Osaka, Mr. Gryffudd. It wasn't my place."

"No, it wasn't." Stan considered the situation. The Normal obviously respected Mai a great deal. And from Thad's scent, he was worried about her, too. "How'd you find out? She's adamant that we keep things quiet."

Thad exhaled, and for a moment, Stan didn't think the enforcer would answer him. "Sam," Thad finally admitted.

Stan frowned. While the death goddess was wary of fae thanks to both queens placing a bounty on her head shortly after her creation, he always suspected Sam's annoyed attitude toward him had more to do with his relationship with Mai.

"Sam and Mai are tight. Why in Morrigan's name would she say anything to you?"

"Because Leslie, Staci, and the baby zombies kept trying to set up Mai on blind dates."

The elevator halted, and the doors parted. Both men headed for the vault. "They did?"

"That's the only reason Sam said anything to me. Me tellin' 'em to lay off wouldn't have the ladies sniffing around to find out who Mai was seeing the way Sam bitchin' at them would."

Stan glanced at Thad. "What did you say?"

"That if they ruined my chances of becoming Las Vegas chief enforcer by harassing Mai I'd use 'em all for artillery practice."

Stan grabbed Thad's arm and pulled the man to a halt. "She's transferring?"

"Get yer hackles down, Mr. Gryffudd. She can't ask for a transfer without telling Master St. James and Mr. Stanton why." Thad shrugged. "But if Mr. Stanton decides to take the cure, the master will most likely move Ms. Osaka to Los Angeles to become co-chief enforcer."

"And why don't you think Master St. James would choose another vampire?"

"Anne's already planning on taking the cure at some point." Thad shrugged again. "Ain't too many other vamps in the coven he trusts anymore."

Stan sighed and resumed walking down the corridor. "You're too smart for your own good, Mr. Wolford."

Thad grunted and followed. "My wife might disagree with you."

Despite his fear, Stan's laughter echoed down the hallway.

Chapter 11

Mai ran, dodging dumpsters and vaulting over shipping pallets. Unfortunately, the men chasing her were faster and nimbler, but they also hadn't drawn their weapons, which meant they wanted her alive. Time to try a different tactic.

She dove behind a rusty grate leaning against a wall and reached into her pockets.

"Oh, little mortal, do you really think the metal hides you from our sight?" the fae in braids said in English.

The other said in their language, "The dumb bitch probably believes as long as she's touching iron we can't kill her."

Maybe Stan teaching her the Unseelie language was a bad idea. The second fae royally pissed her off, and that made him her primary target.

The two separated, each one approaching her from a side. Even though they were fully clothed and wore gloves in this heat, the fae seemed reluctant to touch the metal.

She kicked the grate, a short snappy front kick. Both men jumped back. The grate teetered on its bottom edge before it crashed to the ground.

By then, Mai charged the asshat who had called her a bitch. She scored his cheek with the pointy end of a nail. He doubled over and screamed in pain. She yanked on the collar of his mail and undershirt and dropped the nail down his back. While he blubbered over the steel poisoning him, she whirled and pitched one of the brackets at the other guy's head.

Her fast ball may not be ninety-five miles per hour like it was in college, but her accuracy was still there. The bracket smacked the fae in the middle of his forehead despite their vaunted reflexes. He went down hard.

Mai pivoted and knocked over the man desperately trying to remove his mail and shirt in a bid to get the poisonous nail away from his delicate skin. She raced for the corner ahead. Traffic sounds were getting louder.

Her boots skidded on the concrete as she whipped around the brick and stopped. Hoarancill stood in front of her, a horrible smile on his beautiful face.

Colin had sliced the bastard's head off years ago, but she'd been a member of the St. James Coven long enough to know nothing was totally impossible. She pulled another bracket from her pocket and pitched it at the person in front of her.

The raw steel bounced off his forehead and clattered on the concrete. Hoarancill continued to smile while he stalked toward her. There wasn't a mark on his pale skin.

Oh, she wanted to kick herself for being so stupid. Riley had picked up a steel pipe in the defunct Mexican restaurant, which meant the person who tried to bean her with the damn pipe wasn't fae.

And wasn't Stan's ex-girlfriend Riley.

Any more than this guy was Stan's father.

Mai held up her left wrist, letting him get a good look at her watch.

The dino demon pretending to be Hoarancill paused, and his smile faded. "I haven't done anything to you, Ms. Osaka. I suggest you not do anything nasty. It doesn't have to get ugly between us."

"It's already ugly." She glared at the dino demon. "It got ugly when one of your babies decided to kill three of our employees and put another one in the hospital for two months!"

The dino demon sighed and pretended to examine his fingernails. "I wasn't going to kill you, no matter what the silly fae want."

"No, you want to use me as a pawn against Sam." Mai started to unbuckle the watch strap. "Maybe I can't kick your ass—"

The dino demon rushed her. She managed one decent punch before he locked her in a choke hold and held her left arm well away from her right without touching Sam's gift himself.

All she could think as the blackness closed in was she should have killed Stan's ex in the interrogation room when she had the chance.

CHAPTER 12

Stan and Thad reached the vault, and the enforcer pulled out a bronze pin and a couple of antiseptic wipes.

"I need to get one of these pins," Stan murmured.

Thad frowned as he poked Stan's thumb. "It should be upstairs in the penthouse with the rest of your orientation materials. Staci took everything up the day before you arrived."

"I haven't been upstairs since the first few minutes after my arrival." Stan grimaced and wiped the blood with the pad. He had plans for his first night here. They didn't involve his ex showing up or his girlfriend getting kidnapped.

"Have you gotten any sleep?" Thad didn't move as Stan poked his thumb in return.

"A cat nap in my office." When red blood flowed, he handed the pin back to Thad. The nightmares from those few minutes still haunted him. Jarunmisanrill had wanted nothing more than to prove to their father he was every bit as sadistic as the old man. Stan pushed the images of what his half-brother might be doing to Mai from his mind. If he dwelled on them, he would be useless.

He placed his hand against the biometric pad and said his name. An electric whine raised the hairs on the back of his neck. The giant door swung outward. It was approximately two feet thick.

Inside the vault, full-spectrum lighting mimicked the time of day. Like his enforcers said, the vault wasn't full. The table in front of him held two boxes. One was carved from bone. The other was a standard Styrofoam shipping box, the type the vampires used to transport blood.

Something rustled to his right. He pivoted to find what looked like a potted rose bush in the corner. The plant held twelve perfect blooms. Or they would have been perfect if they'd been any color other than black.

The leaves quivered, and a green tendril reached for him.

"Ah wouldn't let that thing touch you, Mr. Gryffudd," Thad warned.

"He's just lonely down here, aren't you, little one?" Stan held out his hand. The tendril wound around his wrist. Vicious-looking thorns were spaced every few inches. The end of the tendril rose like a cobra, an especially long thorn beneath the last two leaves.

"Uh-uh-uh, we're not going to misbehave, are we?" Stan cooed. "Lady Samantha would be most upset with you. I'm willing to let you out of here for some real sunshine once in a while, but you have to promise not to stab anyone."

The thorns receded into the tendril, and the leaves stroked his palm.

Stan turned to Thad. "When was the last time he was fed?"

"Sunday."

"Would you like a little snack, big boy?" Stan carefully brushed the tendril twined around his wrist. The leaves of the rosebush quivered again. The blooms opened wide.

"Thad, would you please call up to medical and have them send down a pint of O-positive."

"Hu-human blood?" For the first time in the last twenty-four hours, Thad Wolford actually appeared alarmed. "Sam said only to feed it ox blood."

Stan eyed the enforcer. "Would you chain up Leslie in your backyard, leave her there day after day, and only feed her dog kibble?"

"That's wrong—" Thad stopped and cocked his head. "Wait a minute. That thing's intelligent?"

All twelve blooms turned away from the enforcer. One large thorn rose from the foliage, looking terribly similar to a human middle finger.

"Yes, he's sentient." Stan tried hard not to grin at the alarm on the enforcer's face. "That's the reason we're taking him with us to rescue Mai."

———•—•———

Once Stan fed the rose bush a snack of donated human blood, he decided to name him Seymour. As he carried Seymour up to security, Thad grumbled behind him.

"You do know Seymour wasn't the plant, don't you?"

Stan chuckled. "Yes, I know. He's the good guy. Right, Seymour?"

One of the rose blossoms stroked his face.

Everyone in the security office had horrified expressions when he walked in with the potted plant and set it on Mai's desk.

"What the hell are you going to do with that?" a clothed Leslie asked.

Stan ignored her. "Seymour, stay." The rose bush's leaves quivered. "I know I promised you a ride, but I told you I need to do a few things first." He turned to Kunal. "Where's Riley's phone?"

The vampire retrieved the device from an EM-insulated box and handed the device over to Stan.

He thumbed the power button. A four-digit PIN screen popped up. She wouldn't be that sentimental, would she? He typed the numerical equivalent of his nickname on the keypad. The main dashboard appeared.

Regret and pity washed through him while he brought up her recent calls. No names were attached to any of the phone numbers, but the same local number displayed over and over again. Jarun was probably using a burner phone, but Stan thumbed the number anyway and tapped the speaker function. The outgoing call rang once. Twice.

"I wondered when you'd bother, baby brother."

Stan could hear the sneer in his half-brother's voice. "I propose a trade, Jarun."

"You will address me properly," his brother snapped.

Stan willed himself to be calm. Nothing would be accomplished by frying the electronics of Riley's phone. "Very well, Jarunmisanrill. I propose to trade my enforcer for the contents of the Karnak's vault."

"Be specific," Jarun snapped. Did he really believe Stan was bound by the laws of the Courts?

"The current contents of the vault you sent Riley to break into. The same vault holding the property of one Samantha Marie Ridgeway St. James."

"Don't say her name again!"

Stan grinned at his half-brother's paranoia, but he was raised not to say the names of the Tuatha de Danann. Their gods had a habit of showing up when their names were said aloud in such a cavalier manner.

"But that's the property you want, isn't it, brother dear?" Stan practically purred the words.

"I don't. Father does," Jarun answered coldly.

Morrigan help him, things were as bad as Stan feared. After two heartbeats, he said, "Father's dead, Jarun. Whoever's with you is playing his or her own game."

His brother ignored the nickname this time. "Do you want your precious mortal back or not, Stanley?"

Stan closed his eyes. There was no convincing Jarun of the truth. He'd die of old age before he'd listened to his halfling brother. "Where?"

"Fremont Street. The roof of the parking garage next to the zipline."

The place didn't matter so much as the time. Stan was the master of the city now. He needed to keep casualties to a minimum. "Four a.m."

"Until then, brother." As always, Jarun made the word into an insult.

Stan thumbed the disconnect icon.

"You know it's an ambush," Thad said. Worry creased his face.

"Yes, but we need to keep Normals out of the way as much as we can."

"What do you need from us?" Kunal asked.

Stan outlined his plan. It wasn't much of a plan, but it was his only chance to get Mai back from the dino demon.

CHAPTER 13

Mai opened her eyes, a little surprised she could. Her cheek and hand rested on warm concrete. It actually felt good against her aching head.

Warm concrete.

Shit. She pushed herself to a sitting position and found she was in the middle of a blood circle. In the corners of her eyes, orange sparks flashed randomly.

She didn't need to wonder who cast the trap. The color of peripheral light and blood confirmed it. Something else felt wrong and she rubbed her wrists. It took her a moment to realize her watch was missing.

"Looking for something?"

Jarunmisanrill perched on the edge of a swivel office chair a few feet from her prison. If it weren't for the lack of sink and unbroken windows, she would've thought they were back in the room where they had originally chained her. It even had the door with no latch on this side.

"You know, touching my watch wasn't smart." Mai smoothed down her tie. Her bronze pin was still in its hiding place. Since her tie tack was silver and ornamental to them, the fae hadn't bothered with it.

"I didn't touch your timepiece."

Several English and Japanese obscenities raced through her mind, but she couldn't give voice to them. Not if she wanted to gain Jarunmisanrill's trust. Or at least, get him to question his allies.

"Who set the circle?" She looked around the room. Nothing here, but her, Stan's half-brother, and the chair.

"My father."

"But this isn't fae magick." Did he really think she was that stupid? Or was he that desperate to have both his father and his place in the Unseelie Court back?

However, something flickered in Jarunmisanrill's eyes. He shifted in his chair and remained silent. Good. If he was already questioning the situation, she only needed to tweak it along.

Mai watched him. "You don't strike me as the stupid type."

"How generous of you," he sneered.

"Look, I get how annoying younger siblings can be—" she started.

"You know nothing about us, petty worm," he snapped.

"And I also know what it's like to miss your parents regardless of our respective races."

His jaw muscles twitched as he ground his teeth, but otherwise, he was quiet.

"My father was murdered, too. I would do just about anything to get him back."

An ugly look crossed his face. "Then why don't you petition your precious goddess?"

Mai remembered that anger. It had nearly consumed her as a child. But then, she had her memories of her parents after their deaths. Miko only had vague impressions. The anger nearly doubled in force when the necromancer David Head killed Grandpa Kensai and Jamal, but she knew exactly who to blame, and it wasn't Sam.

Funny how she and Stan leaned on each other when they faced the possibility of losing more loved ones after Head's attack at Tiffany and Max's wedding.

"Sam's smart enough not to break certain rules of reality," Mai said softly. "Morrigan wouldn't either no matter how much you begged her, so where do you think this person pretending to be your father comes from?"

Jarunmisanrill leapt up from the chair and roared, "Be quiet!"

"I could say nothing," she admitted. "It's not going to change the fact that your father's dead, and this creature is manipulating all of us to its own ends."

"I don't believe in your alleged dinosaur demons." Jarunmisanrill stalked over to the blood circle, but he stopped himself from smudging the scarlet streak on the floor. "It's all a lie for the vampires to use that bitch to destroy my people!"

She didn't have to ask who he referred to. Selene's crazy scientists had used steel in the nanites that turned Sam into what she was now. The fae assumed first Caesar's twin sister, then Caesar himself, planned to use Sam as a weapon of mass destruction against their race.

Mai shook her head. "Do you really think Sam or Morrigan would break their deal?"

That seemed to sink through Jarunmisanrill's thick skull by his puzzled expression. "What deal?"

"Part of the truce the werewolves brokered between the Vampire Nation and the Courts was that Sam and Morrigan would each keep their people in check. Even the Tuatha realize the dinosaur gods and their demons are a danger to all of us."

He blinked once. Mai wanted to kick herself. Of course. As an exile, he didn't know about the peace treaty.

Or didn't believe it was true considering the reason for his exile.

"Even a lowly Normal like me knows the gods can't go back on their word." She sighed. "Do you think the Winter Queen would be stupid enough to cross Morrigan?"

"She-she wouldn't—" His jaw clenched to keep from speaking the rest of his thought out loud.

"Your queen wouldn't hang you out to dry for attacking Sam?" Mai rolled her eyes. "Are you that naïve about how the Courts function?" She exhaled. She actually felt a little sorry for Stan's brother. "Think about it. If that really is your father, wouldn't he have been exiled too for failing to kill Sam in Ohio?"

She could almost see the little wheels turning inside Jarunmisanrill's brain. Stan was right about his brother's slavish devotion to their father. This was probably the first time Jarunmisanrill was actually thinking on his own.

"He said we could earn the Winter Queen's confidence back."

"If I'm right, your queen probably doesn't know what he's doing." She shrugged. "If you're correct and she does know what you are doing, why would she want you and your supposed father to break the truce? You know what happens when a fae breaks their word."

"And I know how well you Normals lie."

Mai wished she could wipe that sneer from his face, but part of her understood. No one liked being proven they were wrong.

"If I'm lying about the dino demons existence or the peace treaty, surely you have contacts to find out. Like your werecoyote buddies?" Mai cocked her head and regarded him. "Or a friend at the Unseelie Court who would know if your father was still alive and had cut a deal with the Winter Queen? But if you're wrong and the dino demons destroy the world, how can the Winter Queen restore your place in her court if she's dead?"

Jarunmisanrill stared at her, a slight crease down the middle of the otherwise immaculate skin on his pale forehead.

The door opened, and Jarunmisanrill dropped to one knee. Mai's heart caught in her throat. Someone looking exactly like her walked into the room. Blue and gold flashed on the imposter's left wrist. Her watch.

That's how they prevented Sam from showing up when they took it. The damn dino demons didn't just change their shape. They could actually replicate someone's DNA pattern so precisely it took a weapon created by the gods to discern the difference.

Like the bronze pins Ares had acquired for Sam and the coven.

Mai resisted smiling over the fact the demon was so damn confident it didn't bother confiscating anything else on her person. Its mistake didn't mean she wasn't in deep, deep shit though.

Behind the creepy version of her, a figure dressed in a ragged black cloak with a hood shuffled into the room. It didn't shimmer like before. The scent of sandalwood permeated the air.

A vampire? One of Marcus's people? More likely one of the new vampires he's illegally sired over the past five years.

But something was wrong. The vampire limped and its back was hunched.

It pushed back its hood, and Mai couldn't stop her gasp of shock.

Its face was horribly scarred, as if the flesh itself had melted rather than burned. A flap of skin obscured the vision of its left eye. Its lips were stretched into a terrible rictus, and drool oozed down its chin, but it didn't have the pointed canines of a vampire. Sparse, wiry hairs dotted its head.

"Leave us, Jarunmisanrill," the dino demon looking like Mai ordered.

The fae nodded. "Of course, Father." But Stan's brother shot Mai an odd look before he rose and stalked out of the room. The door closed behind him.

"Do you really think you can get into the Karnak looking like me?" she asked the demon.

"All I need are the contents of the vault." It sat in the office chair Jarunmisanrill vacated and spun around. "Which your boyfriend is bringing to us later.

But before we exchange you for the usurper's treasures, Anouk here has a few questions for you." The fake waved at the disfigured person next to her.

"Who are you?" Mai asked.

Anouk made a coughing noise. It took Mai a few seconds to realize the scarred figure was laughing.

"The first question most Normals ask me is what am I." She waved a gloved hand, for the being sounded like a she from her tone. "I am the result of a mutation of the V-virus, or an embarrassment to the pretty vampires, depending on who you ask. What I want is the secret ingredient of the cure to the virus the pretties developed." From her scathing tone, the names she called the vamps wasn't a compliment.

On the other hand, Mai didn't remember any record of this variation of the V-virus. "Why?"

"Really? You would ask that question?" Anouk stepped closer to the blood circle. "You look at me with such an expression of abhorrence, and you ask why my people wouldn't want the cure, too?"

"I can't tell you what all goes into the cure."

"Of course not," Anouk spat.

"Told you she wouldn't help you without a little pain," the dino demon said in a sing-song voice while it continued to twirl in the office chair.

"I didn't say I wouldn't try," Mai held up a hand when Anouk's teeth parted for another retort. "I can talk to the medical team who pioneered the research. If you're suffering from a mutation, they'll need blood and tissue samples from you to develop a cure specific to your condition."

"Or they will twist their research to finish you off for good," the demon said.

What the hell was the demon playing at? Between the Vampire Liberation Front, the creature in front of her, and the fae . . .

Shit. Thad was right, but only wrong about which party was stirring the pot.

Mai stared up at this Anouk. "What do you tell people when they ask what you are?"

"Surely, the vampires still sing songs of their valor against the ghouls." If

Anouk's face weren't so horribly distorted, Mai was sure the woman would be sneering like Jarunmisanrill and the dino demon.

"None of the vampires I know have mentioned ghouls to me during my life. Nor has anyone else." Mai shrugged. "But if your lifespan is as long as the vampires, the length of my life until now means nothing."

"Ah, so they think they've wiped us from memory as well as existence." Bitterness rested thick in Anouk's voice.

"Do you want help developing a cure for your people or not?" Mai cocked her head. "Or is a cure what *she*—" She jabbed a forefinger in the direction of the dino demon. "—promised in return for your help in taking down the St. James Coven?"

The demon stopped spinning on the office chair when the ghoul turned to stare at it with a glint in her eye.

So, Anouk wasn't the fool Jarunmisanrill was. But now, Mai knew who'd been helping the exiled fae and the dino demons keep an eye on the Las Vegas portion of the coven.

"Let the Normal out so I may question her further." Anouk's hand slipped into her tattered robes.

The demon's attention flicked to Mai and back to Anouk. "That would be unwise at this stage of the game."

"Anouk, may I make a suggestion?"

Both of the creatures looked at Mai.

"Whatever you do, don't bite it."

Anouk jerked a long jagged-edged dagger from beneath her robes. She leapt for the demon. The chair flipped and sent the two figures tumbling across the concrete. Anouk gained her footing first. The demon jerked back as the dagger flashed through the spot where its neck had been.

The pair squared off and circled each other. The demon's skin rippled, but it resisted the urge to shift into its natural form of an oversized velociraptor. To do so would mean the end of its game and its instant death.

Even though the demon was forced to fight in Mai's form, it still had a great deal of its speed and strength. And unfortunately, Mai's knowledge of hand-to-hand combat.

With a series of kicks, punches, and blocks, it kept Anouk from landing a blow with her dagger. The ghoul tried, but she was obviously too used to dealing with less powerful foes. A backspin kick from the demon nailed the ghoul in her abdomen. She flew backward and hit the concrete wall with a sickening crack. The dagger clattered from her limp fingers as she dropped to the floor.

Somehow, Anouk forced herself back to her feet though she wobbled. From her rasping breath, a rib or two were broken and had penetrated her lungs.

"Fun time's over," the demon muttered.

Anouk cackled. "I know you're not foolish enough to let me leave here alive."

"You're right. I'm not. But you're still useful." It yanked Mai's sidearm from its back waistband and fired one shot into Anouk's chest.

She sank to the floor. Mai waited for the ghoul's flesh to turn to slime and slide from the bones. Instead, the skin crinkled and dried. A few flakes of scalp drifted to the floor.

The demon turned toward Mai. "Now look at what you made me do."

Chapter 14

Stan waited for Quinn's reaction.

The witches' chief enforcer for Las Vegas simply stared at him. "Please tell me you're shitting me, Gryffudd."

Stan shook his head. "I wish I were."

"Ma'at, take them." Quinn ran both hands over his short dark curls. He paced toward Stan's office window and stared at the city skyline before he turned to face Stan again. "Why the hell would anybody make a deal with these dinosaur bastards?"

"Because I don't think my brother knows he's being conned." Stan shrugged. "He mourns deeply for . . . our father, and he's desperate to restore his honor. Once he realizes the dino demon tricked him, he's going to be ten times more dangerous."

Quinn cocked his head. "That's assuming the demon doesn't eviscerate him as a liability."

"As much as I dislike my brother, I wouldn't wish death by dino demon on anyone." Stan shook his head. "I thought the Winter Queen would bring in those she exiled after the treaty with the Vampire Nation was signed."

"No one likes being told they're wrong." Quinn grimaced and crossed his arms. "Not even a queen. So, what do you need from us?"

"Keep Jarun's people from leaving Fremont without getting yourselves killed in the process. Leave the dino demon for my people."

Quinn nodded. "Sounds doable, but are you sure the vamps can handle one of these bastards?"

Stan grinned. "It was the Normals and werecoyotes who took down the one in the Karnak's kitchen. And it was a Normal who killed my father. Why do you think my half-brother's in such a pissy mood?"

Stan still needed to know a few things. From Alex's status reports, the dino demons could fool not only a person's physical senses, but magickal abilities as well. A year ago, some of them led the Los Angeles enforcers on a merry chase through Southern California after they kidnapped Master St. James's four-year-old niece.

He sent Thad and Leslie back into the interrogation room to question Riley again. Stan watched from the monitor room with Kunal.

Riley's wrists were cuffed to the top of the table, but this time the Karnak's security used a silver-titanium blend. A little bit of sugar to make the next round of medicine go down easier.

Leslie sat on top of the table in her wolf form and glared at Riley while her husband asked the questions.

"Why'd you make a deal with a dino demon?"

"I told you before. I do not know what you are talking about," she said through gritted teeth.

"Did you tell your buddies about the watch?" Thad growled.

"And if I did?" The look in Riley's eyes practically dared them to do something. No, not dared.

Begged.

How bad were things she would rather die than tell them the truth?

"Yer chances are better with us than with the Unseelie exiles." Thad's accent grew heavier. Mai said that happened when he was upset or angry. Despite Stan's rocky start with the enforcer, it was good to know the former sheriff really did care about the people at the Karnak.

Thad leaned his elbows on the table. "Yer only real crime was using magick at a roulette table. We're willing to forgo the charges if you cooperate with us."

"Tell me what these dino demons are first," Riley said.

"You know what a dinosaur is, right?"

Riley rolled her eyes before she nodded.

"These things are the minions of the gods that the dinosaurs worshipped."

"C'mon, dinosaur are just dumb lizards . . ." An expression of horror filled Riley's face. "Lugh take me," she breathed. "The rumors that St. James's wife is a goddess are true?"

Thad grunted an affirmative. "Whatever you think the real Hoarancill might've done to you for screwing up is nothing. Your help in breaking into the Karnak's special vault ain't the real reason these bastards want you. The dino demons'll rape and breed you 'cause you're a super. Only supers can produce a live demon, but you'll die horribly when the damn baby rips its way out of yer womb. Yer past relationship with Mr. Gryffudd and your reputation as a thief were merely icing on the cake."

Riley drew as far back from Thad and Leslie as the chains would allow. "You're lying." The words came out in a choked whisper.

Thad and Leslie exchanged looks before both of them shook their heads.

"A couple years ago, the bastards made a point of leaving the body of a part-fae woman not too far from here. Our coven tried to rescue her and a bunch of other people . . ." Thad looked at the ceiling for a moment.

Stan knew how the enforcer felt. He got sick thinking about the crime scene photos of the massacre at the Sunshine Believers ranch outside of Tuttle Creek, Montana, too. And Thad, Leslie, and their pups had been the ones to find Sharon Tyson's corpse in the mountains outside of Las Vegas.

Tyson had been one of two women unaccounted for at the Sunshine Believers ranch. And the poor lady had probably never known she had fae blood in her ancestry.

"It ain't a gentle way to die," Thad finished. "If yer willing to help us, I can guarantee Ms. Ridgeway will extend her protection to you."

"And if I say no?" Riley's left eyebrow rose.

Stan chuckled. She'd already made her decision, but she still had to push things. She always did.

In the interrogation room, Thad shrugged. "Then we'll cut you loose. When yer contractions start in a few months, just remember we gave you a chance."

He pushed back from the table and stood.

"Wait." Fear made Riley's green eyes so wide the white ringed her irises.

Thad paused. When she didn't say anything after a few seconds, Leslie growled at her.

Riley sucked in a deep breath. "They don't know about Osaka's watch. I didn't have a chance to say a damn word because the spell backlash knocked me out. Jarunmisanrill's not cleverest man around, but he's going to know that watch isn't fae or witch magick."

Thad rubbed his jaw. "Well, he hasn't been stupid enough to take it off of Ms. Osaka."

Riley slowly shook her head. "If these dino demons of yours can challenge a deity, they're powerful enough to block whatever signal the watch puts out."

Stan's gut clenched. The dino demons wouldn't block the signal. One of them would just have to copy Mai's DNA. For all he knew, the love of his life was already dead. And the dino demons were merely biding their time until their trap for Sam was ready.

Chapter 15

The door rattling drew Mai's attention from the dead ghoul. Jarunmisanrill shoved open the basement door and took in the tableau. He glared at the demon. "What in Danann's name have you done?"

It waved at the body. "Thanks to your brother's little girlfriend, the ghoul attacked me."

"Anouk is not stupid enough to attack my father." Jarunmisanrill's eyes narrowed. "What did you do to provoke her?"

Mai held her breath. So, he did believe her, but he'd also revealed his hand.

The demon raised its chin. "I did nothing. She—" It jabbed a forefinger in Mai's direction. "—told the ghoul that a cure for the virus was a lie. And kept insulting the ghoul and blaming me until she attacked me."

It didn't acknowledge Jarunmisanrill's challenge that the demon wasn't his father. That meant the demon was young. Inexperienced. Mai would actually have a chance of killing the damn thing if she could get out of the fucking blood circle.

Shit. Now, her inner voice was beginning to sound as potty-mouthed as her cousin Tiffany.

The fae's lips tightened to a thin line. He looked at Mai before returning his attention to the demon. "There's nothing to be done for it, though I'm loathe to lose one of the few allies we have." His face smoothed. "After considering your suggestion, you should come with us and pretend to be the vampires' lackey. She broke her word to me, so there's no honor to be lost."

The demon smiled. "As I told you, my son."

Jarunmisanrill smiled in return and waved toward Mai. "We take her with us, too."

"Why?" Worry flashed across the demon's face.

An awful grin crossed Jarunmisanrill's beautiful features. "Because I want to see Stanley's expression when he kills one of his own people, thinking she's one of us."

CHAPTER 16

Stan sat in the front passenger seat of an armored SUV from the coven's pool. Thad leaned back in the driver's seat, his thumbs idly tapping a beat on the steering wheel. Vampires, witches, and werecoyotes had been patrolling Fremont Street and the surrounding blocks most of the night. So far, no one had seen a hint of Unseelie activity.

"You sure trusting your ex is a good idea?" Thad asked for the umpteenth time. Thankfully, every time he asked, it had been in private.

"Nope," Stan answered for the umpteenth time. "But I trust Seymore to keep her in line tonight." One thing Riley excelled in was glamours, and not even he could tell where she hid with the rose bush. But he was the one who could communicate with vegetation. An extra pint of human blood, and the plant would have had his babies if he asked.

Thad shifted and stilled. Something else was on his mind, but he'd made his feelings about Stan clear, and he'd be Jarun's practice torture victim again before he'd ask what was on the enforcer's mind.

"Mr. Gryffudd . . ." Thad's jaw worked a few times.

Stan wasn't sure if the enforcer needed a bone or chewing tobacco. A chew toy joke was inappropriate considering Leslie's pedigree. "Yes?" he finally prompted.

"I want to apologize again for my behavior yesterday." The Normal looked at Stan. "I should know better than to judge a man by his family's actions. I wouldn't have three incredible stepsons if I gauged them by their daddy's stupidity."

"Apology accepted." Stan held out his hand. Thad took it, and they shook.

Silence fell over the cab of the vehicle again. Silence except for the grinding of Thad's teeth.

"May I make a personal suggestion?" Stan said.

Thad turned to him, and his eyes narrowed. "Depends."

"Sugarless gum. One of the Normal enforcers in L.A. uses it on stakeouts to deal with nerves. It'll save the wear on your tooth enamel."

Thad grunted, and his attention returned to the zipline building. It would be a perfect place for a sniper, which was why four enforcers were up there with rifles. "Never really liked the stuff, but Leslie and I used the nicotine gum to get rid of the tobacco cravings."

"I applaud anyone who can give that up and stay off it."

"What kind of gum does the L.A. enforcer use?"

"Bubblegum."

Thad chuckled. "What is she? Five?"

Stan smiled at the memory of Tiffany Stephens at that age. "Actually, her daughter turns five this month. She's one of Mai's cousins."

Thad's humor faded. "So you've known the girls since they were born." He wasn't just referring to Tiffany.

Stan considered Thad's position. His daughter had recently graduated from high school according to his dossier. While Stan wasn't a parent himself, he could understand Thad's concerns of an older man preying on his child. The funny thing was the girl Mai had been before her parents were murdered and the woman she'd become seemed like two very different people.

"Yes, I have," Stan confirmed. "Does the age difference bother you that much?"

Thad opened his mouth, but whatever he was about to say, he changed his mind and exhaled instead. He turned to Stan with a wry smile on his face. "I don't have room to talk. Most of the time I forget Leslie's my mom's age."

"But weres and witches don't live that much longer than Normals. Not like vampires and fae do," Stan murmured.

"Don't you dare break her heart by dumping her when she gets old," Thad snapped.

"Sam's already made my punishment clear if I do such a thing." Stan grinned.

"Yer assuming mah wife and stepkids don't rip out your throat first." For an instant, Thad sounded like a werecoyote himself.

"Understood, Mr. Wolford."

Movement caught Stan's eye. "Someone just came out of the stairwell." He popped the latch on the SUV the same time as Thad, and both men stepped out of the vehicle. Shadows didn't match the cavalcade of neon lights dancing around the door that didn't close fast enough for only two people.

Stan glanced behind him. Yep, more shadows near the exit ramp. His brother must have brought his entire team, plus a few extra exiles who weren't fond of halflings. He turned to face the stairwell again.

Honey and apple met Stan's nose before Jarun dropped his shadow veil. He walked across the concrete parking space, dragging a cuffed and gagged Mai. Now, why in Morrigan's name would he bother to gag Mai? She was a woman of action, not words.

Jarun stopped a few yards away. "I brought your present, brother dear. Where's mine?"

"Inside the SUV." Stan took a couple of steps back and opened the rear passenger door. He grabbed the two boxes from the back seat.

Despite their containers, Stan could feel the power of the objects within. He turned to face Jarun. "I hope you know what you're doing."

Jarun scowled. "Where's the third object?"

"What third object?" Stan looked at his brother as if he were crazy.

"Where's the rose bush?" Jarun spat.

"There wasn't a rose bush in the vault when I spoke to you," Stan said calmly.

"Don't play the fool, brother dearest." Jarun jerked Mai's head back and flicked his wrist. A silver knife appeared in his grasp. He rested the edge against her throat. "I want the rose bush Ares of Olympus gifted to that bitch."

A whine came from Mai's throat. Fear and pleading filled her eyes. A single tear trickled down her cheek.

This was wrong. Stan extended his senses, but detected no glamour on the figure his half-brother held. Which meant it had to be a dino demon. So where was the real Mai?

"All right, I won't, but I'll only negotiate with Father over the rose bush." If someone looking like Hoarancill stepped out of the shadows, then they had bigger problems than just one dino demon.

Thankfully, Thad kept silent like he had been ordered.

Jarun smirked. "Really? I heard the rumor your precious vampires and their little pet killed him." He inclined his head slightly to the left.

Towards the creature pretending to be Mai.

Was Jarun saying that the thing with him was the dino demon? It still didn't answer the question of Mai's location.

Stan opened his mouth to answer when a soundless roar and blinding light exploded above him.

CHAPTER 17

Mai jerked free from the fae warrior as he went down to one knee, his hands slapped over his ears and his eyes squeezed shut. She ducked and crouched beneath the wall closest to the zipline tower as chunks of concrete rained on the parking lot. Lights along Fremont flickered and died from the power surge.

A fae and a witch had tossed spells at each other from the explosion in the tower. From the reaction of the fae on the roof of the garage, the magick back-lash would incapacitate them for a few minutes at most.

For once, she was glad she wasn't wearing her special watch.

And the fae were too cocky to restrain her.

Once it got over its initial surprise at the explosion, the demon broke its handcuffs and charged for the two boxes Stan had dropped when the backlash knocked him over.

Mai rushed over to the fae who'd been holding her and snatched a couple of his throwing knives. She bolted for her doppelgänger. The demons may not be able to teleport, but they were damn fast even in human form.

She skidded to a halt beside Stan's prone form. Using the snapping motion her grandfather had taught her, she threw the first knife. The demon kept run-ning and disappeared down the ramp.

Damn. She turned back to Thad who stood at the front of the SUV and held a gun on Jarunmisanrill. "You have some way to restrain all of them?" She waved to indicate all the unconscious or stunned fae.

Thad nodded and whistled. Green tendrils came out of nowhere and wrapped themselves around the five men and women Jarunmisanrill had brought with him. No, not nowhere. From behind the stairwell entrance. A bulky shadow carrying Riley came into sight—

Mai's stomach dropped at the sight of Sam's blood-sucking rose bush. She'd been less than a foot from the damn thing when she ducked for cover.

She whirled to face Thad. "What the hell were you thinking?"

The enforcer shrugged, but he kept his eyes on Jarunmisanrill. "Mr. Gryf-fudd asked Seymour to help us. He agreed."

"Seymour?" She knew Stan had a talent with plants but—

"Do you want me to go after the dino demon, ma'am?" Thad asked softly.

His question shook some sense back into her. She knelt, stowed the fae knife in her belt loop, and grabbed Stan's sidearm. "No. Make sure the boss is all right, and don't let the rest of the fae out of your sight."

As she raced for the ramp, Thad called for backup through his comm unit. She should have grabbed a spare unit herself, but she'd wasted enough time.

Mai rounded the corner to the next level when the stench hit her. Holes dotted the concrete, and steam rose from the damage. No, not steam. Fumes from where the dino demon's acidic blood ate away at the structure. She had nicked it with the knife after all.

Avoiding the fumes, she eased down the ramp at a slower pace. Despite the early morning hour, there were still quite a few cars in the garage, and the only illumination was from ambient city light outside of the EMP's range. Voices came from the opposite end of the level. Familiar voices. The demon was approaching Mike Warner.

"Mike! That's not me!"

The enforcer backpedaled and ducked, but not before the demon flung something at the 'coyote. Mike howled and collapsed to his knees.

Mai took aim at the demon, but it darted behind a sedan. She rushed to Mike. "Hold still."

From the scent, the demon had thrown its own blood at the kid. The 'coyote had burned a couple of his fingers from reflexively grabbing at his face. Mai laid Stan's pistol on the concrete and whipped off her jacket. She carefully patted Mike's skin and pried off his earpiece before the acid eating the casing dripped on him.

"You didn't get any blood in your eyes, did you?"

"No, ma'am." Pain filled his voice. "Just need some red meat."

"Head upstairs and stay with Thad." She tossed her ruined jacket to the side and retrieved Stan's sidearm. She wanted her own gun and her watch back. "He's got the med pack in the SUV."

Mike nodded, but he grabbed her arm and whispered, "I don't hear any footsteps." He inclined his head in the direction the demon had fled.

"What did it do with the boxes?" Mai murmured.

"Boxes?"

"Sam's."

"The demon didn't have them when she, er, it approached me."

Shit. Where had the demon stashed the gifts? Those things were too powerful to leave lying around. Did it have an accomplice it passed them off to? Or was it simply waiting until it was alone to make its escape?

"Get up to Thad," she repeated. When Mike hesitated, she hissed, "Do as I say."

The 'coyote crept toward the ramp. She didn't blame him for not shifting. Sprouting fur around those chemical burns on his face would be painful as hell, and make it that much worse treating them.

Mai ducked and looked under the row of vehicles to her left. No feet or anything else was visible. Either the demon was behind a set of tires, or it had climbed on top of one of the taller SUVs or minivans.

Great. She pursed her lips and stood. Nothing like hunting an injured creature in the dark. And she wanted to kick herself for making a stupid assumption. The comm units would have been disabled by the EMP.

If she yelled mentally for Kunal or one of the other vampire enforcers, the demon would know exactly where she was. And that she was alone.

Mai inhaled deeply and released the air. Maybe she was a fool for hunting this thing alone. But she didn't have a choice. Not when the demon could do a lot of damage with the boxes it stole.

She crept forward, stepping slowly and silently, checking around, below, and above each vehicle as she went. Nothing. There were five empty parking spots before two vehicles and the ramp down to the next level.

A drop of liquid hitting metal and then a hissing sound came from the pickup behind her. Mai whirled and raised her weapon. The demon had tucked itself in the joint of concrete and the steel I-beam above the truck.

Still looking like her.

She squeezed the trigger as the damn thing dropped.

CHAPTER 18

Two figures appeared on the garage's exit ramp. At least, Stan thought it was two figures. He blinked and tried to uncross his eyes. "Thad . . ."

The Normal enforcer looked up from where he was leaning Jarun against the front tire after Thad secured handcuffs on the idiot's wrists. "Shit! Mike, what happened?"

"The demon was disguised as Ms. Osaka," the 'coyote said as he stumbled to the SUV. He groaned and sat next to Stan. "It got the jump on me and threw its blood at my face."

Morrigan! The right side of the kid's face was horribly burned. Stan had a terrible feeling it was a good thing he was having trouble focusing.

Thad retrieved the med kit from the back of the SUV. "Mai followed it down to your level."

"The real one?" Stan asked.

"Yeah, if it weren't for her, the demon would have killed me," Mike mumbled.

Alarm rolled through Stan's aching head. "Where is she?"

"Hunting the demon and the boxes." Mike started to shake his head and thought better of it. "She ordered me to get up here with you guys."

Stan let loose with a string of obscenities. He struggled to rise. When he finally gained his feet, his hand reached for his weapon. His sidearm was missing.

"Where's my pistol?"

"Mai has it." Thad carefully irrigated his stepson's wounds to neutralize the acid in the demon's blood.

"Kunal? Quinn?" Stan tapped the comm unit in his ear. "Anybody read me?"

Thad glanced up at him. "The EMP from the explosion took out communications, sir, as well as knocking the fae and the witches for a loop."

The thought of telepathically reaching out to the other vamp and 'coyote enforcers made Stan's headache worse. Besides, knowing Mai's training regimen, they'd be looking out for the semi-conscious witches.

But no one was watching Mai's back.

He took a step toward the ramp when Jarun called out, "Wait."

Stan turned to watch his half-brother climb to his feet. Jarun looked as wobbly as Stan felt.

"You'll need help. The demon has the ghouls wound up and ready to turn on my people for killing their leader." Jarun tilted to his right and took a halting step to catch his balance.

"You killed the ghouls' leader?" Stan blinked a few times until there was only one version of his half-brother.

Jarun tried to shake his head and fell against the SUV in the process. "No, the demon did while disguised as your lady."

"To get them pissed at the vampires, too," Thad mumbled as he lightly covered the ugly burns on Mike's face. The kid's were abilities should be kicking in to heal the awful wounds, but he needed food and they didn't have much more than emergency rations and jerky in the vehicle.

"Yes," Jarun admitted. "It disguised itself as Father. You will need assistance in taking it down."

Even if Stan couldn't see his half-brother's expression clearly, there was enough venom in his voice to spell out his intention.

"You can barely stand," Stan pointed out.

"Better than you," Jarun snarled and pushed away from the SUV to nearly pitch over on his left side. Only fae grace allowed him to catch himself. "Besides your mortal pet is the only creature capable of watching over both yours and my people while we assist your lady."

Rustling came from behind Jarun. He whirled, lost his balance, and landed on his rump. Seymour quivered.

Stan pressed his own lips together. There'd be hell to pay if Jarun realized the plant was laughing at him.

"Seymour, help Thad keep everyone on this parking level safe and whole."

The rose bush rustled the tendrils holding Jarun's compatriots.

"Yes, them, too." Stan gave Jarun a measured look. "As long as Jarunmisanrill causes me, Mai, Thad, and Mike no harm."

The flowers on the bush bobbed in response.

"Here." Thad held up his sidearm, butt first. "You'll need this."

"What about—" Stan started, but Thad held up his hand.

"Got it covered."

A shot rang out.

"Downstairs," Mike croaked. "Far side, close to the next ramp."

Stan set off at a slow jog. Jarun matched his pace, his sword in his hand.

Chapter 19

Mai dived to the side and rolled. The awful grinding of talons on concrete echoed off the low ceiling.

Onyourfeetonyourfeetonyourfeet. Grandpa's mantra screamed through her head.

She tumbled into a crouch and lined up her shot.

Only to have the demon heave its bloody coat at her head.

Once again, she jumped to the side, her knees reminding her she was closer to forty than twenty. The coat landed with a splat, turning to raw demon flesh now that it wasn't connected to the demon itself.

A backhand blow knocked Mai sideways. She landed hard, all air forced from her lungs, and Stan's gun skittered away across the concrete.

The demon loomed over her, a shade blacker in the darkness. Mai drew her left leg in, and her boot heel shot into the demon's left knee. It howled and fell over.

Her only advantage was the last original dino demon had to breed with supernaturals. Despite prejudice, bigotry, and a greater lifespan, the supernaturals were just as human as the Normals. The new demons had a lot of the same weaknesses.

Mai climbed to her feet. A backspin kick knocked the bitch into a support pillar. It hit with a sickening crack. Fumes floated from the concrete.

The garage's lights flickered back to life.

Her stomach wanted to rebel when the demon carefully relocated its lower jaw. Talons extended from its fingertips. The knife cut on its arm had already healed.

Mai swallowed hard, drew the remaining throwing knife, and dropped into a fighting stance. While it would be great if she could merely cut the wristband so the cavalry would appear, she knew it would take a god weapon to slice through her watch on the demon's wrist.

Nope, this was solely up to her and her own skills. She didn't have the recovery abilities of weres or vampires. She needed to make her first blows count.

The demon stalked toward her. Mai scanned the floor, but didn't see Stan's sidearm. Damn, it must have slid under one of the vehicles.

"You really think you'll win," her doppelgänger spat.

Mai didn't bother to answer. Grandfather always said it was a waste of breath. Instead, she lunged with the knife. The demon moved to block, and

Mai followed with a roundhouse kick. She knocked her opponent a few feet to the side.

Her next kick missed as the demon backed up, a new respect in its eyes and its left arm tight against its ribs. It was also favoring the left leg.

Mai lunged with the knife again, but the demon was ready this time. Talons ripped across her left arm. She gritted her teeth against the burning sensation and ducked under the second slash from the demon.

Her favorite Glock was tucked in the demon's fake waistband.

But the demon was already pivoting for a backslash. Mai dropped and swept the demon's right leg. Both of them went down in a tangle of limbs.

Mai slashed at the demon's Achilles and missed. She rolled free and to her knees to find her own gun aimed at her face.

CHAPTER 20

Stan squinted as the garage's lights flickered back on. Good to know the power company in this city was efficient. Scuffling noise came from the opposite end of the garage. He raced in that direction, Jarun on his heels.

Two women fought ahead of them. At least, he thought it was really two though his eyes kept saying it was four. They hit the floor and parted. The Mais with the gun gained their feet first. The ones on their knees and holding the knives froze, their eyes locked on the barrel of their opponents' weapons.

He slowed, and the women's attention flicked to him and Jarun before they returned to scowling at each other.

"Really?" the standing Mais snapped. "You can't tell it's me, Stan?"

"Ask her for her tie," the kneeling Mais said. "I keep my Olympian bronze pin in my tie clip."

Stan blinked, wishing his headache would go away. If he found out which one of the witches had thrown the spell, he'd definitely bring back the rack.

The standing Mai took her finger from the trigger and held up both her hands, showing a blue and gold band on her wrist. "If my watch doesn't convince you, you need to shoot us both. It's the only way to be sure."

His gut clenched. If he made the wrong choice, the demon would cut down both him and Jarun before it would slaughter Thad, Mike, and the fae on the roof.

An evil smile fell over the kneeling Mai's face. "There's an easier way. Have her say Sam's full name."

The standing Mai blanched.

Stan squeezed the trigger.

And missed.

The kneeling Mai crabcrawled away as the standing Mai brought her barrel to bear on him. The Mai on the floor grabbed a gun next to her, aimed, and fired.

The standing Mai slowly crumpled face-first on the concrete. Red spread along her shirt.

Stan took a step forward when displaced air popped. Samantha Marie Ridgeway St. James, wife of Master Duncan St. James and a goddess of death in her own right, appeared between the two Mais. Of course, she faced the dead one with the watch. Her horrified expression quickly turned to rage.

"Gryffudd! You prick!" Sam's eyes shifted from her human blue until both orbs glowed white.

In that moment, Stan knew he was going to die without knowing if the real Mai still lived.

Chapter 21

"Before you smite my boyfriend for my murder, you could at least make sure I'm dead," Mai grumbled.

Sam pivoted so fast her knee-length black coat flared. "Mai!" The goddess sagged before she turned back and stared at the corpse. As they all watched, the dead demon shifted back to its normal form. Human skin stretched over a velociraptor skeleton. The damn thing was eerie as hell.

Mai wearily got to her feet and shuffled a little closer while Sam knelt beside the dead dino demon.

"There's more and more human in the DNA in these things," she murmured.

"Too much for you to . . ." Mai glanced at Jarunmisanrill. "You know," she finished lamely.

"Eat it?" Sam stood. Even though her eyes had returned to human blue, her skin had a distinctly greenish cast that had nothing to do with her powers or the garage lights. "Yeah, but I'll take the body back to Los Angeles, and let Bebe and Ray examine it."

She glared at Jarunmisanrill. "Before I jump to any more conclusions, what's that asshat doing here?"

Of course, the fae's expression turned haughty. "Cleaning up your mess."

"Dude, I'll give you a mess—"

"Wait." Mai grabbed Sam's sleeve, though there wasn't a damn thing she could really do to stop her friend. But she could try to diffuse the situation and salve the fae's pride. "The dino demon tried to con him by pretending to be his father."

"His father?"

"Hoarancill."

Sam's head whipped back to Jarunmisanrill so fast her blond ponytail smacked Mai in the face. "So this is a revenge thing?"

The fae lifted his chin. "As delightful as such vengeance would be, the dino demons are a threat to all of us. It wanted my assistance in stealing your property from the Karnak."

Mai resisted the urge to smile at Jarunmisanrill repeating her words. She made the right call.

"My property?" Sam frowned.

Mai cleared her throat. "The gifts."

Sam groaned and rolled her eyes. "I wish there was a universal dump for this type of shit."

"It would help if you'd create your own heaven and keep them there," Mai said dryly. It was the same old argument they'd had for the last five years.

Peter stuck his head out of Sam's coat pocket. The phantom rabbit squeaked his agreement.

"I'll get around to it." Sam looked down at her pet ghost. "And I don't need any lip from you two."

Peter sniffed and retreated back into the pocket.

"Speaking of which . . ." Mai slowly pivoted. "We need to find the boxes. The demon had to have stashed them somewhere in the garage."

Sam sighed. "As long as it was just the boxes . . ."

Stan and Mai exchanged looks.

This time, he cleared his throat. "Seymour's with us. I thought it would be good to give him a job."

"Seymour?" Sheer disbelief filled Sam's face. "You named that damn rose-bush *Seymour*?"

Stan shrugged. "Names make a difference."

Thank goodness, Jarunmisanrill was smart enough to keep his mouth shut, even though he smirked.

"Can you sense those boxes anywhere in here?" Mai asked. Best to keep Sam focused on the immediate problem.

The goddess closed her eyes for a moment, then opened them. "They're up in the corner where the ledge merges with the upper level." She blew out a deep breath. "Do you need help getting them back to the Karnak?"

"No, thank you," Mai said. "We'll get everything back in the vault."

"Uh-huh." Sam's right eyebrow rose. "Who's driving? You have a concussion, and those two are suffering from magick backlash."

"Thad's on the upper level, keeping an eye on Seymour," Stan answered.

"You left Thad alone with the killer plant?" Sam's eyes started glowing white again.

"Seymour's not going to hurt him," Stan said sternly. "He's been a big help in exposing the demon."

"And the Swedish Bikini Team wannabe?" Sam inclined her head toward Jarunmisanrill.

"He sent in an old friend of Stan's to make contact with us and warn the coven of the demons' plot," Mai said. "And he helped set up the demon for us to take down." She glanced at the fae. Yep, he was too proud to ask for himself. "Could you pull some strings with Morrigan to get him and his team from the Ohio incident back into the Unseelie Court? The Winter Queen needs to understand we're all in this together, like it or not."

Sam's eyes narrowed. "Done." She jabbed a finger in Jarunmisanrill's direction. "That doesn't mean you're totally forgiven for your share of the crap you pulled in Ohio."

"Understood, m'lady." The idiot gave Sam a mocking bow.

Luckily, she merely rolled her eyes before she popped out of the garage, taking the dino demon corpse with her.

Chapter 22

It took the rest of the week for them to clean up the mess from the night before. Stan offered the high roller suites to Jarun and the cousins while they waited to hear from Sam about the negotiations, or more likely Morrigan's threats, with the Winter Queen. Amazingly, they took him up on the offer with no snide comments. Even weirder was his half-brother keeping company with Riley. However, if they kept each other occupied and out of his hair, all the better.

The two boxes were returned to the special vault. Seymour volunteered to stand guard over them in return for an hour of sunshine a day and a pint of human blood once a week.

None of the fae or witches admitted to throwing spells. Quinn must have suspected it was one of his people because their high priestess offered the use of their top healer free of charge for Mike and Mai's injuries.

The ghouls simply disappeared after the magick explosion downtown. None of the phone numbers or e-mail addresses Jarun had in his phone worked anymore. And the house where he originally met the ghoul leader burned to the ground the same night as the confrontation with the dino demon. Master St. James sent an alert to the other vampire leaders, but no one had a clue the ghouls were still around.

Or so all the coven masters claimed.

Stan donated money to the company who ran the Fremont Street zipline for repairs to their tower. The Karnak got more back when everyone assumed the damage was caused by unknown terrorists. Staci and the marketing department ran with the Vegas Proud promotion. Within a week, the hotel was filled to capacity.

Once they got everything squared away, Stan was a little surprised when Mai agreed to move into the penthouse over their first non-working dinner since his arrival in the city.

"Don't get me wrong." He leaned forward. "I'm ecstatic! But what made you change your mind?"

Mai poked at her broccoli, her lips pursed. Finally, she laid down her fork and looked at him. "Leslie tattled to all the dealers."

"Leslie?" Stan blinked. "How did she find out?"

A disgusted look filled her face. "Apparently, Thaddeus Wolford talks in his sleep."

"Is it just the dealers?"

"Not anymore," Mai said sourly.

"Is people knowing about us so bad?" He reached across the table and took her hand in his.

She sighed. "No, I guess not. No one has been stupid enough to say anything directly to me. It's just—"

The elevator whirred to life. Mai looked in the conveyance's direction and back at him, frowning. "Were you expecting someone?"

"No," he said softly.

They both pulled weapons and took positions near the elevator. There was a ding, and the bronze-colored doors slid open. Black rose blossoms leaned through the opening.

Stan breathed a prayer of relief. "No, it's only me and Mai." He rose and holstered his weapon. Mai did the same. "Next time, call me first."

The blooms drooped.

"Seymour, it's as much for your safety as everyone else's."

The rose bush held out a stem with a tiny pin prick in it. Thorns grew around it.

"No, you can't poke Sanjay in return." Stan said sternly. "He's doing his job by making sure you're not a demon."

Seymour quivered before he shuffled to the sliding glass doors. He pushed one open and went out on the patio to enjoy the sunset.

Mai's grunt sounded a lot like one of Thad's. "I thought we had him on a schedule."

Stan chuckled. "Kids are always changing."

"Kids?" Mai stared up at him with an alarmed expression.

"Seymour isn't that old. Not quite two hundred."

Mai shook her head and watched the plant. "I never thought I'd have a sentient, blood-sucking rosebush as a stepson."

"Well . . ." Stan wrapped his arms around her, pulled her back against his chest, and nuzzled her neck. "We could start practicing. So he has a brother or sister to play with."

"You're pushing, Gryffudd." But there was laughter in her voice as she tilted her head to give him better access.

"I'm sorry. How about we finish dinner in the bedroom?" he murmured against her skin.

"Are you sure Seymour will be all right out there?"

He reined in his impatience. For all her claims she didn't have a maternal bone in her body, Mai Osaka cared an awful lot.

"How about I give him a bottle?" He turned her to face him. "Then I'll meet you in there."

"Fine." But the look she gave him was sultry as she sauntered down the hallway.

"And don't forget to remove your watch."

Feminine laughter echoed from the master bedroom. While he appreciated Sam's concern, and Mai loved the Mulan replacement watch, he didn't need the goddess popping in while they were in the middle of making love again.

Stan crossed to the kitchen and retrieved a blood bag from the refrigerator, B-negative, Seymour's favorite. He warmed it under the hot water tap before heading out to the patio.

"Here you go, buddy."

The rose bush stroked Stan's cheek with a blossom before Seymour seized the bag. He shook a couple of stems.

"Yes, you can watch some TV, but you need to keep it down." Stan leaned against the railing. "Mai's moving up here."

Two green tendrils twined around each other.

"I don't know yet." Stan smiled. "Maybe."

The tendrils unwound and waved.

"Thank you for promising not to drink her."

Seymour stabbed a thorn in the plastic bag and happily slurped his treat.

Stan carefully patted the bush and headed back inside. Yeah, he missed San Francisco, but it looked like everything would work out in Las Vegas after all.

GHOULS IN THE GROCERY STORE

───◆───

Author's Note: This story takes place approximately six months prior to the events in *Resurrected*.

Chapter 1

The werewolf in front of the entrance to my in-laws' Beverly Hills estate poked my left index finger with an Olympian bronze pin, one of many my foster grandfather had finagled out of his brother Hephaestus. When I didn't scream, burst into flames, or otherwise croak from the injury, the were signaled his partner to open the gates.

I guided my SUV up to the portico of the main house and climbed out. Enough sunlight from the early April evening remained to show the flower beds had been redone.

Again.

My mother-in-law Elizabeth didn't have much else to do these days. She was damn lucky she had only been sentenced to house arrest after her treason. All of the St. James Coven enforcers, except one, wanted the privilege of whacking off her head, which was why Uncle Duncan had to trade favors with Los Angeles's packmaster. Elizabeth thought she'd been saving Max's life when she went behind our backs, but she started a cold war between the North American vampire masters that had threatened to turn hot for the last eighteen months.

A brief twinge of grief jerked at my soul at the thought of my late husband as I jogged up the steps to the front door, not the all-consuming blackness that had coated every waking thought the first year after his death. I stabbed the doorbell. Max was the reason I agreed to our daughter spending a day of her Spring Break with her grandparents. The extra time to work on my masters' thesis was only a bonus.

The door swung open for my second surprise. Susannah Epstein stood there in a gray housekeeper's uniform way too big for her petite form and an expression that could only be described as a mix of amusement and annoyance. "Hey, Tiffany!"

"Should I ask what happened to Juanita?"

The teen witch smirked and flipped her ponytail. "Besides the fact she could deal with the weres and the vampires, but dealing with your mother-in-law's cabin fever wasn't worth her green card?"

Shit. Elizabeth must have been on one hell of a roll this week. If our vampire coven didn't need her so bad, Uncle Duncan would have dug the family broadsword out of storage and cheerfully beheaded her himself, even though she was his mother-in-law as well as mine.

"Come on in." Susannah waved. The polish on her fingernails matched the aqua streaks in her dark curls. The bright color distracted from the even darker turn my own thoughts had taken. "Ellie's putting on a performance for the family."

As much as I wanted to ask the witch how her step-grandmother conned her into working as a housekeeper for the craziest Normal on this side of the Mississippi, I managed to remain quiet. Instead, I followed her. Strains of Vivaldi grew stronger as we approached the formal living room.

A pained smile was plastered on Elizabeth's face when she glanced at me from where she sat on one of the couches with her toy poodle, Mr. Cuddles. As I entered the living room, I saw why.

Kabuki theater makeup decorated my baby's face. She was dressed in her black leotard and tights, hot pink tutu, and the black toe shoes she'd demanded for her fifth birthday six months ago. The sweet tones of the composer's "Spring" concerto were at odds with the mix of ballet moves and kata forms Ellie demonstrated in time to the music.

While Elizabeth tried, and failed, to hide her dismay, Ted was enthralled. Given Ellie would be his one and only grandchild, I suspected Ted would support her even if she decided to become a contract killer. As the last notes of the violin died, he launched into enthusiastic applause.

"Bravo! Bravo!"

Half-blind, the thirteen-year-old Mr. Cuddles barked at Ted's clapping.

"That was very nice, Eleanor." Elizabeth was the only person who called my daughter by her full name, probably thinking it would irritate me. Hell, I was just happy my own mother hadn't given me one of my ancestors' more frumpy names.

Like Mathilda.

"Spectacular, sweetie!" a garrulous voice said.

I walked a little further into the living room. Grandma Neel, Elizabeth's mother and one of my daughter's namesakes, sat on the raggedy recliner she insisted on bringing with her when she moved to Beverly Hills from Ridgeway, West Virginia.

Well, forced to move to keep Dare Coven, which controlled the U.S. east of the Mississippi River and north of the Mason-Dixon line, from murdering the old lady out of spite.

"Hi there, shrimp!" She grinned, showing more than a few missing teeth.

"Back atcha, munchkin." I leaned over to give her a hug.

From the hot pink and black track suit she wore, I knew what had inspired Ellie's performance attire. It also explained why Susannah was now working here. Max's grandmother and the high priestess of the Los Angeles witch co-ven had hit it off from the moment they met.

Including wearing any and all outfits Elizabeth deemed tasteless.

"Mommy! You need to see my new show!" Ellie raced toward Ted's expensive stereo.

"Hold up there, young lady!"

She paused, her index finger inches from the "Play" button, and looked at me, her big blue eyes narrowed for daring to challenge her.

I gave her a stern look. "I told you this morning before Grandma Phil brought you over here we would need to leave at seven."

Ellie lifted her chin in a defiant gesture. "You said we could stop at McDonald's for dinner."

I squelched my urge to vomit. These were the times I missed Max taking on certain household duties, and trips to that particular fast food joint was one of them. "And I also said you needed to be ready. If you wash your face, put on your street shoes, and don't argue with me, we will still go to McDonald's."

"Yay!" She tore off for the stairs.

Susannah laughed. "I'll go help her."

Once they disappeared, Ted quietly said, "Why don't you two stay for dinner?"

"Because god knows she doesn't have any food in the house?" Elizabeth sneered.

Figured my own kid would tattle on me. Next, Elizabeth would start on my camouflage tactical pants, black t-shirt, and jean jacket. I didn't meet her frumpy skirt and pearls sensibilities.

However, before I could come up with a good retort, Grandma Neel came to my rescue. "When you bother to get something higher than an M.R.S. degree, you can bitch, Lizzie. Until then, shut the fuck up and leave the girl alone."

Elizabeth's mouth open and closed a few times, but the glares both Ted and her mother aimed at her convinced Elizabeth she was on the losing side of this battle. Or maybe she realized I hadn't accepted Ted's invitation.

Mr. Cuddles growled in my general direction, all too happy to give voice to his mistress's displeasure.

I smiled at my father-in-law. I may totally detest his wife, but they were Ellie's only living biological grandparents, and for her sake, I made the effort. "I appreciate the offer, but I've got a couple of errands I need to run tonight. How about we come over for Easter dinner?"

People would've thought I'd given Ted the fucking Holy Grail the way his face lit up, but he immediately sobered. "Is it okay if Duncan and Sam are here?"

My eyes narrowed at the mention of *her* name.

"Please, Tiffany. It's been a year and a half since I've had my family together for a holiday." His big blue eyes looked so much like Max's through his glasses. The same eyes as our daughter's.

Did my hate for the bitch who'd condemned my husband to death outweigh Ted's need for his family?

"Can I second Ted's request?" Grandma Neel asked. "Not trying to play the guilt card, shrimp, but I'm eighty-years-old, and Lord knows how many Easters I have left."

Elizabeth rolled her eyes. "Samantha would know."

And that snotty comment tilted the emotional pile in my head despite my feelings about my sister-in-law. "It's cool, Ted." I held up a finger before he could say whatever he was about to say. "On the condition that *she* is never alone in a room with Ellie. Got me?"

He didn't even ask me who I meant. He simply nodded.

Ellie raced back into the living room, her black bangs damp from her face scrubbing and her jacket on. "Ready to go! See?" She held up her right foot to show off her matching hot pink athletic shoes.

"All right then." I gave Ted and Grandma Neel hugs. "We'll see you Sunday."

"At noon," Ted added.

Ellie's eyes widened. "We're coming here for Easter?"

I nodded.

"Yay!" She hugged everybody before she tore off for the front door.

Part of me rejoiced a smear of red face paint Ellie had missed now decorated Elizabeth's off-white skirt as I turned to follow my daughter out to my SUV.

After getting us both buckled in, I waved to the weres at the gate as I pulled onto the street. A glance in the rearview mirror showed my daughter while she rattled on about bringing her eggs over to hide. Behind her, headlights snapped on, and a Jeep pulled into traffic.

A familiar red Jeep that was often parked in my driveway. Rather than guess and take chances with my daughter's life, I tapped the hands-off button for my phone and said, "Call Alex."

Two rings later, my boss's cheerful voice filled the compartment. "Hey, darlin'! What's up?"

"Hi, Grandpa Alex!" Ellie yelled from the backseat.

In addition to being my boss and surfing buddy, Alex was also married to my foster mom. All of my family relationships would give a genealogist a nervous breakdown. But that wasn't why I called Alex.

"This is business, young lady," I said sternly.

"Sorry, Mommy," Ellie faux-whispered.

"What's wrong?" Alex's voice turned serious at my words.

"Was there a change in guard rotation?" I bit out.

"Oops! Sorry, Tiffany." Computer keys clicked in the background. "Mattie had a last minute family thing. Jake's on tonight."

"You're lucky I recognized his vehicle."

Alex groaned. "Please tell me you didn't shoot him."

"Hell, no—" I started.

"Mommy, language!" came an angry five-year-old's voice from her car seat. Alex's stifled laughter echoed through the speaker.

"Sorry," I muttered and cleared my throat. "No, I didn't shoot him. He's supposed to help me swap out our garbage disposal tomorrow." Part of me felt guilty for depending on Jake's knowledge of household repairs, but I wanted Ellie to learn to fend for herself. That meant I needed to learn. Neither my uncle who raised me or my husband knew basic household shit. They always hired other people to fix their stuff.

"I promise I'll call you next time there's a schedule change," Alex swore.

"Only because you know I'll tell Phil, and she'll barbeque your ass."

"Mommy!"

Alex chuckled. "She will, and, Ellie, don't give your mom a hard time."

"I won't! We're going to McDonald's!" she yelled.

"Thanks, Alex. Talk to you later." I ended the call. It wasn't his fault I had turned into a raging paranoid. The same assholes who had beaten Max to death had kidnapped Ellie, and despite their efforts, I managed to get her back alive. I'd already lost my husband. I sure as hell wasn't losing my daughter, too.

Chapter 2

"Mommy, why does everyone call Uncle Duncan 'master' now?"

I glanced at Ellie as I yanked the shopping cart out of the row. The overhead fluorescent lights turned my daughter's pale skin into a ghastly gray-blue tone even with the kabuki makeup washed off. And while the days were getting longer, dark had already fallen by the time we reached the grocery store in our Tarzana neighborhood.

Frankly, I would have given anything to light some candles and soak in a hot bath than deal with grocery shopping, but we literally had nothing for dinner in the house except juice boxes and peanut butter as Ellie had already blabbed to my mother-in-law.

Hell, we had nothing to spread the peanut butter on. We ate it straight out of the jar last night.

I passed the cart I had to the woman behind me, dressed in a full burqa. Our gazes met. Her eyes were arresting, such a light hazel that they stood out against her black lashes and dark skin.

"Here you go," I said with a friendly smile. Okay, I did it more to buy time to answer my daughter's question than any shred of politeness.

The woman nodded and murmured, "Thank you." She pushed the cart into the main part of the store while I grabbed another one.

"Because he's the boss now Uncle Caesar has retired, sweetie," I said, coming up with the simplest explanation I could. The entire fucking vampire coven were honorary aunts and uncles. I hoped it made up for Max not being in her life. I pushed the cart forward, and the second set of double doors into the supermarket hissed open.

Innocent blue eyes stared up at me. "My teacher says it's a bad thing that we call him 'master.'"

I froze half-way through the doors. Mrs. Hill was a dream, kind and patient with my daughter and her fellow kindergarteners. Lydia Hill was also black. And even though I was mixed, she probably didn't realize it because of the predominant St. James genes. I fumbled for what to tell Ellie.

I settled on clearing my throat as I pushed the cart past the open doors. "Did she say why it was a bad thing?"

Ellie skipped beside me. "She said it meant his family owned your family."

"Where on earth did she get that idea?" I had a pretty good notion, but I wanted to hear my daughter's side of the story.

"She said the only way minorities came to America was because white people bought and sold them." Ellie frowned. "I tried to tell Mrs. Hill Grandpa Kensai came here because he wanted to, but she said I was wrong."

Technically, Kensai Osaka, his descendants, and his retainers had been forced to leave Honshu after he'd butted heads one too many times with the vampire master who ruled the island. And technically, he'd worked for an African prior to Caesar becoming Normal and ceding the coven leadership to Duncan. But trying to explain the complexities and subtleties of ancient family lines in today's politically correct climate was damn near impossible. Add in the vampire portion, and we were looking at pretty, white straightjackets.

I paused next to the flower department while I fumbled for my shopping list and a pen in the knapsack that doubled as my purse as well as the words to explain things at a kindergarten level. The multitude of Easter lilies overpowered every other bloom in the vicinity. A quick glance said no one was nearby. No one except the dark-haired man in sunglasses and a tan windbreaker, standing behind a towering display of houseplants. For the love of Murphy, did Jake Wong realize how much he stuck out in a crowd?

At least, he'd learned not to wear hoodies after an encounter with department store security when I was buying Ellie new shoes for school. Now, he looked like a middle-aged perv stalking us instead of a purse snatcher.

I returned my attention to Ellie and lowered my voice. "Sweetie, did you tell Mrs. Hill Uncle Duncan was a vampire?"

"No!" Her eyes widened. "You and Daddy told me never to say that word to anybody who's not Family."

A pang hit my heart. Part surprise she remembered something Max had said, part guilt I hadn't thought much about him lately. And we were coming up on the eighteen-month anniversary of his death.

"Thank you for listening to us." I smiled at her. "I'll have a talk with Mrs. Hill, but in the meantime, let's not use the word 'master' around anyone at school since it bothers your teacher."

"Okay, Mommy."

I envied the simplicity of my daughter's world. I didn't have the same luxury when I was her age. My mother and all other remaining relatives descended from Duncan's sister Margaret had been slaughtered shortly after I was born. The fact Dad could trace his line back to Caesar's sister and Kensai had been icing on the cake for the rogue vampires who murdered him while they sought to overthrow our previous coven master nearly twenty-five years ago. As a result, I'd been constantly watched and guarded nearly my entire life. And now?

Now, thanks to Max's genetics, Ellie was even more valuable to various parties who wanted to destroy our coven.

Which was why my fellow enforcer was following us.

"Why don't you pick out a couple of nice tomatoes for us?" I pointed at the low display Ellie could reach.

Suspicion narrowed her eyes at my request for fresh produce. "We're still going to McDonald's tonight, aren't we?"

Once again, my stomach rebelled at the thought, but I couldn't blame the fast food restaurant. My extreme morning sickness when I'd been pregnant with Ellie was thoroughly at fault. Because of the memory, I hadn't been able to eat there since then.

So, of course, it was my daughter's favorite.

"As soon as we get our shopping done. We don't have any coffee either," I reminded her.

"No grumpy mommies!" She tore off for the tomato display.

I didn't bother to turn around. "Come out from behind the plants, Wong."

"Wow. Ellie is right. You are a grumpy mommy." He appeared in my line of vision and peered at me over the rim of his sunglasses. "Do I need to get you some coffee now?" He gestured toward the in-store café on the other side of the produce section.

"You're lucky I didn't shoot you. Mattie was scheduled to be on duty tonight."

He shrugged. "Her great-something-granddaughter's play is tonight. She asked if we could trade shifts."

I crossed my arms and tapped the toe of my right boot. "And Alex approved this?" Like I said, our coven's chief enforcer was married to my foster mom, which kind of made him my step-foster father as well as our boss. Vampire families are complicated even when you're Normal.

And just because I'd already talked to Alex didn't mean I wouldn't give Jake some shit for not calling me himself.

"Why wouldn't he?" Jake frowned, but even while talking to me, his eyes roamed, examining the other shoppers for signs of danger. "In case you haven't noticed, he's been on an unpredictability rampage lately. He wants to keep the bad guys guessing."

The last things I wanted to discuss was work or Alex's tactics, much less the fact I'd been placed on desk duty for the last eighteen months because of the threat against Ellie. My only consolation was Elizabeth was even more restricted in her movements than I was.

"Next time, call me and confirm even if Alex contacts me," I muttered. "You know these dino demons can pretend to be anyone."

"Yes, ma'am." Jake flashed me a grin that sent inappropriate feelings through me. Why on earth *she* dumped him was beyond rational understanding. Hell, if I'd met Jake before Max and I became a couple, I might not have hooked up with my husband.

But then, I wouldn't have Ellie either.

"Uncle Jake!" Ellie raced back with two tomatoes in a clear plastic bag.

He caught her as she leapt at him. "What's up, munchkin?"

"You're not doing a good job of hiding," she whispered. Or tried to. Everyone in the flower department and produce section could hear her. "I saw you behind those plants."

"Yeah." He gave me a dirty look. "Your mom pointed that out, too."

I grinned. "Dude, I wasn't the one made by a five-year-old."

"How about we get your mom some coffee so she won't be so grumpy?" he said.

"Uh-huh." She nodded her head vigorously. "Can I get some milk, too?"

"That's up to your mom."

They both looked at me and said, "Ple-e-e-ease!"

I shook my head, trying not to laugh at their antics. "Fine. I'll be in the deli."

Ellie handed me the bag of tomatoes before the pair headed for the café. Jake and Max had been friends for years before I met my husband. Hell, their friendship had even survived—

Her.

Old rage welled, and I roughly shoved the cart toward the deli department. She could have saved her brother. She had the power. But she hadn't lifted a finger.

And now, my little girl didn't have her father. Even worse, Duncan had sided with *her*, which was why I only spoke with him when necessary. Even as my grief for my deceased husband eased, the fury remained.

Maybe agreeing to go to Ted and Elizabeth's for Easter dinner wasn't such a good idea. I might get *her* blood all over their expensive berber carpet.

"Can I help you?" The hair-netted store employee peered over the counter. She smiled brightly. Her medium brown complexion didn't look any healthier under the grocery's lights than Ellie's had. Murphy only knew how bad my skin looked.

"Yes, please." I tapped my pen against my chin. "A half-pound of Swiss, and a half-pound of Colby Longhorn."

I stared at the rolls of lunch meats, trying to decide between pesto ham and black pepper turkey, when the sandalwood hit my nose. I looked up. The slip of paper and pen fell from my hands.

The deli lady's brown eyes had the faintest gold sheen. She wasn't anyone I knew from the coven. It didn't matter if my body language or my thoughts gave me away. She leapt over the counter, fangs gleaming in the awful grocery lights.

I stumbled backward, yanking the cart with me as I went down and drawing my Glock at the same time. The rogue vampire landed in the cart. She smashed Ellie's carefully selected tomatoes before her landing bent and stretched the heavy wire bottom. Thankfully, she didn't tear through the steel. I kicked the cart away from me.

The sudden jerk and roll caught the vampire off guard. She struggled to maintain her balance, which meant she was a newborn. I lined up the heart shot and squeezed my trigger twice.

I didn't wait for her to dissolve into a puddle of goo. I rolled to my feet and took off for the café. "Ellie!" Behind me, there was a loud splash.

A middle-aged lady wearing a business suit in the produce section screamed, "Gun!" She and the other shoppers took off in all directions.

All of Alex's lectures over the last year and a half about altering my routes ran through my mind. I only hit this grocery once a month at most. Was it Marcus Giovanni and his rogues who'd allied themselves with the dinosaur demons, or was it the Vampire Liberation Front? How long had these assholes been planning their attack?

Someone tackled me, and I hit the thin veneer of linoleum over concrete hard enough to knock the wind out of me. My Glock skidded away, coming to a rest beneath a display of oranges.

Rage came roaring back, even if my breath didn't. I twisted onto my back, flicked my wrist, and shoved my silver-coated, and very illegal, stiletto into the temple of my attacker. His shocked expression came an instant before he slumped on top of me.

Unfortunately, the stiletto blade wasn't long enough to penetrate his chest wall all the way to his heart, much less big enough to cut off his head. I jerked out the blade and stowed it inside my jacket sleeve again before I wiggled out from under him and crawled over to my handgun. Air came back with little fits and gasps, and my chest ached like a son of a bitch.

Another vampire dressed like a suburban dad rounded the bin of Idaho potatoes, a sick, fanged smile on his face. I squeezed off one shot. He wavered for a moment before the flesh slid from his bone and landed on the floor with a loud *splooch*. His skeleton collapsed a moment later.

I rose to a crouch and made my way back to the asshole who tackled me. He could have been any day worker in the greater Los Angeles metropolitan area. He was also trying to regain his feet when I finished what I started.

GRANDPA ARES! I silently yelled. I hated depending on anyone, but Ellie was in danger. I wanted my foster grandfather to fry these bastards before our luck ran out.

More shots echoed against the cavernous ceiling, followed by the screams of more shoppers. There was no *pop* of displaced air. No sudden appearance of the god who claimed me as a granddaughter. He would have done anything for Ellie, so why wasn't he answering me?

Another shot, much closer to me. Jake.

With a wary eye for more rogues, I crawled toward the café, but apparently, I'd taken care of the ones meant to keep me out of the way while they kidnapped my daughter. Dammit, I was not going through this bullshit again!

Outside of the rails around the café area were two reeking puddles of goo. Jake used broken legs of a wooden chair to keep a third vampire at bay near the register. Ellie was nowhere in sight.

I rose to my feet and took aim. "Hey, asshat!"

Jake dove for cover, but the rogue vampire turned toward me as I planned. I squeezed off two more shots. The first took out an unhealthy chunk of skull. Bright red blossomed on the white t-shirt where his heart was from the second shot. Once again, my target wavered for a moment before the flesh and organs slid from his bones. Two seconds later, the skeleton collapsed in the gross, spreading remains.

I stalked over to Jake who climbed to his feet. "Lose your weapon?"

"Nope. Found it." He held up his own gun and flashed a bright grin.

"Where's Ellie?" I bit out.

Jake stuck his index finger and thumb between his lips. His whistle sounded like a bird call. An answering whistle came from one of the cabinets behind the register counter. Jake changed his bird sound.

The door of the cabinet eased open, and Jake gave the dark space a thumbs-up. Ellie crawled out. She ran to me and wrapped her arms around my waist. I tried to block her view of the two kids who had been working the café. I couldn't think about their parents waiting for them to come home for the rest of eternity. If I did, I'd freeze with panic.

"Good girl," I whispered into Ellie's hair. "We need to leave, sweetie."

She nodded.

I'd only taken one step toward the closest exit when the entire store plunged into darkness.

Chapter 3

All three of us dropped to the floor.

More surprised shouts echoed from the high industrial-style ceiling. The cries shifted to howls of pain and shrieks of terror. One last scream abruptly cut off. An occasional moan swept from other parts of the grocery store. Otherwise, it was eerily quiet.

"Shit," I muttered. *Ares!*

Still no answer to my silent prayer.

"Mommy, language," Ellie chided under her breath. I should never have let her watch Captain America movies. She was turning into a goody-two-shoes.

Waiting for my eyes to adjust, I wrapped my left hand around her right. We crept to the edge of the railing and peeked between the slats around the back wall of the café. Outside the main doors of the grocery store, the security lamps for the parking lot were off, too. Against the ambient light from the stores across the street, tall shadows shuffled in front of the glass. Whatever they were, they didn't move with the speed and elegance of vampires or fae, nor with the purpose of healthy Normals.

"I count a dozen outside," I whispered.

The warmth of Jake's body against my back was comforting as he peered over my head. "Same. They probably have more waiting for you by your SUV and at the pharmacy entrance. What the hell are they?"

So he noticed the discrepancies, too.

"Don't know," I breathed. "Don't want to find out either." The emergency generator still hadn't kicked on. Whoever was after us had done their research on the building's power supply.

"There's a door to the storage area in the dairy section," he whispered. "Maybe we can go out the delivery bay."

"If they have the main entrances and my vehicle staked out, then they'll have someone watching the back," I pointed out.

Ellie tugged on my hand. "Mommy, I don't see any vampire eyes."

She was right. Most of the rogues we'd encountered over the last few years were newborns, like the ones who initially attacked us. Baby vamps couldn't keep their emotions in check while hunting. When my uncle Duncan was Turned in the sixteenth century, those glowing eyes caused terror. Now, the signature glow made the younger vampires a convenient target.

So either really old vampires stalked us with Murphy only knew what those shadows outside were, or whatever was after Ellie were things we'd never encountered before. I hoped, anyway. If they were dino demons, we were seriously fucked.

"Dairy section then," I breathed the words to Jake. "Ellie—"

"I know the drill, Mommy," she whispered back fiercely. "Stay quiet and do what you and Uncle Jake tell me."

The cavernous interior of the store was pitch black. We carefully backtracked out of the café. I crept down the closest aisle, trying not to breathe too loud. Ellie's damp hand clung to mine as she matched my steps. My boot brushed something, and it rolled away with a clatter that sounded obscenely loud compared to the silence of the rest of the store.

Dammit! Leave it to me to select the canned fruits and vegetables aisle in the dark.

Snuffling sounds came from all around us. My heart pounded.

"Up," Jake whispered. He grabbed Ellie and boosted her to the top shelf. She kicked the shelf below her in her effort to climb up, and more cans hit the floor in a series of bangs and clangs.

A shadow slightly darker than our surroundings moved at the end of the aisle. It stumbled on other cans probably knocked over by panicked shoppers. And the monster reminded me of how I'd captured a certain red-coated, home-intruding elf who wasn't as harmless on Christmas Eve as everyone thought.

I holstered my gun and ran toward the shadow, sweeping my left arm along the fourth shelf. More cans landed on the linoleum tiles, the sound reminiscent of a horrendous hail storm. The noises drew the shadow closer, and it sniffed loudly at the cans rolling toward it.

Taking advantage of the distraction. I scrambled up the shelving and reached the top. Teeth snapped behind me. I looked down, but I couldn't make out much in the dark. It was about the size of a large St. Bernard. Or a small Volkswagen Beetle. Its smell wasn't remotely canine though. Pulling up my legs, I knocked over some more cans. The monster below grunted when they hit it, but otherwise, the blows didn't seem to faze the creature.

Instead, the thing raised its head, or what I thought was its head, and let loose a rising and falling whine that sounded suspiciously like an emergency vehicle siren. Snuffling from the other things got closer.

"Stay here." The shadow that was Jake had clambered to the top of the shelves on the opposite side of the aisle. His silhouette stood out against the red lights of a cereal display a couple of aisles away that must have been battery-powered. He race-walked along the narrow tops of the shelving units, trying not to knock anything over and attract the monster's attention, before he faded into the rest of the darkness.

Below us, the creature leapt and snapped in Jake's general direction before it resumed its call. Without knowing how to kill these creatures, shooting them could be a waste of bullets. Not to mention, the noise of the gunfire would attract the others, and we'd be surrounded within seconds.

"Mommy?" The one word from my daughter could barely be called a whisper.

"I'm right here." I crawled toward her, desperately trying to think of a way to get her away from these creatures. I trusted Jake, but I'd learned a long time ago not to put all my faith in other people's great ideas.

"We need to make it be quiet." Ellie lifted a can and threw it in the direction of the siren call. Another grunt followed the dull thud, but it did stop its weird wail.

Instead of restarting its call, it jumped toward the source of the projectile. The shelving unit wobbled. A muffled shriek came from my daughter's direction. But her action and the creature's response gave me an excellent idea.

I reached for her, and she shivered beneath my touch. "You had the right idea, sweetie." I didn't bother keeping my voice down anymore and peered over the other side into the health foods aisle. Two darker shapes snuffled and prowled the floor. "Throw cans at the ones over here." I drew her hand to where I wanted her to aim.

"But two monsters will knock over these shelves—ooooo! We jump to the next shelves and the other monster will get squished!"

"That's my girl." I squeezed Ellie's hand and released it. A little prayer escaped me. Ares still didn't appear.

There was a time I would have banked my daughter's life on a response from one of the gods we personally knew, but not anymore. Not after what happened to Max.

"Ready," I said. "Go!"

We threw can after can at the two creatures below. The grunts of pain turned to growls. At the same time, the first creature started its siren wailing again. Finally, the two we were trying to antagonize threw themselves against the unit.

The shelving started to rock, but it wasn't enough. "Keep throwing, sweetie," I ordered before I launched a couple of cans at the first creature. Its alternating howl cut off, and it leapt at me. The unit swung wildly. Ellie squeaked and I grabbed her.

The monsters after us must have instinctively decided to work in tandem to knock us off our perch. Or they were just dumb enough not to realize the units were close enough for a domino effect if one was knocked over. The shelves swayed with their rhythm as they took turns ramming the steel, each oscillation bringing us closer to our target.

I rose to a crouch and pulled Ellie to her feet. "When I say go, jump as high and as far as you can."

"Yes, ma'am." Her palm was definitely sweaty, or mine was. Maybe it was both of us.

The unit hovered over the single monster in the canned goods aisle before it did a slow swing back. Had I miscalculated?

As the shelves became perpendicular with the floor, the other two creatures must have sensed they were close to capturing us. They slammed into the steel rack.

"Go!"

Cans rained to the floor. The single monster's howl of pain abruptly cut off when the unit we leapt from slammed into its counterpart. Our landing spot slid away beneath our feet. The acceleration made us overshoot both the opposite side of the canned goods and the international foods aisle.

I curled around Ellie, hoping beyond hope I didn't break any of my own bones or hers when we landed. We crashed into another rack before we dropped. Plastic bags and cardboard boxes exploded beneath me. The scent of wheat, corn, and sugar filled the air.

"Up, Mommy!" Ellie yanked on my arm once, but I couldn't move fast enough. I covered my daughter as more cardboard boxes pummeled me from above. A series of successive clangs followed by a tsunami of products crashing to the floor rattled my eardrums as each row of shelves tipped over into the next.

When quiet settled over the store again, I relaxed my tight grip on Ellie and listened. No snuffling or siren wailing pierced the silence. It was too much to hope the monsters had been crushed under the falling debris, but we definitely couldn't stay here.

"Follow me," I whispered before I brushed aside boxes and loose cereal and crawled toward the reddish lights gleaming at the end of the tunnel formed by the tilted shelves. Glow-in-the-dark yo-yo's hanging from the endcap marked the right side of the aisle. Those might come in handy for a distraction later if more creatures prowled the store.

A soft crunching came from behind me that sure as hell didn't sound like it was caused by hands and knees. It was too . . . wet. I paused. Murphy, please tell me my baby wasn't doing what I thought she was doing.

I didn't want to ask, but I had to. "Ellie, are you eating cereal off the floor?"

"Just the pieces on top of the piles," she whispered. "I'm hungry."

Only my daughter would be worried about food while we were in mortal danger. "If you're too full of cereal to go to McDonald's . . ."

The crunching stopped. "I'm not."

"Follow me." I gritted my teeth and crawled toward the red lights and glowing yo-yo's again. I really couldn't complain. I'd done far weirder shit when I was a kid. At least, my daughter wasn't being raised by vampires.

A shadow appeared between the glowing cereal display and the yoyos. I stopped and drew my sidearm. We had no place to go if another creature stalked us from the opposite end of the makeshift tunnel.

"Tiffany?"

I relaxed at Jake's whisper and started to stow my gun when an awful thought occurred. The dino demons, the ones who helped the rebel vampire Giovanni beat Max to death and kidnap Ellie, could shapeshift beyond a were's two forms. They could become anyone. And you wouldn't know until they were ripping out your heart.

I aimed at the shadow. "What were you planning to help me with this weekend?"

The shadow shifted before he said, "Your damn garbage disposal. When was our first kiss?"

"You've never kissed me, asshole." But I relaxed and holstered my weapon.

"I think you two should," my daughter piped up from behind me.

Thank Murphy, it was dark. From the heat in my face, my lily-white skin would be glowing like the freaking cardboard tiger beneath the battery-operated Christmas lights.

"No one's kissing anyone," I muttered. I crawled toward Jake.

"Why not?" Ellie asked. "You like each other."

Jake helped me to my feet. "Yeah. Why not?" His dark eyes glittered red from the cereal display.

He was funny and cute, and he doted over Ellie. As much as I hated to admit it to myself, he'd replaced Gerard Butler in my fantasies. And with that silent admission, old guilt crashed over me.

"Don't make me break my promise to Alex," I hissed.

"And what's that?" Jake asked as he pulled Ellie from under the fallen shelving and lifted her onto his hip.

Ellie cupped her hands around his ear, but I could hear her anyway. "Grandpa Alex told her she's not allowed to shoot you."

Jake's teeth flashed scarlet in the token light. "I'm glad Grandpa Alex is looking out for me. I wouldn't want to be shot."

She nodded solemnly. "I won't let Mommy shoot you either." She patted his cheek.

"I'm glad somebody has my back." His voice grew serious. "We're not getting out the rear entrance. There's a dozen of those things prowling the unloading dock."

"What about the, um . . ." I didn't want to ask about the grocery employees who should have been in the store room in front of Ellie.

"There's a lot of frozen pizza and sausage on the floor back there," Jake murmured. "Nothing we could really use."

For an instant, I wanted to hug him for his discretion. Ellie didn't need to see the mangled bodies of the employees. "So why haven't they come in after all the racket we made?"

"Same reason the ones in the front haven't come in." His voice turned grim. "They got us trapped, or they think they do."

I glanced around us. Still quiet. "So what are they waiting for?"

"I don't think we want to find out," he said.

Faint snuffling came from a few aisles away, followed by the pop and crunch of a bag filled with more air than snack food.

Jake nudged me in the opposite direction. "Let's head to the manager's office. It's defensible and we can call for backup." He left out that the land lines had probably been cut the same time the power had been. But talking on a cell phone before we were out of the monsters reach wasn't smart either.

The better question was whether my cell phone still worked after my awkward landing in the cereal aisle.

I grabbed a couple of the glow-in-the-dark yo-yo's and shoved them into my jacket pockets before we crept through the dairy section, keeping low against the waist-high refrigerator units in the middle of the floor. Ellie stayed silent. If it weren't for the adrenaline rush, my heart would have broken. I didn't want my daughter to grow up like I had, her life in constant danger.

Max and I tried so fucking hard to give her a normal life. But here we were—hunted through the damn grocery store.

Crawling behind the floor units in the dark kept Ellie from seeing the bodies. There weren't many though, not for the amount of people in the store when we arrived. And they sure weren't killed by falling cans or broken wine bottles.

Unfortunately, the super-dim secondary emergency bulbs kicked on around the perimeter of the store as we neared the end of the dairy section. The battery-powered lamps were designed to give shoppers and employees enough light to evacuate the building in the event of an earthquake. It also meant the things hunting us wouldn't have to rely on their noses anymore.

The shelving units we'd tipped over came to a rest against the first section of upright freezers. Movement flickered inside the endcap unit. I hissed, and Jake halted his crawl. Using hand signs, we argued about checking the unit.

He wanted to take care of the creature inside. Logically, I pointed out why the hell would one of them open the freezer, much less crawl inside?

"It's a kid," Ellie whispered.

We both looked at her. Pantomiming us, she emphatically jabbed a thumb at her chest before pointing at the freezer.

Jake and I exchanged looks. Something rustled a few aisles away. Cereal crunched and popped, followed by a snuffling sound. One of the creatures had picked up our trail.

Shit. We couldn't leave a child in the damn freezer. The mom had probably shoved him or her inside before a vampire or a canine monster gutted her.

I ignored Jake's gestures and crept around the corner of the floor freezer. His loyalty to Max meant he'd keep Ellie safe. Holstering my sidearm, I checked the dairy aisle. Nothing in sight. More crunching came from our landing spot in the cereal.

There wasn't any time left. Condensation fogged the interior glass of the upright freezer. I eased the door open and laid my finger over my lips. The boy didn't look much older than my own daughter. Thankfully, terror kept him from even whimpering.

I beckoned for him to come out. He shook his head wildly. Even in the dim emergency lighting, the whites of his eyes stood out against his dark skin. I couldn't leave him in there. He was dressed in a t-shirt and shorts. Even if the monsters couldn't find him, the hypothermia would kill him.

From halfway across the store, the crunching came closer. Choosing your battles is part of parenthood, but this wasn't a battle I could let the child win, even when the kid wasn't mine. Not for the first time, I wished I was telepathic.

I stuck my head in the freezer. The little boy tried to meld his back into the plastic shelving.

"I can get you some place safe and help you find your mommy and daddy." My whisper turned into a cloud inside the unit. I hoped I hadn't just lied to the kid. "But we have to go now."

Finally, he nodded. The shelf creaked as he crawled out of the freezer. I took his chilly hand and turned.

A dark shadow emerged from the tunnel that used to be the cereal aisle. It immediately howled its companion's siren-like wail. Or maybe it was the same damn monster.

Whatever. The fucking thing stopped calling for backup and barreled straight for me and the kid.

Chapter 4

I reached into my jacket pocket for one of the yo-yo's. With a snap of my arm, I tossed the toy. The beast skidded and leapt for the glowing piece of plastic. With a crunch, the yo-yo shattered and bits pinged off the floor, but it gave us the moment we needed.

"Office!" Jake shouted.

"Ellie to me!" I screamed.

She raced in my direction as I drew my own weapon. My baby kept her head, but the boy went rigid. These damn things probably could smell his fear. She shook him and shouted, "Follow my mommy!"

We took off through the frozen food section for the pharmacy. A shot came from behind us. The shriek of pain wasn't Jake's. At least, the monster wasn't howling anymore.

I waved the kids to stop and peered around the corner. Another body lay in the pharmacy waiting area along with a skeleton in a puddle. Someone else managed to take out a vampire. I was impressed since the only two ways to kill one was destroying the heart or beheading the vamp.

While the coast was clear inside, we were near the second main entrance into the superstore. I counted another ten figures shuffling outside. I leaned over a bit further. A couple of dark shadows shambled near the pharmacy drive-thru window. Damn, they really did have all the exits covered as Jake feared.

I motioned for the kids to follow me and crept past the pharmacy, keeping below the service counter. We reached the hallway to the public restrooms and ran. Steps sounded behind us. I whirled and raised my gun.

And lowered it at the sight of Jake.

I turned back to the last door in the hallway and twisted the knob. Of course, the entrance to the stairs was locked. The actual store offices and employee break room were a story above the main shopping floor. They kept the safe up there, among other things.

"Tiff," Jake hissed.

"Gimme a minute. And don't ever call me Tiff again," I retorted as quietly as possible and holstered my weapon once more.

"Two unfriendlys entered the produce section from outside," he whispered.

So, whoever was after Ellie expected the vamps and monster dogs to either capture her or flush her out.

And kill Jake and me in the process.

I retrieved my lockpick kit from a pocket on my camouflage pants. Most of my classmates thought the garment was a fashion statement. A couple believed my clothing choices were a holdover from military service. In reality, they were simply the most practical things I could find to wear when it came to being a St. James Coven enforcer.

Truth? I hated the tailored suits the rest of the enforcers wore. My cousins

Mai and Miko looked like they came straight from the movie set of *Men in Black*.

On the other hand, Uncle Duncan was ecstatic I didn't wear leather skirts and fishnet stockings anymore. We both knew they were my attempt at rebellion during my teen years.

I selected two of the picks and whispered, "Silent count, kiddo." She'd tap my shoulder every ten seconds.

This damn lock was nothing special though. The release clicked before her first tap, and I tossed my tools back in the kit and stowed it in my pocket. Pulling out my gun and my flashlight, I eased the door open.

A quick look revealed nothing on the stairs or landing. And nothing hanging from the ceiling. I flicked off the flashlight and waved for the kids to follow me.

Behind us, Jake stepped into the stairwell and relocked the door. The shitty lock wouldn't hold for long, but it would buy us a little time. Unfortunately, there was no emergency lighting in the stairwell.

The little boy whimpered.

"Hold my hand," Ellie whispered. "Mommy's taking us to place that's depensible."

If my heart wasn't pounding so hard, I would have laughed at her mispronunciation. Caesar insisted Ellie improve her vocabulary daily. It had become a game between the two of them.

"What's 'depensible'?" the little boy whispered back.

"Someplace where Mommy and Uncle Jake can whack the bad guys without us getting hurt," she told him as they climbed the steps behind me.

I reached the landing and had to pull out my flashlight again. There was an indent about four feet long to the left between the top step and the next door.

This lock was a little more serious than the one downstairs. At least, the company that owned the store realized an electronic lock would have either disengaged with the loss of power or trapped employees up here. But even this deadbolt was no match for my skills.

I eased the door open and was immediately blinded. When I blinked the tears out of my eyes, I noticed the gun barrel pointed at my nose.

Shit.

CHAPTER 5

"Who are you?" A man's voice came from behind the flashlight in my eyeballs.

"You first," I snarled back.

"Terry Goodman, off-duty LAPD," he barked. That explained both his pistol and the dead vamp downstairs.

"Tiffany Osaka, head of security for Brent Poole and Jessie Alton." It wasn't too often I used my celebrity cousins' names, but it was better than claiming I was in law enforcement. Goodman wasn't on the list of local officers who were Family and could be told the truth of who and what we were dealing with.

And I sure as hell couldn't use my real surname or my late husband's. In case Goodman blabbed to the wrong people, it was an extra level of protection for me and Ellie, no matter how little it was.

"I've got two kids with me," I added. "Can we please not point guns at each other?"

The flashlight abruptly cut off, making me blink again.

"Their eyes aren't glowing," a woman's voice said. Crap. That was not a good sign. Maybe this was another Vampire Liberation Front stunt after all. All of the coven masters, including my uncle Duncan, worried about the terrorist organization revealing the vampires' existence to the general public. Those assholes formed because we'd discovered the cure for the disease that caused vampirism, and they wanted to stay at the top of the food chain.

"Get in here," Goodman ordered.

We entered the office area. Massive windows on my right faced the parking lot and street. The ambient light from the home improvement store across the boulevard showed a cubicle setup.

And lots of scared people.

Goodman had been smart. He'd kept the survivors away from the one-way mirror looking over the sales floor as well as the UV film on the outside windows where their shadows could be seen. Everyone hunkered in the middle aisle formed by the two lines of cubicles.

The LAPD officer's sidearm came back up when he spotted Jake, who was still holding his gun. Jake slowly raised his hands.

"That's Jake Wong," I said. "He works for my family's security firm."

"Tristan!" one of the women cried out.

"Mommy!" The little boy I'd found in the freezer tore away from Ellie and raced into the woman's arms. Ellie ran after her new friend.

"Do either of you two know what those things inside the store are?" Goodman asked.

"If you mean the animals? No." I clenched my fists. "I think the other assholes are what's left of the Sunshine Believers."

"The ones who kidnapped your client?" Goodman stared at me. "I heard the whole cult died in a mass suicide up in Montana a few years back."

That had been the official story. What no one knew, outside of the supernatural community anyway, was the founder of the Sunshine Believers had been a demon. And not an ordinary run-of-the-mill type from any of the human religions. No, he was a minion from the gods the dinosaurs had worshipped millions of years ago.

And they wanted the planet back.

A handful of the dino demon's inner circle had been illegally Turned by Giovanni, a defector from our own coven, that night in Tuttle Creek. Nearly everyone else became snacks for the fledgling vampires and the demon. Everyone except a few female supernaturals the demon had raped to breed more of his type.

Goodman didn't need to know all of that shit.

"Unfortunately, not all of them drank the Kool-Aid," I murmured instead.

"But these guys here had glowing eyes and pointed teeth." The large woman next to Goodman had been the one who stated my eyes didn't glow. From the style of her vest and her necktie, she was one of the store managers. However, I couldn't make out her nametag in the low lighting.

"Special contacts and fake teeth," Jake said. "I use stuff like that all the time when I do stunt work."

Goodman cocked his head. "You're a stuntman *and* a security expert?"

Jake's teeth gleamed orange thanks to the outdoor halogens. "Planning ahead. I can't fall off buildings forever."

"I'd prefer it if you didn't fall off buildings at all," I mumbled. Regret filled me the instant the words spewed out of my mouth.

"I wouldn't want my boyfriend falling off buildings either, girl," the store manager said.

Thank goodness, Ellie was occupied and didn't hear her. I wasn't sure where her matchmaking came from, and I sure as hell didn't need more of it.

"Can we talk about more important things?" Goodman snapped. "Either of you have a phone on you?"

I pulled mine from my back pocket and hit the power switch. It flickered once, which was all I needed to see the fractured screen. The device made a sound like a dying seagull before it went black. "Well, this one wouldn't survive jumping off a building if it can't handle jumping off store shelves."

"You jumped off my store shelves?" the manager said. I imagined she had the same appalled face Elizabeth would have if I were jumping off her living room furniture.

"I didn't want me or my daughter to become monster chow," I snapped.

"The land lines—" Jake started.

"Dead as the power lines," Goodman answered. "And none of the rest of us up here can get a signal."

Jake pulled his phone out. "No service for me either," he muttered and shoved it back into his pocket. He lowered his voice. "Officer Goodman, did you get a count of the Believers on this side of the building besides the one you shot in the pharmacy?"

The cop shook his head. "I didn't shoot anyone in the pharmacy." Jake and I exchanged looks, but Goodman continued. "I did wing one of the two who were near the checkout lanes. Then the lights went out, and the dog things came into the store. Two of the dog things took down the guy I did shoot as well as his buddy."

That didn't make sense. Why would the vampires' weird pets attack the vampires? A chill ran through me. It made sense if the dog things didn't belong to the vampires. It also meant we had more than one group inside the store after Ellie.

"Both the people and the dogs are probably so whacked out on drugs they can't tell who's friend and who's foe," the store manager stated.

We didn't need the people up here to ask more questions. What we needed was a way to contact assistance. And get my daughter and the civilians out intact.

"Where's the fire alarm," I asked. "It should be on a separate circuit than the main power supply. Or at least a battery backup."

"Downstairs," the store manager said dryly. "Where the people should be."

"What about the burglary alarm?" Goodman asked. "Does it go to the closest police station?"

"Yes, sir. There's a button at the service desk and one up here in the general manager's office." The store manager shook her head slowly. "I don't think Lisa had a chance downstairs, but I punched the one up here when everything started." She gestured at the outside windows. "Not to be going on about your brothers-in-blue, Officer Goodman, but that was almost ten minutes ago."

"Um, what's your name?" I asked.

"Marla. Marla Enriquez."

"Marla, show me the alarm button," I said.

"What are you going to do?" At least, Jake's voice didn't have that quality of disbelief that Max's had so often carried.

"See if I can jury-rig some power to the police alarm." I turned to Ellie who still sat with Tristan and his mom on the floor. "Sweetie, stay here with Uncle Jake while I check on something."

"Affirmative." She nodded her head emphatically.

"I know it's none of my business, sweetheart," Marla said quietly as we headed for the GM's office. "But it's never a good idea to have your kids call your boyfriend 'uncle.'"

"He's not my boyfriend," I ground out as we walked through cubicle land.

"Uh-huh," Marla muttered.

"He is, was, one of my husband's closest friends."

"'Was'? Because you two hooked up—"

I grabbed the bitch's arm and yanked her to a stop. "My husband Max died eighteen months ago." The realization this was the first time I'd said the words out loud jolted through me. I released her arm and sucked in a deep breath. I couldn't lose it. Not here. Not now. Not with Ellie's life on the line again.

Marla patted my shoulder. "First time you said it, huh?"

"Yeah," I whispered.

"I had the same problem when my granny passed. She'd always been there for me, my brothers, and my sister."

"She raise you?"

"Yeah."

"My uncle raised me after my parents were murdered," I said softly. "I didn't want that for my daughter."

"Mind if I ask what happened to your man?" Marla said.

"Disgruntled ex-employee. Tried to make it look like a home invasion." Bitterness coated my voice.

"Because you wouldn't bend over?" She resumed walking to the back of the cubicles.

"He did it to get back at one of my uncles who founded our firm." I sighed. "He's attacked various family members over the last five years."

"And the cops aren't doing anything about this asshole?" Marla's voice got a little louder.

"They almost had him, but he managed to get out of the country. A place with no extradition." She didn't need to hear how Marcus Giovanni had kidnapped Ellie. How he'd escaped with a dino demon through a dimensional portal to what the witches and fae called Otherwhere. I hoped some critter in that wasteland ate Giovanni, body and soul.

"I'm sorry, sweetheart. That's a shitty deal."

I sighed. "Max insisted I go to college and get my degree. Between my classes and Ellie starting kindergarten, Jake's been helping around the house."

We reached a real door at the end of the cubicle aisle. Marla removed the lanyard from around her neck, picked a key, and unlocked the door. I followed her inside.

"You know that boy isn't hanging around you out of respect for his dead friend," Marla said.

I ignored her comment. It was bad enough Jake invaded my dreams, and I kept waking up feeling guilty as hell.

Instead, I examined the decent-sized office. Stacks of paperwork covered most of the desk. All of the equipment on the desk and a nearby table was dead. The built-in safe in the corner farthest from the outdoor windows had an electronic keypad, also dark. However, this room had a solid wall instead of a one-way mirror overlooking the sales floor.

"What happens with the safe when you lose power?" I knew damn well this wasn't a robbery, but I was hoping to distract the manager and her astute observational skills.

"It deadlocks," Marla said. "The only way you're getting into it right now is with a blowtorch and two tanks of acetylene." She crossed to the opposite corner of the office from the safe. "Here's the panic button."

I pulled out my Swiss army knife and pried off the panic button's cover. Replacing the knife in my pocket, I pulled out my penlight, turned it on, and stuck it in my mouth before I retrieved my small circuit tester.

"What are you? A female MacGyver?" Marla said as she stood between the window and me. Definitely too smart for her own good by keeping anyone in the parking lot from seeing my tiny light.

"Something like that," I mumbled around the penlight. Touching the appropriate wires produced no indicator light on the tester. "Damn." We were on our own unless I could jury-rig an AC/DC converter.

"You sure your tester's working right?" Marla asked.

I bit my tongue to keep from saying something snarky to her. She was only being sensible and a bit hopeful. I popped out the battery on the penlight and connected it to the tester. The indicator lit up.

"Yeah, it's working." I returned my equipment to my pockets and popped the cover back on the button's electronics. When my eyes adjusted to the darkness, I crossed to the desk.

"The panic buttons are supposed to be on a different line than either the main power or the telephones," Marla muttered.

"I'd say someone did their homework here." I traced the computer's power supply by touch. "Did any new employees join the staff in the last two months?"

Marla chuckled. "Oh, sweetheart! You've never had a real job in your life, have you?"

I winced because I knew exactly what she was thinking. Classism was alive and well in our country. The uncle who raised me was once an English duke. Even my cover story about working for Brent and Jessie meant I had money. Marla would totally flip if she learned I had a trust fund that outstripped my cousins' net worth by several trailing zeroes.

"You're right," I said calmly. "I haven't had what you would consider a regular job. But someone had to have been casing your store for a little while in order to know where the burglary alarm is located."

"Except the perps didn't touch the registers." Marla crossed her arms. "I also saw Polly in the deli attack you."

Shit. I took a deep breath before I did something really stupid. Like shoving Marla through one of the office windows.

"Then you know I shot her in self-defense." I eased my hand toward my sidearm. "Are you planning on attacking me? Is that why you wanted me back here alone?"

"No. I want a straight answer." She dropped her arms and propped a hip on the one bare corner of the manager's desk. "Polly's flesh slid off her bones like Jell-O off a hot plate after she was shot. I grew up in Watts. I know what someone getting shot looks like, and that wasn't it."

I shrugged, trying to play it cool. "I didn't see anything like that."

"You, your boyfriend, and Officer Goodman all went for heart shots."

"And?"

"That's the only way to take out a real vampire. You gotta destroy the heart." I laughed. "Come on. It takes a wooden stake, not a bullet."

She blew out an exasperated breath. "You gonna tell me again vampires aren't real?"

"You're kidding me? I really have to say that?"

"Just because I don't have your kind of money doesn't mean I'm stupid, sweetie."

"Vampires aren't real," I said as calmly as I could.

"Are you saying that because you really believe that, or because you're a Normal?" Marla crossed her arms again.

"My family would be the first ones to tell you I'm not normal." I chuckled, deliberately playing dumb, as I went back to tracing the computer cords by touch.

"Your pants are going to catch fire, girl—"

With a *crash*, one of the outside windows shattered.

Chapter 6

Marla and I both dived behind the general manager's desk as the object that had broken the window tumbled across the industrial carpet. For a woman nearly three times my size, she could move damn fast. But it was still human fast, not supernatural fast. Nor did she make any sound.

When the expected explosion didn't come, I peered around the corner of the desk. Something lay in the middle of the office. It looked suspiciously like a hunk of broken concrete.

The office door eased open, and a familiar voice whispered, "Tiffany?"

"We're fine," I whispered back. I turned to Marla. "You are fine, right?'

She nodded, not talking. Like I said, smart lady.

"We're going back to the other room before someone decides to rappel down from the roof," I said quietly. "Stay close to the floor and against that wall." I pointed to our right.

"Below the windows." She nodded sharply. "I got it."

We crouch-walked out of the general manager's office. From this angle, I got a better look at the object that had broken the window. Definitely a chunk of concrete, probably from the parking lot. Once we reached the cubicle section, Marla relocked the door.

Officer Goodman was with Jake just outside the GM's door. "What the hell happened in there?" the policeman snapped.

"Our friends were trying to flush us out," I murmured.

"What about the security alarm?" Jake asked.

I shook my head out of habit though he would barely be able to see me in the dark. "All we've got are batteries. I need a power converter, some duct tape, and wire to jury-rig the system. Even then, that's no guarantee we'll get a signal out, considering the cell phones are being jammed somehow."

A dull thumping echoed from the direction of the stairwell.

We were out of time.

My heart pounded as fast and as hard as the noise below us. Breaking the window was meant to drive us back here, but Marla had blocked the light. How did they know? I wanted to kick myself.

Because vampires were telepaths. After twenty-six years, you'd think I'd have learned not to underestimate my foe.

"The main floor entrance to the stairwell," Jake murmured.

"What if we push the refrigerator from the breakroom to block the upstairs door?" Marla whispered.

"That's fine as long as they don't decide to throw something more dangerous up here than broken concrete," I muttered.

"They already know we haven't left the building," Jake pointed out.

I swallowed hard. He was right. And everyone up here could die because these goons wanted Ellie's blood.

"I'll go downstairs," I said. "Try to negotiate."

"What? Are you insane?"

I could feel Jake's gaze bore into me despite the darkness. "Think about it. We're dealing with two different groups. If Goodman, you, or me didn't shoot the attacker in the pharmacy, who did?"

"But they both want the same thing," Jake said.

"I know, which means they need an alternate target." I grabbed his forearm. "No matter what happens to me, I need you to get Ellie to safety."

He must have guessed my plan because he muttered "You can't hang Elizabeth—never mind." It finally registered he was the only St. James enforcer who gave a shit about my mother-in-law's well-being after she betrayed us to Dare Coven.

And she did it all for nothing because Max was immune to the V-virus. He couldn't have been Turned even if he wanted it. Which he didn't, but that hadn't mattered to Elizabeth at the time.

"What are you two talking about?" Goodman sounded perplexed.

"*Madre de Dios*," Marla breathed. "Your family is the carrier of the cure."

"Carrier?" Goodman said.

Marla looked around and lowered her voice. "There's a disease related to Ebola. Some scientists recently found out there was a family here in Los Angeles who are immune to it. Some rivals of the people developing the vaccine and the cure killed one of the family. There's only three known carriers of the immunity left."

Goodman turned toward me. "Your security company is protecting that family, aren't they?"

"Mommy."

With a start, I looked over my shoulder, grateful for the interruption. Ellie stood behind me.

"Are you going to leave me like Daddy did?"

The scars on my heart split open. "No, sweetie," I choked out while I knelt, pulled her into my arms and hugged her tight. "I'm just going to try to talk to the people downstairs."

"The ones who tried to take me?" Her voice quivered.

"Ah, shit," Goodman muttered as he understood what was going on.

"Language, Officer!" Ellie blurted.

Jake shook his head. "Without backup of any kind, we're trapped up here. You need to call your grandfather." He hesitated for a split second. "Or Sam."

"No," I spat.

"Is Ellie's life worth your pride?"

Of course, he went there. Except I couldn't deck him because I was holding my daughter.

"None of the phones work," Goodman said, not understanding what Jake and I were talking about.

Marla ignored the officer. "Your man's right. These bastards aren't going to let us go until they get what they want, even if you trick them into going wherever this Elizabeth is."

"I have to try," I said. "I can't let any more people die."

Ellie framed my cheeks with her tiny palms. "Mommy, you don't listen to Aunt Bebe. It's the bad men's fault Daddy died. Not yours."

My eyes burned, and my throat tightened. I couldn't say all the things I wanted to. It was too big of a burden for a five-year-old.

"Sweetie, these people are in danger because I chose this grocery store. What have I said about taking responsibility for your own decisions?"

"The bad people would have tried to take me no matter which store you went to. They could have tried at McDonald's for all you know." Ellie released my cheeks and wrapped her arms around my neck. "I'm more mad they ruined our night for going."

I laughed. I couldn't help it. Marla and Goodman snickered.

Jake knelt beside us. "Ellie, do you trust me to take care of you?"

"Sure," she said.

"Then we're going to do this your mom's way." Jake didn't touch me, but I felt hugged by him nonetheless. I was too used to everyone else treating me like a china doll. An unintelligent china doll.

The banging downstairs changed as the door splintered under our opponents' onslaught. I pulled my weapon from its holster and the extra clips from my left-side thigh pocket, and I handed them to Jake.

"Do what Uncle Jake tells you," I murmured in my precious baby's ear.

"I will." She kissed my cheek. "Be careful."

She released me and turned to Jake who whispered, "Stay with Ms. Marla for a minute, Ellie."

He rose and followed me to the upstairs door.

"Get the fridge over here as soon as I leave," I muttered. "And . . . I'm sorry for snapping at you. I've been yelling for Grandpa Ares since everything started downstairs. He's not answering." I couldn't call for *her*. Not with Ellie's life on the line. I just couldn't.

Besides, if Ares wasn't responding, odds were *she* couldn't hear me either.

"It's okay. I know you wouldn't risk Ellie's life like this if you had a choice," Jake murmured.

"If this goes sideways, I promised Ted I'd bring Ellie to Easter dinner."

"Things always go sideways on us, but we still come out on top," he said.

"Not always—"

Jake's kiss caught me totally by surprise. It started simply, but my lips parted. I grabbed his windbreaker and poured everything into returning his kiss. My regrets. My hopes. My terror.

And guilt smacked me upside the head as soon as we parted.

"I-I'm sorry," I murmured.

Jake leaned his forehead against mine. "It's my fault. I-I wanted you to be thinking positive thoughts."

He unlocked the door. As soon as I had my flashlight in hand and pulled my silver knife from my right boot sheathe, he yanked the door open.

I stepped through and peered around the corner. Two of the dog things perched only three steps below me.

Jake slammed the door shut before I had a chance to change my mind.

Chapter 7

I held up my knife and edged forward. The two beasts snuffled. One of them whined as I approached the steps.

With the flashlight, I got a better look at them. Over-sized teeth kept them from closing their mouths properly. Saliva dripped from the corners of their muzzles. Their flesh was oddly distorted. Sparse bristly hair covered them. They reminded me of dogs with severe cases of mange and too much inbreeding.

From their size, it would be difficult for me to kill one before the other tore my throat out. Despite their frightening visage, there was something oddly familiar about them. The flashlight reflected orange back from their eyes.

Like weres when they were in their animal forms.

The same beast whined again as I carefully lowered my boot to the first step. "I'll make you two a deal. You don't rip out my throat or any other internal organs, and I won't stab you with silver."

Both beasts bobbed their head before they slunk backwards down the stairs.

I shouldn't have been surprised, but I was. There was a hell of a lot more intelligent species on this planet than anyone knew. It was simply easier for them to let humans believe they were the prima donnas of Earth.

The dull glow of the emergency lighting came from the doorway below. It seemed pretty damn bright after being stuck in the offices for so long. The beasts continued backing out through the splintered wood, but they stayed within my sight.

I reached the edge of the destroyed door and took a good look. About five yards back from the end of the hallway stood three people. The dog things backed down the hallway. I eased down the corridor at the same pace.

When I reached the end, there were more than three people. A group of twenty humans stood in a ring around the entrance to the hallway.

Or I thought they were human. Some were dressed in rags. Others were clothed in modern apparel. All of them showed similar physical deformities as the dog creatures, except the humans' issues were a lot worse.

With a lurch of my stomach, I realized I was surrounded by ghouls.

CHAPTER 8

Ghouls. The ancient, deformed eaters of human flesh. All of my Family and coven had thought they were extinct, hunted down and slaughtered in the Middle Ages.

Until they showed up in Las Vegas six months ago. My cousin Mai said their leader had been searching for information about the V-virus cure until the ghoul was murdered by a dino demon wearing my cousin's face and using her own gun. Just another attempt by Giovanni's allies to pit the supernaturals against each other.

Was that the real reason the ghouls were here? Revenge against the St. James coven for their leader's death?

When one of the people in the center of the group stepped forward, I jerked and raised my knife a little higher. It was the woman in the burqa who I'd given the cart to when Ellie and I entered the store. "No closer. From your buddies' reactions, you're as vulnerable to silver as vampires and weres."

She pushed back her hood and pulled down her veil. Despite her beautiful eyes, the rest of her face was as deformed as the other ghouls' visages.

"And yet, you only have one silver knife, and there are many of us." The woman gestured at her compatriots on both sides of her. I couldn't quite place her accent though. It almost sounded Egyptian.

"That's because I left my gun and silver bullets upstairs to protect the innocents," I answered. "How about a show of good faith?" I lowered my knife.

"Tell me who you are and why you're threatening the people here. Maybe we can work something out. Something we can all walk away from."

"We only battled the vampires who came to this grocery," she said. "None of the Normals were harmed by us."

I glanced around. Three relatively intact corpses sprawled within my view. "That's an awful lot of killing even for a couple of vamps."

"It was more than a couple."

She had a point, considering how many Jake and I had killed by ourselves.

I shrugged. "You already know I'm Normal. If all the vamps are dead, why are you still here?"

"We're not here just for the vampires," she said.

"You play word games, madam," I said. Sometimes, using Uncle Duncan's old-fashioned phrases could provoke a response.

"We want the St. James child. She carries the cure to our disease."

A chill ran through me. Time for a more direct conversation. "Let's start from the beginning. Did you originally plan on kidnapping my daughter tonight?"

The ghoul raised her chin. "We have been monitoring the rebel vampires. The ones who call themselves the Vampire Liberation Front."

She didn't deny wanting to take Ellie, so I decided to play along. "How? The North American covens have been searching for those asshats for the last year."

"They were hiding from you, not from us."

I got the distinct impression she was secretly laughing at me though her expression didn't change. "Why? Because you told them you'd team up until it was convenient for you to kill them?"

"No one pays attention to the dead," the guy next to the ghouls' spokeswoman said. "We have watched and waited and lived."

"Waited for what?" I asked. It seemed as if I were on the cusp of some truth.

"A cure for our children," the woman in the burqa said.

"You can have children?" I swallowed hard. Sweat slicked my palms, and I tightened my grip on the knife handle. Infertility had been one of the worst effects of the V-virus. The reason so many jumped on the cure wagon, even though Bebe wasn't sure yet if the infertility could be totally reversed.

"Yes. However, they are born with our disease." The woman in the burqa dropped her shoulders. "Wouldn't you do anything to save your child?"

"That's why I'm here," I said softly. I nodded toward the dog beasts. "Is your version of the virus communicable to other creatures?"

"You could say that," the woman in the burqa said. "Neither the witches or the werepeople are immune to our form of the V-virus."

Bile burned the back of my throat as I put two and two together. That's why the dog beasts backed away from my silver knife. They were infected werewolves. It also explained why no one upstairs could get a cell signal either. At least one of the ghouls was a witch.

"What about the fae?" I asked.

"Their deaths from this disease are even uglier than ours," the male ghoul said. "They kill us on sight."

"I don't understand. You die from the disease?" My gaze swept across the entire group.

Burqa Lady nodded. "How old do you think I am?"

I shrugged. "I honestly have no idea. You could be my age. You could be one hundred. Or one thousand years old for all I know."

"I am twenty."

"Twenty what?"

"Twenty years old," she clarified.

I shook my head. "No way. You're younger than me?"

"We only live to be forty." She shrugged as well. "Fifty in rare cases. We are born dying. Eventually, the disease will progress to the point that my people will become extinct. So you see, we need that cure. For our children's sakes."

It made sense. If the V-virus sped up a patient's rate of healing, why wouldn't a mutation speed up the entire maturation cycle of the infected host? It also made sense why the ghouls came out of hiding. Bebe's research and my daughter's DNA were their children's chance at living normal lives.

Time to take a chance. I slowly bent over and slid my knife into my boot sheathe while keeping an eye on the ghouls. "You do realize my daughter's not the person St. James Coven is harvesting blood from to cook up the cure, don't you?"

The ghoul cocked her head. "But she survived the bite without Turning..."

Damn. They knew way too much about us. Things that we thought hadn't left Caesar's, now Duncan's, inner circle.

"Yes, but she's too young for the amounts needed to test and create the cure," I said as I straightened. "The genetic immunity comes from my husband."

"His tomb was empty." The ghoul would have grimaced if the right side of her lips didn't droop past her chin.

"That's because our coven master is married to a goddess. She destroyed my husband's body for that very reason. I didn't want my husband desecrated."

The ghoul snorted. "We would have consumed him honorably. He could have cured—"

"You don't know that for sure," I snapped. "The research team needed were, witch, and Normal immunity genes to formulate the V-virus cure. If all of us are susceptible to your variation of the disease, there's no guarantee my husband's DNA would have cured you." I sucked in a deep breath of humid air to calm down. Without the A/C running, it was starting to get uncomfortable in the store.

I licked my dry lips. "Let the folks upstairs go. They're innocent. I can put you in contact with the coven's research team—"

"No!" The male ghoul grabbed the female's arm. Whatever he said was in some kind of Arabic dialect, probably an older version. I couldn't understand a word. Dammit, if Grandpa Kensai's boyfriend Jamal were still alive, he could probably tell me.

"My son is correct." The woman stared at me, her golden eyes unreadable. "Why should we trust you?"

Son? Shit, how fast did ghouls breed and mature? We could be in a huge amount of trouble far beyond the lives of everyone upstairs if I couldn't negotiate some kind of deal.

"As far as my coven is concerned, any dispute between the vampires and the ghouls was over centuries ago—"

"Because you thought you exterminated all of us," the male spat.

"—and because an enemy to both our peoples resurrected the feud by setting you against our people in Las Vegas," I finished.

"The fae who was not fae?" the female asked.

I nodded. "So you know about the dino demons?" At Burqa Lady's slight nod, I continued, "The coven prisoner Anouk tried to question was my cousin."

All of the ghouls showed signs of surprise that I knew their compatriot's name.

"Your cousin killed her," the male snapped.

I shook my head. "No, the dino demon did when Anouk realized it was attempting to pit our people against yours. They've already tried something similar with the vampires and the fae by using an eclectic necromancer.

"In addition to shooting Anouk, the demon wore my cousin's form in an attempt to murder the coven's new lieutenant master of the city and to steal items of great power from Master St. James's wife. These demons can look like anyone. Sound like anyone. Smell like anyone. You could have one in your group, and you wouldn't know."

"Are you saying your precious goddess can tell the difference?" The male ghoul had a pretty good sneer, especially with his left eye about a half-inch lower than the right.

The last thing I wanted to talk about was *her*, but I swallowed my anger and grinned. "Yep. The demons smell about as tasty to her as human corpses do to you. But she can't be everywhere at once. At least, not yet. My grandfather, Ares of Olympus, gave us a way to detect the demons."

I reached slowly into my pocket for the case holding my lockpick tools. I unzipped the case and produced my pin. The Olympian bronze glowed slightly in the low light.

I held up the bit of god-forged metal. "These pins were forged by Hephaestus of Olympus. On you, me, anyone, it would be a simple pinprick. On the demons, it hurts them bad enough they can't keep their disguise. I'm willing to give this one to you as a sign of good faith—"

"For all we know, it will kill us!"

The male ghoul was getting on my last nerve.

His mother held up her hand. "We will accept your gift. However, you will also take us to the person your coven is harvesting the blood from for your experiments. We want our own unadulterated samples. Given the history between the vampires and us, you understand why we want our own for testing."

A lump in my throat threatened to choke me. "In return for letting the people upstairs leave peacefully."

She shook her head. "Not yet. They will remain here until we come back to this store."

"You have me." I tapped my breast bone with the head of the bronze pin. "Why do you need more hostages?"

The ghoul shrugged. "If this is a trick, we still have your daughter. And if we kill her, your coven will have nothing, but my people will have their revenge for being hunted by yours for centuries."

Chapter 9

Burqa Lady was elected to go with me to my in-laws. I tried mentally shouting for Grandpa Ares again during our drive, but he still didn't appear. Either Burqa Lady was a witch, or she had a charm on her that prevented me from gaining Ares's attention. So, I was on my own until I could come up with a way of alerting the enforcers at the in-law's estate.

While I guided my SUV through the evening traffic toward Beverly Hills, I glanced at the ghoul siting in the passenger seat. She had replaced the hood and veil of her burqa.

"Do you mind if I ask your name?"

She turned toward me. "So you can cast a spell?"

"Normal, remember?"

"Not if your grandfather is a Greek god," she countered.

"Not biologically," I said. "One of his daughters was my foster mom after my parents were murdered."

I hadn't truly understood what Phil was during my childhood. She was as strong and smart as Uncle Duncan, but she could go out in sunlight. I found out she was older than Caesar the only day I tried to skip school when I was twelve. Before that, all I really cared about was her warm hugs.

Uncle Duncan didn't deprive me of physical affection or neglect me in any way. Nor were any of the other vampires emotionally distant, though some-how I understood not all people had their chilly skin. It was more that they regarded me as some special treasure because I was the last uninfected member of Uncle Duncan's biological family line. None of my other cousins were treat-ed like I was, and it made me damn uncomfortable.

Okay, more like outright fucking resentful during my teen years. Which is why I slept with Max when I was nineteen. He was the only person I'd ever met who let me be me. Damn, I missed him.

My eyes burned, and I blinked away the blurriness.

"Why do you grieve?" the ghoul asked. "I assure you my people will not harm your child unless you betray us."

I swallowed hard to get the lump out of my throat. "I was thinking about her father. He died eighteen months ago."

She was silent for a moment before she said, "When the rumors about the cure started." When I didn't answer, she added softly, "My name is Tanis."

"Like the ancient capital of Egypt?" I asked.

"You know of the city?" She seemed genuinely surprised.

"I know a little bit about Egyptian history." Another pang went through my heart. I had a major league crush on Caesar's younger brother Ptolemy when I was a teenager. He could be a royal asshole, but once I grew up and got some perspective, I was relatively certain he acted like a dick to drive me away. I'm sure he thought he was protecting me from my own idiotic hormones at the time. He had to have known how I felt because all vampires were telepathic, though he was never deliberately cruel to me. And he certainly didn't deserve to be shot through the heart by his sister Selene.

I seriously had sucky luck when it came to men. Maybe that was part of the reason I was reluctant to pursue anything with Jake.

"A little bit of Egyptian history?" Tanis's amusement drew me back to our conversation.

"You have no fucking clue of which vampire used to rule this territory, do you?" I asked.

"The middle son of the last pharaoh," Tanis replied. "Before Elizabeth of Britannia's spy took over your coven."

Okay, maybe she knew as much history as I did.

"Why didn't you approach Caesar about a cure for your people earlier?" I didn't need to look at Tanis to see her answering glare. I felt it to my bones.

"You know even less history than you claim." Bitterness coated her words.

I didn't want to ask, but I had to. "What are you talking about? Caesar's fair. He's taken in many outcasts—"

An ugly laugh erupted from the ghoul. "He was awarded his North American territory for his role in what the vampires thought was their final battle with us."

My heart tried to lodge in my throat. "You're mistaken."

"Ask him about our children. The ones his army slaughtered."

I didn't want to believe it. Caesar, hell, even Duncan and Phil, had done some shitty, bloody things in their lives. But there were lines.

Lines that shouldn't be crossed no matter what. Lines that once you crossed them made you no better than the people you fought. That's what the three of them had taught me my entire life.

And I was furious with Sam because she understood that lesson. She hadn't brought Max back because doing so would've broken the very universe. I should have understood, given the zombies a necromancer unleashed on my wedding guests. I still had nightmares about the shambling corpses.

About how close I came to losing both Max and Ellie that night.

The realization didn't really lesson my anger over Max's death, but it made me consider Tanis's words as I braked at a stoplight.

"Are you sure?" I asked her softly. "Because if you really believe Caesar murdered your people's children under any justification, and you hate him for it, I have no reason to believe you will keep my daughter alive."

Instead of defending herself as I half-expected, she said, "Why do you believe in his innocence without proof?"

"You've given me no proof he did it other than your word. But—"

Her teeth clicked, but she held back her argument. At least, she was listening to me.

"—the real reason I believe he didn't do is because he's tried so damn hard to keep the peace between the supernatural communities. He listened to his advisors no matter what they are, including me. He made sure to put a strong vampire in his place as master, someone who counts gods as friends—"

"And a spouse?"

I sighed. "Her, too. Unfortunately, you need power to keep the people you love safe."

"Including your husband?"

That particular wound burned as Tanis dug further into the scab. I braked at another stoplight and looked at her. "Why are you doing your damnedest to turn me against my own coven?"

"Because you are merely food to them."

"I am to you, too," I replied.

"We only eat the dead," she snapped.

"And vampires don't feed directly from humans. It's illegal."

"But using them as milk cows is?"

I returned my attention to the street when the light turned green, and I pressed the accelerator. "Donated blood saves lives, regardless if you're Normal, vampire, were, or witch. Besides, with a cure, the vamps won't need to consume blood anymore."

"Not every vampire wants the cure." Another glance revealed Tanis staring at the walls of the estates we passed. "Why do you think this Vampire Liberation Front formed?"

"You're right. Which is why some are volunteering to live with the damn disease to make sure everyone else can live a normal life." I tightened my grip on the steering wheel. "My in-laws' place is ahead. The guards on duty will prick both of us with an Olympian pin. If you resist, they will kill you. Their bullets are a silver and steel combination with a couple of special ingredients."

"And if I pass their tests?"

"I'll introduce you to my mother-in-law Elizabeth Howell." My lips stretched into a vicious grin. "She hates Caesar about as much as you do."

Chapter 10

I swallowed a groan as I braked to a stop in front of the gates. Just my fucking luck, Cara Lannigan was on duty tonight. She stepped closer to my vehicle, and I hit the control to lower the driver's window. Despite the pack beta's recommendation Cara be removed as an enforcer after she'd repeatedly discharged her firearm at the wrong person inside Caesar's house, the Los Angeles pack master insisted his niece needed to learn discipline.

So far, we'd been lucky it wasn't at the price of any lives.

"Is your Uncle John hoping you'll accidentally kill Elizabeth?" I asked the werewolf.

Cara blushed under the security lights and mumbled, "I haven't screwed up in over a year. Who's your guest?"

"Tanis ibn Abdullah," I lied. "She's a reporter friend of Max's from Egypt, and she wanted to extend her condolences."

Cara's eyes narrowed as she examined my passenger. "That was over a year ago."

"Have you tried to enter the U.S. lately when you're from a Muslim country?" Tanis said lightly.

I made a show of closing my eyes and rubbing my forehead.

"I-I-I apologize, Ms. Indullah," Cara choked out. It wasn't worth correcting the anxiety-ridden werewolf over a fake name.

"Blood test?" I prompted.

Cara produced her bronze pin and stabbed my little finger. She handed me an antiseptic wipe package before she crossed to the other side of my SUV. Tanis pulled off her glove, but I could feel her tense beside me.

Thankfully, Cara said nothing about the ghoul's blemished skin. The were pricked Tanis's little finger, and nothing happened besides a little drop of blood.

Cara handed Tanis a wipe before the were nodded and signaled her partner on the other side of the barrier. The iron gate swung open, and I guided my vehicle up the drive.

Tanis placed her antiseptic wipe in the little box I used for trash. "Someone could pick up my disease from that pin."

I shook my head. "The holy bronze destroys microorganisms like the V-virus or your mutation. We checked and double-checked. Believe me, my uncle Duncan doesn't want that shit spread around."

"Even though he likes his power," Tanis said.

I parked in front of the house and shot her a glare. "If his wife weren't immortal, he would have been the first one in line for the cure."

She shook her head slowly. "We often cloak our own lies to make them easier to swallow."

I yanked the latch and shoved the door open. We just needed to harvest the blood and tissues samples from Elizabeth, I'd get my baby back, and we'd all go our merry ways into the night. I circled my SUV and retrieved the med pack from the equipment compartment.

Tanis slid out of the passenger seat and followed me up the portico steps. I rang the bell.

This time, Ted opened the front door. I breathed a little sigh of relief it hadn't been Susannah. Only the gods knew what a ghoul's aura would look like to a witch.

He frowned. His attention flicked in Tanis's direction and back to me. "Tiffany? We weren't expecting you until Sunday."

I played an air of boredom. "I know it's late and not Elizabeth's normal time, but Bebe needs some samples. It's an emergency. She's found a mutated strain of the virus."

Ted's eyes narrowed behind his glasses. "Where's Ellie?"

"Jake's watching her." I shrugged and gave him a wry smile. "We flipped a coin for who had to come over. I lost."

Ted shook his head. "Duncan should have—" He stopped himself as he realized how stupid the thought of sending an enforcer other than Jake or me was. "Come on in, girls."

"This is Tanis," I said as we stepped into my in-laws' home for the second time tonight. "She's learning how to draw samples."

"Elizabeth needs to come with us."

I gritted my teeth at the ghoul's contradiction. "No, we discussed this in the car on the way here."

Ignoring me, she tilted her head before she strode toward the living room. I recognized the behavior, seen it on the vamps and weres too many times. She was sniffing out my mother-in-law.

Swallowing my irritation, I tightened my grip on the med bag and followed Tanis.

"Excuse me? Who—" Elizabeth's voice had her snooty, high-pitched tone.

Until I entered the living room, and my mother-in-law's expression turned confused. She'd changed her clothes, which meant she found the stain on the skirt she'd been wearing earlier. "Tiffany? What are you doing back here?"

I sucked in a deep breath. A bit of guilt trickled through me at agreeing to let the ghouls harvest Elizabeth's DNA. "We need some samples."

"That's not what we need from her," Tanis snapped.

Elizabeth rose to her feet. "Now, wait just a minute here—"

Susannah chose that moment to come into the living room with a tray with steaming cups, Mr. Cuddles trotting behind her. Everything turned into the proverbial slow-motion train wreck.

Susannah took one look at Tanis, and the tray flew through the air. Hot chocolate splattered and stained the thick cream Berber carpet, but the cups didn't break. Somehow everything missed the elderly poodle as he scented the stranger. His little legs carried him as fast as his arthritis allowed toward his foe, and he yipped his fool head off. Susannah's fingers curled in a peculiar pattern. Ozone filled the air.

Tanis raised her own hands. I recognized her gesture for a defensive shield.

And Elizabeth was right in the middle of the magickal battle.

So I did something I've been wanting to do for years. I hit my mother-in-law with a flying tackle.

CHAPTER 11

Contrary to movies and TV series, there's not a lot of noise in a magickal battle between witches, but they do put on one hell of a lightshow. The sound comes when certain spells hit a physical object.

Like when Tanis deflected Susannah's offensive spell. Green and red exploded in my vision. The plasma bolt barely missed Ted, blew apart a chunk of drywall, and ignited the expensive, designer wallpaper.

I rolled off of Elizabeth, crawled closer to Ted, and yanked him to the carpet.

"You lied to me!" Tanis shrieked. The unbroken cups and any objets d'art made of ceramic or stone flew in our direction.

Great. My ghoul was an earth witch.

People were more afraid of the fire witches like Susannah due to human's innate fear of flames. And they were more respectful of water witches since so many of them were healers. But pound for pound in a fight, earth witches were the power houses.

We were in deep trouble, even though Mr. Cuddles was doing his best to chew up the hem of Tanis's burqa.

I yanked the couch cushions over our heads. It didn't stop other items from hitting exposed limbs. My shins were going to have some healthy bruises in the morning. I needed to figure out a way to stop these two before they brought Ted and Elizabeth's home down on our heads.

Another plasma bolt smacked the wallpaper. The damage would give my mother-in-law something to do during her house arrest if we survived this.

"Susannah! Tanis! Stop it!" I screamed.

The two women ignored me. Sure. I was a lowly Normal. No reason to listen to her at all.

The sharp report of a firearm, however, stopped the witches' spells in mid-casting. Both Susannah and Tanis shrieked in pain. I raised the couch cushion to see what was going on.

Amidst the smoke from the smoldering wallpaper, little dots of scarlet marred Susannah's uniform and arms. Tanis's black burqa disguised any hint of blood, but the way she held her right arm, she'd been hit, too.

Grandma Neel stepped into the living room, dressed in the lavender terry-cloth bathrobe Ellie had given her for Christmas, with an antique double-barreled shotgun propped on her shoulder. "You two witches gonna behave or do I have to unload another round in ya?"

Susannah and Tanis looked cautiously at each other before they both shook their heads.

"Shrimp, get the fire extinguisher and put out the wallpaper before we all die of smoke inhalation."

"Yes, ma'am." I shove the couch cushion back and jumped up to retrieve the device from the kitchen. I took one step when the front door busted open. Fellow enforcer Connie Torres entered, her eyes gleaming neon yellow and fangs extended. Behind her was another vampire I didn't know and Cara Lannigan. The werewolf sprouted fine fur all over her exposed skin, but her side arm was drawn.

"*Madre de Dios!*" Connie looked around. "What the hell?"

"I've got these two, sweetheart," Grandma Neel assured the vampire. "But for cryin' out loud, would someone get the blasted fire extinguisher!"

—•—

Once Connie secured both witches with spelled handcuffs on my recommendation, she sent the other two enforcers to open the windows through the house to clear out the smoke.

"Why am I handcuffed?" Susannah protested. "I'm supposed to be watching out for Mrs. Howell!"

"Because you threw the first punch!" I raised my arms in the air. "You didn't check with me. You didn't even try to read my mind to find out if Tanis was a real danger."

"And you lied to me!" Tanis shouted.

"I didn't—" Susannah began.

"She means me." I crossed my arms and glared at the ghoul. "And I said samples, Tanis. Not the whole hog."

She snorted but didn't say anything more.

"You got this for a few minutes, Cara," Connie asked.

"Yes, ma'am," the werewolf said crisply.

"She's got me for backup," Grandma Neel proclaimed. She was tucked in her recliner once again, but she refused to give up her shotgun. Luckily, it had only been filled with rock salt.

Connie looked at me and inclined her head toward the kitchen. I followed her.

Our elderly relative notwithstanding, that was the most self-confident I'd ever heard Cara Lannigan, and I said as much to Connie once the door swung shut.

"The kid just needed a little reassurance." Connie shrugged. "The boss's wife scares a lot of people. Now, what's really going on?"

The enforcer stuck with business. Business was good. The last person I wanted to talk about was Sam. I laid out the events that occurred after Jake, Ellie, and I left Ted and Elizabeth's place earlier.

"So that's a ghoul, huh?" Connie stared at the swinging door to the living room.

"Yeah, I'm still hoping for a diplomatic solution to this mess."

"I'll call Alex." When I glared at Connie, she gave me a rueful smile. "We need a backup plan just in case this goes sideways."

She was right. I knew she was right. I would have suggested the same thing even if it weren't my daughter in the fucking crossfire. So, I did what I normally do when things are out of my control. I bitched at the nearest person.

"When did Alex start assigning vamps to watch Satan Spawn?" I hissed under my breath.

"I volunteered," Connie said. "I don't have anything against your mother-in-law."

"In other words, your sponsor told you—"

The kitchen door swung inward. "Uh, Ms. Torres?" The other vampire stepped into the kitchen and raised his hand like he was in school. His eyes glowed a shockingly intense blue against skin that had been deeply tanned before he became a vampire. "I'm sorry, but I really need to step outside."

"No problem, Derek." She smiled at him. "I'll yell if I need you."

"Sorry." The guy gave us a rueful look before he ran out of the house. My ponytail fluttered against my cheek with the speed and draft of his passing as he darted out the patio door.

"Derek?" I pinched the bridge of my nose. "We have an enforcer named Derek?"

Connie chuckled. "He's not technically one of ours. Master Rousseau's people have been volunteering to watch your in-laws. A lot of them want the cure as much as all the other vampires."

I smiled at her. "I still can't believe you turned it down after Colonel Smith offered to get you back in the Army." Connie had been a sergeant and one hell of a sniper in the service. Or she was until she drove out to Death Valley to kill herself after she lost her entire unit in an attack overseas.

"We can talk about personal shit later," Connie said. "Right now, we need to get Ellie back, and—" She made a face at me. "I'm having a terrible feeling of déjà vu."

Chapter 12

I let Connie take over the situation when we returned to the living room. I was compromised because of my worry over Ellie and Jake, and I knew it.

But then, maybe Connie enjoyed being on the giving end this time. When her maker Marcus Giovanni beat Max and kidnapped Ellie, we'd forced Connie to help us.

After I'd shot and stabbed the former army sniper turned vampire.

Actually, it was a wonder Connie talked to me at all after what I'd done to her.

Connie asked Tanis for her version of our deal. Even though the ghoul tried to say we owed her Elizabeth, Tanis finally admitted the samples were all I had promised.

"I'll honor Enforcer Stephens' bargain with you and your people," Connie said. "But you need to understand one thing. My sponsor within the coven is Master St. James's wife. What do you think she'll order me to do to you if your people harm a hair on her niece's head? What do you think *she* will do to you?"

Tanis remained silent for a long moment. So long, I worried she'd forfeit her own life and my baby's out of sheer spite.

Finally, she bowed her head. "I agree."

"Well, I don't!" Elizabeth shrieked. "You can't barter me like—"

"A luscious fat pork chop?" Grandma Neel offered.

"You're under house arrest until the end of time," I reminded her. "And if you ever want to see Ellie again, you will do exactly as we say."

"I will not—"

"There are better punishments, Tiffany." Connie smiled at Elizabeth. "If you don't cooperate, Mrs. Howell, I'll make sure you have an orgasm in front of everyone for every vial,"

"You can't control my mind," Elizabeth spat back. Which was true. Not even Caesar could penetrate her psychic shields. Bebe thought it had something to do with the Ridgeway DNA.

"Who said anything about mind-fucking you?" Connie made a point of licking her lips very slowly. Her perverse act to get under my mother-in-law's skin made me like my fellow enforcer even more.

Grandma Neel, Susannah, and I snickered at the shocked look on Elizabeth's face. Ted turned the proverbial beet red. Tanis looked at us like we were all insane.

Maybe we were.

Elizabeth gasped for air and words a few times before she bit out, "Fine."

—•—

We uncuffed Susannah and Tanis once they promised no more magick.

Connie left the room while I took the blood and tissue samples from Elizabeth. The vampire claimed my actions were triggering her hunger. I knew damn well she was calling our situation in to Alex. Coven backup would be on its way to the grocery store.

Tanis watched closely, but she didn't interfere. Maybe she realized she couldn't help her son if she adulterated the source of the vaccine.

"What happens if we use these samples up without finding a cure?" Tanis said.

"How about trying to ask for more instead of kidnapping my daughter?" I muttered.

"She took Ellie?" Elizabeth's eyes narrowed as she faced Tanis, and her voice lowered an octave. "You took my granddaughter?" She started to stand.

"Sit still," I snapped.

Ted pressed his wife back into her seat on the couch. "You are not doing anything, Elizabeth. The last time you tried to fix things, you almost got your head chopped off."

I pulled out the last full vial and gently tipped it back and forth before I set it in the rack with the others. I grabbed a piece of gauze and pressed it against the crook of Elizabeth's elbow as I withdrew the needle. I dropped it in the red plastic sticks box before I tore off a bit of surgical tape and sealed the gauze to her arm.

"Where's Ellie?" Elizabeth growled at me.

I looked at Tanis while I stripped off my bright purple, non-latex gloves. "You want to tell her?"

Even though I could only see the ghoul's eyes, she actually appeared uncomfortable for the first time tonight.

"She's with the rest of the hostages at a grocery store in Tarzana," she murmured.

"Hostages?" Ted's cheeks blazed with his fury. I could count on three fingers what it took to get him mad. Touching his precocious granddaughter was one.

"Jake and an off-duty police officer are with the Normals at the grocery," I said before Ted joined Elizabeth in the doing-something-stupid department. "They're both armed, and unless Tanis's people didn't follow her orders, everyone's fine."

"I'm assuming you two are rendezvousing with her people at the grocery store," Grandma Neel said. When I nodded, she added, "You need some backup?" She lifted the end of her shotgun and pointed it at Tanis.

Thank goodness, Connie came back in the living room. "That won't be necessary, Mrs. Neel. We've got it covered." She turned to Tanis. "This has been settled correctly?"

The ghoul nodded.

"Good," Grandma Neel stated. "I'd hate to have to shoot you again."

—— • ——

Tanis took Grandma Neel's threat seriously. She meekly climbed in the back seat of my SUV, clutching the reinforced transport box filled with frozen gel packs and the precious vials of Elizabeth's blood and cell samples.

We were halfway back to the grocery store when Connie muttered, "Crap."

"What?" I glanced at her before focusing on traffic again. The last thing I needed was a fender-bender tonight.

"My sponsor got wind of what's happening." The faint glow of neon yellow from Connie's eyes filled the passenger compartment.

"Shit." My fingers tightened on the steering wheel and my foot pressed the accelerator. "If she fucks this up—" I left the rest unsaid. There wouldn't be any more family dinners if that bitch got anybody killed tonight.

CHAPTER 13

My SUV slid around the right turn into the parking lot. It was already well after ten p.m. so most of the stores on this stretch of street were closed for the evening.

A familiar red pickup was parked next to Jake's Jeep. I recognized Phil's vintage Mustang along with a couple of other vehicles. The other four in sight were the standard issue armored black SUVs most of the coven drove.

With the attempts on the lives of several high-ranking members of the North American covens by the Vampire Liberation Front, nearly everyone ordered the specialized vehicles. No sense taking chances on our wards' existence especially since the bastards liked to use bombs.

"Where are my people?" Worry filled Tanis's voice.

"According to our boss, they retreated inside when our backup arrived five minutes ago," Connie said.

"And how do I know you simply haven't disposed of the bodies?" Tanis snapped.

"Because we would've just fucking killed you by now," I shot back as I parked next to a knot of people. Alex's blond hair stood out above the crowd. Phil stood next to him along with Ray Xavier, a vampire who normally worked as a medical examiner at the Los Angeles County morgue.

Those three faced Grandpa Ares and *her.* From all their expressions under my headlights, the five of them were in the middle of a major argument.

I cut the engine and slid out of the driver's seat. Connie and Tanis exited my SUV and followed me over to the huddle.

"Do you have contact with anyone inside?" I asked Alex.

"No." Alex frowned at me. "If ah'd known we were dealing with rogue witches on top of ghouls—"

My hand slashed through the air to stop him. "The ghouls are the witches." I looked at Tanis before I added, "No one's immune to their version of the virus."

"If that's the case, it's imperative we help them find a cure—" Ray started.

"Are you mad?" Ares roared. "These bastards slaughter innocents and steal children—"

"Stop it!" I shouted. It had already been a long day before I dropped by this stupid grocery store, and my patience snapped. "Just stop it."

Surprisingly, he did.

"Tanis here—" I gestured at the ghoul beside me. "—and I cut a deal. As Ray said, the ghouls need a cure as much as the vamps do. This disease is killing them, and it's contagious to everyone, including the fae. We are going to cooperate with them, whether the rest of you like it or not."

"What about Ellie, Jake, and the rest of the people inside?" *she* said quietly.

I didn't want to talk to her, but since I had no patience left, I got ugly. "Are you here to take their souls? Is that the real reason you came?"

She merely looked at me as if I were a cockroach. However, I'd lay good money Tanis's sharp inhalation meant she realized how piss-poor of a position she'd put her people in, especially her son.

"I'm here to help." *Her* words were calm, but her eyes flared from blue to a soft white glow. Good, I'd gotten under her skin.

"Then you will stay outside with everyone else," I said equally calmly. "Tanis has what she needs, and she's going to collect her people. You are going to let them leave peacefully." My gaze swept our little group. "The same goes for the rest of you."

"May I give Tanis my business card?" Ray's little smile display the tips of his fangs.

I nodded.

He pulled out his wallet and extracted the cardboard slip with his name, business address, and phone number. "I'm one of the research team. If you change your mind about wanting our help, contact me."

She stared at the card as if it were too good to be true. "Why?"

"Because once upon a time, a ghoul saved my life."

Everyone stared at Ray.

"You knew they were still out there?" Alex finally asked.

Ray shrugged. "It was not my secret to share, *amigo*."

Tanis gently took the proffered card. "Thank you." She looked at me. "We will go peacefully."

"Let me see the card."

She cocked her head, but she handed it to me.

I realized my bag was still inside the store. "Anybody got a pen?"

Ray handed me one from his breast pocket. He was such a nerd despite his Hispanic top model looks. It was one of the reasons I liked him.

I scribbled my number on the back of his business card and handed it to Tanis. "In case, you have any questions or you need more samples."

She nodded again. "Let's get my people out of your way."

We walked side-by-side toward the pharmacy entrance to the store. I realized for the first time, Phil hadn't lectured me about acting foolishly. Maybe I was finally getting some respect from the rest of the coven after all this time.

The glass and steel automatic doors were still parted by a finger-width, exactly how we'd left them. Someone had posted a hand-written sign on the door, stating it was closed due to loss of power.

I had to give the ghouls credit for coming up with a plan to keep additional shoppers out of the building. Together, we pulled one of the doors enough for us to slip through the gap.

Someone should have been guarding the entrance. Silence reigned inside the store. The emergency lights still glowed, but they'd noticeably dimmed since we'd left for Beverly Hills.

"Vald? Esau?" Tanis called softly.

When no one answered, she strode briskly towards the hallway leading to the staircase up to the second-floor offices. I pulled my silver knife from its right boot sheathe. My gut said something had gone very, very wrong. Had the VLF sent reinforcements to the grocery store and murdered Tanis's people when they saw their dead comrades? Worse, had they killed Jake and taken Ellie?

My heart pounded. A sharp gasp from Tanis stopped me in my tracks. One of the werewolf ghouls lay in front of the splintered door to the stairwell along with two other ghoul bodies that weren't there when we left. All three had bloody holes on their necks.

Right where the jugular vein passed underneath the skin.

She whirled to face me. "What is this? What did your people do?"

"This wasn't us." I knelt next to the closest body. I recognized the female ghoul dressed in a business suit. Her wig rested a few feet away, splayed like a dead animal.

"Really? You expect me to believe—"

A sharp female scream from upstairs cut off Tanis's tirade.

CHAPTER 14

Tanis raced up the stairs. I ran after her, but she was definitely faster. With my heart in my throat, I realized my fatal mistake. On the landing, someone had punched through the drywall opposite of the intact door and into the store's breakroom.

The ghoul ducked through the hole.

Crap. I didn't want to yell for the cavalry. Not until I knew what was happening, but I wished I hadn't given my sidearm to Jake.

I hoped he was all right. I hoped I hadn't really screwed up, and he and Ellie were dead.

I ducked through the hole and charged around the corner toward the offices. Tanis's son stood near the refrigerator blocking the upstairs door. In his hands was a long, dark object. A rifle, my brain forced me to acknowledge.

"Vald?" Tanis whispered. "What are you doing?"

This wasn't making sense. Ghouls didn't have fangs, but something with fangs killed at least three of Tanis's people. How did Vald end up here unscathed? And where were the rest of the ghouls?

The civilians crowded in the space between the two rows of cubicles. Jake and Officer Goodman stood in front of them. Ambient light glinted off the barrels of their weapons, and I recognized the one Goodman held as my own Glock.

"The St. James bitch deceived us," the male ghoul hissed. "Vampires came and, and . . ." He was shaking. Whether it was rage or grief for his friends didn't matter. Not when his rifle was pointed at the people I loved.

Everything clicked in my head. This had Giovanni's prints all over it. Instead of the rage I normally experienced when it came to that bastard, I felt icily calm. There was no way I was going to let history repeat itself.

"It's a set-up, Tanis." I stepped between her and the thing pretending to be her son, keeping an eye on him the whole time. "The VLF let you follow them because they've been infiltrated by the same assholes who tried to trick Anouk and the fairies into attacking our coven members in Las Vegas." Sam knew. That was the real reason she was here at the store.

"What?" The dino demon pretended to be incredulous. "Mother, are you going to believe such a ridiculous story?"

I had to give the demon credit. He, or rather it, played their part well.

"Is the real Vald even still alive?" I said.

A sound suspiciously like a sob came from the ghoul behind me.

"Why do you lie?" The dino demon shook its head. "You think they will reward your service with eternal life?" It pointed in the direction of the parking lot with the end of the rifle. "You think those things you worship can return your husband?"

"You saying you can?" I mocked it. I wanted its attention on me, not the innocent civilians. Maybe what I really wanted was to be wrong and to talk down Tanis's son. Murphy knew where the real Vald's body was, but I was pretty damn sure he was dead despite my wishing.

"I have what we came for." Tanis stepped around me and approached the dino demon.

I nearly panicked until I saw the glint of a long, thin piece of metal in her left hand.

"I want revenge for our people we lost tonight as much as you do," she continued. "But if we kill the hostages, neither of us will make it out of here alive. We cannot win today's battle, my son. There's always another day." She reached for its upper arm. In one motion, she stabbed the Olympian bronze pin into its flesh, and with her right hand, she threw up a shield spell in front of Jake,

Goodman, and the rest of the civilians. Ozone stank up the air in the relatively small space. Flashes of green appeared in my peripheral vision.

The dino demon shrieked, and its skin rippled in reaction to the god-forged metal. Tanis grabbed the rifle and leapt back as the demon continued to contort its body in ways mortal muscle and bones couldn't imagine.

"Bitch!" It screamed a few other things I'm sure were equally insulting, but I didn't recognize the languages. Claws sprouted from the tips of its phalanges, and its mismatched human and lizard eyes focused on Tanis. It took a halting, off-balance step toward her.

I yanked her backward. "Tanis! Drop the shield!"

She muttered something in Arabic. The scent of ozone disappeared. Jake and Goodman both fired.

Any wishful thinking on my part disappeared when the demon pretending to be Vald dropped to the floor. The acidic blood of the demon melted the artificial fabric of the industrial-grade carpet. The chemical reaction started to fill the offices with choking fumes.

"Mommy, is the first floor clear?" Ellie asked.

Alex?

You're good, Tiffany.

Of course, he'd been listening through me. Surprisingly, neither he nor the gods with him had interfered in the showdown.

"Downstairs is clear, sweetie," I said.

"Everyone, follow me." Ellie shook off Marla's grip on her shoulder and charged toward the breakroom. Thankfully, the civilians didn't question why a five-year-old had taken charge of the evacuation. They simply followed her.

Goodman shook his head as he passed me. "What the hell do you teach your kids?"

CHAPTER 15

Ares and Sam got the supernatural corpses out of the grocery store before the fire trucks, ambulances, and LAPD arrived. Our people restored the power and phones. Luckily, both had been stopped via the emergency cut-offs, and not actually slicing the lines.

Alex had a little talk with Goodman, Marla, and Sergeant Olivera, the senior LAPD officer at the scene. Olivera was one of the coven's Family contacts. Both civilians had witnessed too much, and I could see their expressions the moment Alex, Jake, and Olivera told them the truth. Goodman looked like someone had cold-cocked him. Marla laughed so hard she bent over double in order to catch her breath.

I had to give Goodman credit. The officer had seen some seriously freaky shit tonight. But he'd handled it well, and he saved a lot of lives. Being a former Texas Ranger, Alex had a soft spot when it came to memory-wiping fellow law enforcement. It looked like the recruitment talk with Goodman was going well.

I hoped Alex recruited Marla, too. She'd obviously picked up enough of the real story long before tonight and hadn't freaked with the ghoul/vampire/demon invasion. It would be nice to have a safe place to shop for groceries.

Trudging across the parking lot, I spotted Connie with Ellie and Tanis. The ghoul sat on the curb and clutched the bag holding Elizabeth's bio-samples tightly to her chest. She'd gotten what she wanted, but from the angle of her head, she realized how much it had cost her. Ellie sat on her left and stroked Tanis's arm.

My daughter, however, was much more animated than I expected given the time of night. "Hey, Mommy!" She waved as I joined them. "Can Tanis spend the night with us? She lost her family tonight, and she shouldn't be alone."

Tanis's head jerked at my daughter's words. Connie frowned. Somehow, I wasn't surprised by Ellie's request. From the strong scent of sandalwood mixed with something I couldn't identify, even us Normals could understand Tanis's pain.

I sat on the curb next to Ellie. Deep down, I didn't like the idea of the ghoul in my house, but I understood her agony. I'd faced it myself too many times.

"That's up to her." I hugged Ellie. "She's had a very bad night."

Tears glimmered in Tanis's eyes. "After everything that's happened, you would offer me a place in your home?"

I shrugged. "As long as you understand coven security will be at my house with or without you."

"If our situations were reversed, I don't know if I could be that gracious," Tanis murmured.

"That's what I thought, too." Connie smiled down at the ghoul. "But these are good people. They gave me a chance after my involvement in Ellie's abduction a year and a half ago."

"You didn't hurt my daddy, and you didn't stick me in a cage," Ellie said fiercely.

Her words wrenched my gut. I had thought, hoped really, she didn't remember much of what happened that awful time. Everything had gone down a couple of days before she turned four. No one should have her father die the day before her birthday.

"Um, thank you for defending me, Ellie," Connie said. If she'd been Normal, I had no doubt her face would be a dark red right now.

Tanis exhaled, a deep breath that fluttered the edges of her veil. "Unless you are holding me, it would be best if I contacted my associates. I have no wish to restart our peoples' war."

"Can we ask a favor first, Tanis?" *Her* voice made all of us jump. She glided out of the shadows formed by the remaining vehicles and cart corrals in the parking lot.

"Aunt Sam!" Ellie leapt up before I could stop her and ran straight to *her* arms. I found myself a little too weary and sad to protest. She picked up Ellie and kissed her on her forehead before they both faced Tanis again.

"Do I have a choice?" Despite the ghoul's defiant words, a thread of primal fear penetrated her tone.

"Yes. Contrary to popular belief, I'm not a total asshole." She shot me a look as if expecting me to say something snarky.

Which I normally would have, even when we were still speaking, but too many people had died tonight for any flippancy from me.

"What do you wish?" Tanis murmured.

"The locations of the VLF bases and members your people have been tracking," Sam said. "Jake mentioned that's how you knew they planned to take Ellie tonight."

For the next five minutes, Tanis spilled. I reached for my backpack, but

I remembered it was still somewhere in the deli section of the grocery store. Neither Sam or Connie wrote anything down. They didn't need to.

Jake walked up as Tanis finished her recitation, my backpack in his hands. "I hate to break up the party, ladies, but I'm under orders to escort two of you home."

"What about McDonald's?" Disappointment filled Ellie's big brown eyes.

"It's late—" I started.

"The drive-thru's still open, and I'm a little hungry myself." Jake gave me an odd look. One I couldn't quite decipher. Or maybe I was too tired to even try.

"Fine." I held up my hands in surrender. My stomach burbled its own opinion of the idea.

"Can I ride with Uncle Jake?" Ellie batted her eyes at me.

I hesitated for an instant. So of course, Jake and Ellie chorused, "Ple-e-e-ease!"

"All right. All right. You win." I stood and accepted my backpack from Jake. It was a little heavier than normal. About the weight of a Glock and its clip. Glad one of us remember to retrieve my sidearm from Officer Goodman.

Ellie kissed Sam on the cheek before Sam set her down. My daughter ran over and hugged Connie and Tanis, then she took Jake's hand. "See you Sunday, Aunt Sam!" She waved cheerily and skipped away with my fellow enforcer.

Sam waited until they'd climbed into Jake's Jeep before she turned back to me with a quizzical expression. "Sunday?"

"Don't make a big deal about it," I snapped.

"All right." No snarky comeback from her either. If we could keep up this brittle politeness, maybe we'd both survive Easter.

CHAPTER 16

I hit my favorite hole-in-the-wall sub and pizza place not too far from our house. I hadn't been there since the night Giovanni invaded my home and destroyed our lives. A veggie sub was my healthiest option this late. And we still didn't have any food in the house besides a jar of peanut butter and a pack of juice boxes.

Hell, I didn't have any coffee for tomorrow morning.

Jake's Jeep was already parked in our driveway when I turned onto our street. I waved at Saif Al-Issa as I passed his SUV parked by our curb, but I didn't recognize the other enforcer with him. There'd been so many changes within the coven since the night Bebe discovered the cure.

Since the night Max died.

I pulled into our garage. I'd given Jake a set of keys for my place since he picked up Ellie from school at least twice a week. This stupid thesis was kicking my ass, but dammit, I was almost done with my masters' degree.

I felt I owed Max that much. He'd been the one who pushed the most about me going to college. Figuring out what I wanted to do with my life beyond my allegiance to the coven. Beyond my hero worship of my uncle who raised me.

The garage slowly lowered. I slid out of my SUV, slammed the vehicle's door and locked it. My late husband was right. Ellie needed to see there was more to life than monsters and terror and death. I needed to change. Needed to live so my daughter could.

Maybe it wasn't just for Ellie. I turned twenty-six last week. I was hardly an old fogey. And Jake . . .

Part of me wanted to explore what was behind that kiss he gave me in the grocery store's office. The rest of me started piling on the guilt.

I entered the kitchen with my sub. Jake was still pulling food items from their bags. Poor Ellie was sticking fries in her mouth as fast as possible.

"Slow down there, sweetie." I set my sub on the table.

"But I'm starving!" she said, giving me a full view of half-masticated fries. "We should have had supper hours ago!"

"I'm hungry, too." I shed my denim jacket. My index nail caught on cotton threads, and I realized I had a serious rip across the back. My favorite jacket. Ruined in the deli and produce section fight. Or maybe the rip occurred when Ellie and I jumped from our perch on the shelves. I should just be happy it wasn't my skin.

I sighed and slung it and my backpack across the back of my chair before I sat down. "All I'm saying is slow down and chew your supper because I don't want to spend the night in the ER because a fry went down the wrong pipe."

She wrinkled her nose and rolled her eyes, but she answered, "Yes, ma'am."

Jake retrieved a couple of bottles of water for us from my refrigerator. I eyed the cup and straw Ellie was enthusiastically sucking on. I really hoped he bought my daughter milk to go with her fast food. My constitution for dealing with a sugar-hyped kindergartener was non-existent.

Ellie took a bite of her cheeseburger, chewed it thoroughly, and swallowed before she asked, "Are you two going to kiss again after I go to bed?"

Water sprayed from my mouth and caught Jake in the face and chest. It looked like he was trying not to laugh as he reached for the napkins lying on the table next to his Quarter Pounder. My throat burned, and I hacked and coughed, my body trying to get the water out of my own windpipe.

"Why are you so vested in your mom and me kissing?" he asked while he wiped off his face and shirt and mopped the water from the table. Thankfully, neither of us had opened the wrappings on our sandwiches, and I had totally missed his own fries.

"Because you both have been really sad since Daddy died." She steepled her fingers and rested her chin on them. Her pose was reminiscent of Caesar's don't-mess-with-me attitude. With a start, I realize Duncan had picked up the same mannerism since he became master of the coven. "And you're here a lot. Aunt Anne and Grandma Phil said you wouldn't come to our house this much unless you really liked Mommy."

I buried my face in my hands. I really needed to have a talk with my fellow enforcer and my foster mom about gossiping in front of my daughter.

"Would it be that bad, Tiffany?" Jake asked softly.

I looked up at him. My throat ached, but not from the recent choking fit. Despite my pep talk to myself in the garage, I owed him the truth. "I'm not sure I'm ready."

"I can wait."

And I knew he meant that as a promise.

CHAPTER 17

Just before noon on Sunday, Jake eyed my in-laws' McMansion as he drove through the gates in the bright Easter sunshine. "This wasn't what I had in mind for a first date."

"Unfortunately, they come with the package." I couldn't laugh at his discomfort. I shared it.

"Is this just your attempt to piss them off?" he asked me for the third time in as many days.

"Language, Uncle Jake!" Ellie's sharp reprimand from the back seat only reminded me that this may be a huge mistake.

"Sorry, kiddo," he replied.

He parked behind Ted's mid-life crisis toy. If the black Corvette convertible was out of the garage, Sam and Duncan were already here.

Jake turned to me. "Please tell me you're not bringing me to Easter dinner to throw sh—" He sucked in a deep breath and rephrased his words for Ellie's sake. "—stuff in everyone's faces."

I smiled at him. "No, I'm depending on you to keep me from killing them, and that's only because Ellie's not big enough to stop me."

"Yet," my little combat ballerina said.

We all got out of the vehicle. I smoothed down the skirt of my pale green floral dress. It felt a little weird with the slight breeze blowing up and around my legs. I hadn't worn a dress since my wedding day. Jake insisted on wearing a suit and tie. The electric blue silk knotted at his throat looked smart against the medium gray light wool.

Black velvet formed the bodice of Ellie's new dress. The floaty tulle skirt was slightly less pink than her athletic shoes. The dress matched her Easter basket full of dyed hardboiled eggs. Eggs that also matched her dress.

Jake chuckled as we climbed the three steps to the front door. "The only reason I'd stop you is because I need this job."

I didn't answer. I'd learned the hard way from Max that you don't insinuate a guy can't pay his way. Instead, I lifted my hand to press the bell when the door flew open.

Ted grinned like a fool. "You came!"

"Hi, Grandpa!" Ellie, on the other hand, grinned like a maniacal Easter bunny. She hugged him before she tore into the house.

"I said we would." I kissed him on the cheek.

Ted held out his hand. "Good to see you, Jake."

Jake shook it. "Thank you for the invitation."

Ted lowered his voice as he closed the door. "Honestly, I'm happy you're still going to be part of the family."

"Whoa!" I held up my hands. "Let's not jump ahead of things. This is just Easter dinner."

"You're the one that said Max's family is part of the package." Jake grinned at me.

"Max's family is part of what package?"

I turned to find Uncle Duncan. His black hair was far shorter than I ever remembered it being, more in the style of a modern businessman than a sixteenth-century border noble. It went along with the dark gray suit and the emerald silk tie he wore.

He eyed me, then Jake. The hint of a smile played at the corners of Uncle Duncan's mouth. Of course, he read our minds. He turned to Ted. "May I speak with Tiffany and Jake privately for a moment? Coven business."

"Sure." Curiosity filled Ted's expression, but he knew better than to ask. He headed towards the living room where I could hear Ellie showing off her eggs to Grandma Neel.

"Do not start with me—"

Duncan held up his hand to stop my rant. "I merely wanted to update both of you. Alex and a team raided the last of the VLF locations Tanis gave us before dawn this morning."

Jake's grin disappeared. "Same as the others?"

Duncan nodded. "All dead. Both the vampires and the humans they fed on. From appearances, it was the combination of the two diseases again. Bebe and Ray are in the process of confirming it."

I shook my head. "The dino demon had to know what would have happened if it sicced the VLF on the ghouls."

"That is the general consensus," Duncan said. "You should also know Tanis has reached out to Ray."

"That's . . . sooner than I thought she would." I shrugged. "It's a good start for normalizing relations with the ghouls."

"Jake, may I speak with Tiffany alone for a moment?" Duncan asked.

"Sure." Jake squeezed my hand and headed into the living room.

Duncan motioned with his index finger to follow him. He retreated into the dining room. I entered, half-expected a chewing out from him about dating a co-worker. Instead, he folded his hands behind his back and smiled.

"Ten years ago, I wouldn't have dreamed you would become the ambassador you are now."

"Thank you." I frowned at him. "I think." For an instant, I questioned whether a dino demon replaced my uncle. He was rarely this complimentary.

"Feel free to prick me with an Olympian pin if you wish, little one." He held out his right hand.

I grimaced and shook my head. "Stay out of my brain, and just tell me whatever it is you wanted to tell me."

"I am requesting you take the lead in negotiating with the ghouls."

Ellie could have knocked me over with one of her bizarrely colored Easter eggs. "I seem to recall a lecture five years ago about overstepping my authority regarding the treaty with the fae."

His smile disappeared, and his usually perturbed expression reappeared. "I display confidence in your abilities, and you must argue with me?"

"Sorry," I muttered. For once, I really did regret my words. Something had shifted in everyone's attitude toward me. I should be thankful of that little fact.

His right eyebrow rose. "Do you want the job?"

"Yes, I do." I cleared my throat. "What made you ask me?"

"You developed a rapport with Tanis." But there was something in his face. I would almost say it was discomfort. I didn't need telepathy to know there was more to the story.

"Wanna try again?" I crossed my arms and tapped the toe of my right sandal against Elizabeth's custom cut hardwood floor.

"Samantha pointed out I was still treating you as a child."

I blinked, a little surprised she would take my side. Especially after the ugly things I said to her after Max died.

And the fact I literally stabbed her in the back at Max's wake.

I glared at Duncan. "Was this before or after she found out Jake has a thing for me?"

"After."

I inhaled deeply and released the air. "Are you going to lecture me about dating him?"

"No." Duncan relaxed a fraction. "I am grateful to him for watching out for both you and Ellie. I was . . . worried about you both after our loss."

Our loss. Murphy help me, I was truly a selfish bitch at times. The last thing I wanted was to hurt Duncan. It never registered how Sam's changes, him becoming coven master, watching everyone else being cured, how everything was affecting him.

"You know I'm here if you need to talk." I stepped forward and wrapped my arms around him. He hugged me in return.

"I know," he murmured in my hair. "Would it be acceptable if I came to visit once in a while?"

I leaned back and looked up at him. "Of course! I was . . ." I swallowed hard. "I didn't mean to drive you away. I was . . ."

"I know." He hugged me tighter against his chest. "I know."

For the first time in a very long while, the universe didn't feel like such a horrible place.

THE LAST STORY

Author's Note: This story takes place sixty-two years after the events of *Resurrected.*

Fog.

Everywhere Caesar Augustine looked there was fog. So much for the stories of a bright light at the end of a tunnel. Or the sound of wings. No, after death, there was simply fog and silence.

He turned around. Or he thought he did. There had been light and the sound of wings when his baby brother Ptolemy died the first time. He wasn't sure why he assumed it would be the same for him. Hades, after meeting so many gods the last century of his life, he wasn't sure what, or who, he believed in anymore.

Caesar held his hand in front of his face. Or did he? Technically, he shouldn't have a physical body. He touched his nose with his palm. Ran his fingers over the bridge and across his lips.

It definitely felt like his face. Or the face he'd had for the two thousand-plus years of his life. The last sixty years had left him with his face, but different. Would his father have had the same wrinkled visage if he hadn't died so young?

The fog was starting to get on his nerves. He started walking. Or he thought he did.

Sam said a person picked their own heaven or hell when they died. She didn't say a damn thing about fog. So why would he want fog?

There was a sound. Caesar paused. He couldn't hear his own breathing.

Of course, he couldn't. He was dead. He wasn't breathing.

"Take my hand."

Cold swept through him at someone speaking Latin in a familiar Japanese accent. A voice he hadn't heard in nearly seventy years. "Kensai?"

"Take my hand, Master Augustine."

Caesar reached out. Fingers wrapped around his own and yanked him forward, but not into light. It was night. Waves splashed against solid materials. Lines tugged on cleats, making the wood beneath his dress boots creak and groan. Saltwater and dead fish scented the air. He was on a dock.

Kensai Osaka stood before him. The samurai dressed as he had when Caesar first met him centuries ago. A formal black and white kimono. The long and short ceremonial swords tucked into the wide black belt. He wore a modified version of the Japanese warrior's updo.

Caesar frowned and switched to English. "Your hair's different."

"The chonmage? It's not shaved back like it was when we first met." Kensai ran his index finger across his natural hairline. "She asked me not to. Said it reminded her too much of her brother."

Caesar didn't have to ask who Kensai meant. A traditional chonmage would have resembled Max Howell's male-pattern baldness, except Max didn't keep his hair in an updo of any sort. Caesar had always given the man credit. He owned his looks until the very end, never trying to be something he wasn't.

Caesar looked down at himself. He was dressed in an early twentieth century traveling suit. Reaching up to check his own hair, his hand hit a hat. He removed it and examined the fine felt. A bowler.

Oh, how Selene had nagged him for wearing something second class, no matter how many times he pointed out that top hats were going out of style. Only snobs wore them back in—

Thoroughly confused now, he looked around him. It was still slightly foggy, but not like it was before Kensai grabbed him. A gigantic cruise ship moored nearby along with all sorts of other boats.

Southhampton. England. The last time he'd been here was . . .

He peered up at the cruise ship.

H.M.S. Titanic.

His twin sister Selene had desperately tried to talk him into taking the brand-new luxury vessel back to the United States. But even their younger brother Ptolemy had noted it wasn't a good idea. The owners and engineers had called the ship "unsinkable," which was an invitation to the gods to strike it down, he said.

A few days later, Ptolemy had been proven right.

Caesar turned to Kensai. "Is she insane?"

The samurai chuckled. "No, her sense of humor simply hasn't changed a bit. It could have been worse. She could have sent the *Black Pearl*."

Caesar groaned. "How did I end up here?"

"You chose this afterlife," Kensai said. "Frankly, none of us were sure which way you'd jump. You literally left it to the last second. However, we can't wait here too long." He beckoned Caesar to follow him.

They walked down to where the first-class passengers would have boarded in really life. There was no one around.

"Shouldn't there be more . . . ghosts?" Caesar asked as they climbed.

"You're the only new guest tonight, Master," Kensai replied.

"Don't call me that," Caesar chided. "I haven't been a vampire master in sixty years."

"I haven't been a vampire longer than that." Kensai grinned as they climbed the gangway.

Caesar considered his next question. "So, she employed you?"

"You could say that." Kensai grew serious. "The way Jamal died . . ." He shook his head. "It broke me. I refused any who could have claimed me until she found me drifting in the void."

"Allah preserve us, are you telling that sad story again?" Jamal stood at the top of the gangway, his lips pursed in disapproval. Unlike his life partner, he was dressed as a ship's steward. However, his hair was still in the braids he wore when he died, tied back with a gold ribbon.

"It's good to see you again, Caesar." Jamal hugged him and slapped him on the back. "She's waiting for you in the VIP lounge." Jamal released Caesar and jabbed an index finger in Kensai's breastbone. "And you better get dressed for dinner. You know she'll get snippy if you're late again. You almost missed the damn boat as it was."

"And she would have been more perturbed if I hadn't brought Master Augustine to the ship at all," Kensai responded.

Jamal stuck his tongue out at Kensai and grabbed Caesar's elbow. "Come on, she's waiting for you at her table."

"What made her choose the *Titanic*?" Caesar murmured.

"It could have been worse." Jamal grimaced. "It could have been the *S.S. Pacific Princess*."

They passed people laughing and gossiping, all dressed as if this really were 1912 and the ship was about to set sail for the United States. Caesar swallowed hard. If he'd given in to his twin sister's demands, they and Ptolemy would have died the moment the sun struck them on the deck of one of the rescue ships or floating in the Atlantic. Or worse, they could have been sucked down with the ship to be driven mad by drowning for an eternity.

"Who are these people?" Caesar looked around while they walked, not recognizing any faces.

"She's taken a page from your book." Jamal grinned at him. "She takes in strays."

They entered the first class dining room. She stood out, and not just because the guests gave her a wide berth. She wore an elegant formal dress for the era in the blackest of blacks. Even the decorative lace and buttons were the same color. Her skin took a pearlescent gleam against the dark fabric. Her hair could have been spun gold, swept into a crown of curls on top of her head. But it was her eyes that caught him, gleaming sapphire blue as he and Jamal approached her.

This wasn't the scared girl Duncan had brought to him decades ago. Nor was she the friend who said good-bye hours before his passing. This was Death in her own domain.

Samantha Marie Howell Ridgeway-St. James stood and grinned. "Told you I'd see you on the other side."

Caesar decided the safest response was to bow. "A pleasure to see you again, m'lady," he said as he straightened.

"Dammit, Caesar!" Her grin shifted into a scowl. "We've been friends too long to stand on stupid etiquette."

Now, that sounded more like the woman he knew.

"So much has changed for both of us." He shrugged. "I decided to err on the side of stupid etiquette."

That drew a chuckle from her as he hoped.

"Is there anything I can get you and your guest, boss?" Jamal said.

Caesar opened his mouth before he realized Jamal wasn't referring to him.

"A bottle of tequila, limes, and salt for me." Sam looked at Caesar. "This is your last voyage. You can eat or drink anything your heart desires tonight."

"Anything?" Caesar quirked an eyebrow.

"Anything," she repeated.

"There was a little tavern three streets from the main gate of Caesarea in Mauretania that had the freshest figs and the finest wine west of Alexandria." Caesar leaned closer to Sam. "If you can produce those, you will have my allegiance forever."

She shook her head. "Be careful saying things like that around me. You've seen the consequences." She turned to Jamal. "Get the man what he wants."

Jamal laughed and jogged toward the servants' entrance to the kitchens.

Caesar automatically held out Sam's chair for her. Once she was seated, he took the chair across from hers.

"You don't seem surprised by what you're seeing," she murmured. "Did Bebe make you watch the movie too many times?"

"No." He grinned despite the wave of sadness. As a witch, his wife would easily live another fifty years beyond him. "I toured the docks when it was being built. White Star was looking for additional investors."

"What made you not put your money into the ship line?"

Caesar looked at the chandelier above them before he returned his attention to Sam. "For once, I listened to Ptolemy instead of Selene. He was right. The engineers were too cocky. And innocent people paid the price." He took a deep breath before he said, "So, how does this work?"

"You asked Jamal about the other people." She waved at the other diners around them. "Some are strays as he said. People who died rejecting any allegiance to any particular pantheon."

Caesar frowned. "You told me atheists and agnostics go to your friend Norman."

"That's the problem." Sam leaned her elbows on the table. "They believe. Just like Kensai and Jamal believed. But the way they died made them so angry that when my counterparts tried to collect them, they both refused to go. For most of the others, it's fear that makes them reject their final destination."

She sighed. "Then you have the folks like Ptolemy who weren't or couldn't be given proper rites so they become stuck." She looked around the room before turning back to Caesar. "A few here believe in me, but they refuse to pay the toll."

"The toll?" For an instant, a chill ran through him.

"They have to tell me the story I ask them for." Again, she shrugged. "The ones that don't, they stay on the ship. Usually, they're ashamed, or they think I'll punish them for their sins." She chuckled. "I worked for the *Scoop* a little over seven years. There isn't a damn thing that shocks me anymore."

Caesar had to laugh at that comparison as well. Sam had been one of the top reporters at the celebrity rag he had once owned. Back when he was still a vampire and she was a Normal.

"What story haven't I told you?" he asked.

Sam propped her chin on her fists. "Don't be a tease, Caesar. You know the one I'm waiting for."

He should have known. The one tale of his past he hadn't told her because part of him was ashamed as she suspected. Not because of what he did, but because of what he selfishly wanted from a teacher in Galilee. A teacher who wanted nothing more than peace.

"All right." Caesar settled back in his chair. "Ironically, I first met Jesus of Galilee on my seventieth birthday . . ."

DECEMBER 25TH, 30 A.D.

Dust coated every inch of Alexander's exposed skin as he and his retinue rode north along the Jordan River. As much as he wanted to leap into the water and bathe under the moonlight, they had leagues to go before dawn.

He hoped the Olive Branch was still in Nazareth. The inn was owned by Family and would be a safe stop for any vampire traveling through the Levant. However, any attempt at gleaning information about the Olive Branch from travelers coming in the opposite direction was met with suspicion. Traveling at night was bad enough, but from the whispers when the other travelers thought he was out of earshot, he was far too Roman for their tastes.

"You're a fool," Selene muttered beside him for the umpteenth time. She'd taken to dressing like an Amazigh youth. As she pointed out, her appearance caused far less trouble than if she dressed like the Kemetan princess or Mauretanian queen she truly was. Not to mention she was a far better horsewoman than most of their guards.

"You could have stayed in Kemet," he said.

"It's better that Drusilla and Marcus rally those who believe in restoring the Thirty-second Dynasty. Isn't that why you left Ptolemy behind to protect them?"

Her words made sense. As far as the world knew, all the children of Cleopatra VII, the last pharaoh of Kemet, had been dead for decades. There was no way he could explain why a soon-to-be seventy-year-old man looked like he did when he was twenty-four.

Soon-to-be? No, as of midnight, it was December 25th.

"Happy Birthday, dear sister."

His twin snorted, a very unladylike sound. "You're trying to change the subject."

He laughed. "Can you imagine Octavian rolling over in his tomb if he knew we were still alive?"

Her expression turned thoughtful, which meant she was about to say something he couldn't stomach. "We could ignore the edict of the vampire masters. Considering what we can do now, it wouldn't be that hard to sneak into the Imperial Palace and kill Tiberius."

"And we would be breaking the ancient treaty."

Once again, she made a derisive sound. "Humans don't even remember the treaty any more."

"The masters do," he replied. "Do you really want to be crucified in sunlight?"

Selene made a disgusted expression, but she remained silent. His way was better. Incite Rome's client states to rebel. The more he and his Family could convert to their cause, the less the masters could do about stopping them.

And the last scion of David of Israel might just be the ember he needed to turn the entire Levant into a raging blaze.

———•———

At sunset the following evening, Alexander set out through the city. They'd been lucky. The Olive Branch was still in business, and the innkeeper Simon knew the location of Yeshua the Nazarene.

Selene had argued Alexander should take a small escort with him, even going so far as stamping her foot. But as he pointed out, he didn't want a show of force scaring the last prince of the Israelites before Alexander had a chance to convince the man to join them.

Besides, too many people running around Nazareth at this time of night would attract unwanted attention. They didn't need the governor of Syria receiving reports of unusual happenings within the province. Not to mention, Alexander could move faster than their human guards or even most of their vampire ones.

In less than a candlemark, Alexander found the small carpenter shop. Like most places of businesses, the proprietor and his or her family lived in an apartment at the back of the shop itself. He approached the family entrance and knocked.

An elderly woman carrying a lamp opened the door. "I'm sorry. The shop is closed. Please come back tomorrow." Behind her, people spoke jestingly of the local gossip.

Alexander held out his hands, showing he was unarmed. "Forgive the late hour, mistress. I'm looking for the rabbi called Yeshua the Nazarene. It is important that I speak with him."

She lifted her chin. "And what business does a Roman have with my son?"

At her words, the amicable discussion at the table stopped.

"My father may have been Roman, but my mother was not." Alexander tried to make the appropriate pleading expression. He couldn't trust mind-touching the woman. While he was confident in his physical abilities, his mental ones needed far more practice. The rabbi wouldn't be happy if Caesar accidentally turned his mother into a slavering body with no spirit left.

"The empire is eating its own. Your son has nothing to fear from me. Please may I speak with him?"

When the old woman quavered, he reached into his purse and withdrew two Imperial gold coins. "For interrupting your evening and for your son's time."

Finally, she nodded and accepted the currency. "You may join us at our table. However, your money will go to the needy." She stepped back to allow him to enter.

Alexander ducked his head and entered a small living quarters. The rabbi and his family were by no means wealthy, but their home was neat and clean. And the mother was telling the truth from her surface thoughts. His money would go to people far worse off than this family was.

Three men and two women sat on cushions around a table. The food smelled delicious, and part of Alexander wished he could partake of a solid meal again. One of the men rose. He had the same dark curly hair and warm brown eyes as the elderly woman and other two men. But it was his smile that set him apart from the others.

"Welcome to our humble abode, stranger." He gestured at a pillow next to him. "Please join us."

Alexander swallowed hard. For the first time since Octavian marched Selene and him through the streets of Rome in gold chains as children, nervousness consumed him. "Are you Yeshua the Nazarene?"

"I am." He gestured at the pillow beside once again. "Sit. Break bread with us, and tell me your tale." He turned to the woman. "Mother, would you please get another skin of wine for our guest?"

Alexander carefully lowered himself next to Yeshua and murmured his thanks to the rabbi's mother when she handed him a cup. The other woman started to dish up a bowl of lamb stew, but Alexander held up a hand. "You show me honor by treating me as a guest, but I've already eaten."

One of the other men puffed up his chest, but before he could start on his offended tirade, Yeshua held up his palm. "Stay, brother, he means no offense. He is ill, and eating now would only make him more sick."

"How-how did you know?" Alexander stared at his host.

"I've encountered those who have the blood sickness. There's something about the way lamplight reflects in the eyes, like a jackal or a lion." Yeshua shook his head. "I walked into the desert with one like you. I tried to convince him that he could live an honorable and full life. But he chose to lay down in front of the sun."

Yeshua smiled again. "However, you do not strike me as the type who has given up."

The third man leaned over the table. "Do you wish my brother to heal you?"

Alexander chuckled. "Not even the magi healers can reverse my condition. I have come to accept it in a manner of speaking."

"Yet, you do seek something from me." A mischievous twinkle flashed in Yeshua's eyes.

"You are the last eldest son of the line of David and Solomon."

Everyone at the table went perfectly still, like antelope when they know a cheetah is near. The ashy scent of human terror filled the little room.

"You need to leave," the mother said.

"I have no love for the Romans any more than the Hebrews do." Alexander would have to speak fast and convincingly, or else, this situation could get ugly. He met Yeshua's gaze squarely. "We have a similar position. I am the eldest surviving son of the last pharaoh of Kemet."

"That's impossible!" the first brother growled.

Again, Yeshua held up a palm to stop his brother's tirade. "Tell me this. Did you make yourself sick to seek revenge on the emperor?"

"No." Alexander clenched his fists to keep his own temper under control. But from the way everyone but Yeshua himself drew away from Alexander, he knew his eyes were glowing. "My youngest brother and I were infected when Augustus Caesar's sister sent *empusae* to assassinate us."

"You survived the attempt to kill you and the blood sleep?" For some strange reason, that seemed to impress the Hades out of Yeshua.

"I walked into my younger brother's bedchambers when they were attacking him and raised the alarm. They fled when the guards responded. My brother by marriage believed they were under orders not to get caught and to make our deaths look like accident or illness."

"Still." Yeshua clapped Alexander on the shoulder. "It takes a strong will to wake up from the blood sleep."

"This life would not be my first choice, but I have no wish to die."

Yeshua cocked his head. "And what is it you want from me if not to call upon my God to heal you?"

The words rushed out of Alexander. "I wish to combine our forces. I have allies along the Mediterranean who chaff under Rome's rule just as your people do—"

Yeshua's two brothers began shouting that Alexander had lost his mind. Both women began crying.

"Silence." Yeshua barely raised his voice above a murmur, but everyone in the room went silent. He turned to Alexander.

"My friend, I don't know what stories you might have heard, but I have no wish for the throne of old Israel." He smiled gently. "A new time comes, a time of peace, and with it, new attitudes and a new Israel."

"But—" Alexander started.

Yeshua clasped Alexander's cheeks between his hands, his palms callused from honest work. "As I have told others, the emperor may reign in this realm, but my concern is my Father's Heavenly realm. I seek to show truth to the people that they can live honest, righteous lives. I have no argument with Tiberius. And if you're honest with yourself, neither do you. He's not the man your parents fought. He's not the one who humiliated you and your sister in Rome all those years ago."

"You don't understand." In Alexander's irritation, his canines elongated and his eyes glowed a brilliant yellow, casting odd shadows in counterpoint to the oil lamps.

"I understand more than you think, my friend." Yeshua released Alexander. "I hope in time you'll understand as well."

"Then we have nothing more to say." Alexander rose and bowed. "Thank you for the lecture, rabbi."

"Until we meet again, my brother." Yeshua's smile was secretive, but Alexander had more than enough. If the rabbi didn't care about his people as much as he claimed he did, there wasn't a damn thing Alexander could do about it.

His heart sank. How many more people would die under Rome's heel before Yeshua would take the danger seriously and join the alliance Alexander was creating?

December 25th, 31 A.D.

Alexander found himself riding in Galilee for his second birthday in a row. He wasn't sure what exactly prompted him to make this trip. No, that wasn't true. The stories of Rabbi Yeshua had reached him in Alexandria. For a man who said he wasn't a leader, he'd amassed a great many followers since the last time they'd met.

Maybe, just maybe, Yeshua would listen to him this time.

Above them, the thin arc of Artemis's bow hung, a clean counterpoint to the dust they and their retinue stirred on the road.

"My ass hurts," Ptolemy complained.

"You're not riding an ass, brother. You are riding a horse."

"Have you thought about a living as a professional fool?" Ptolemy shot back.

"You would be far better at it than I, dear brother."

Ptolemy grunted. "It's only been a year. What makes you think he has changed his mind?"

"He has many more followers now." Alexander stared at the road, seeking holes or divots that may trip his steed. "Followers can inspire a lust for power."

"And what if he decides he doesn't need us in his so-called lust?" Ptolemy said sourly. "Selene said you revealed our true nature to him."

Alexander considered his brother's question. There was a time when he believed their parents and their older brother were the most powerful people in the world. Those assumptions were dashed to bits when he was nine. He sucked in a deep breath.

"That's a chance I'm willing to take." He eyed Ptolemy. "Go home if you're concerned about your safety."

Ptolemy scowled back at him. "Oh, for the love of Horus, that's not what I meant, and you know it. This Yeshua and his family may be the last descendants of the Israeli kings, but from everything you told me, he's a pacifist. And we both know what happens to pacifists in a Roman world."

"Rome doesn't control the whole world," Alexander bit out.

"Then why are you building your alliance?" Ptolemy's tone wasn't his usual snide one. His was a serious, heartfelt question.

"I want Rome to pay for our parents' deaths." Alexander's words were so quiet only Ptolemy would hear them.

"They killed themselves, brother, not Rome." The wind carried Ptolemy's sigh into the wilderness.

———•———

Only a faint pinkish glow showed on the western horizon when Alexander and Ptolemy approached the Nazarene's camp along the shores of Lake Galilee. From Alexander's rough count, there had to be nearly three thousand people. Most asleep. Over half of them were women and children. No one stood guard. It was a slaughter waiting to happen.

Ahead was a campfire. The men around it spoke quietly. Alexander approached them, and they went silent. A familiar figure rose, one of Yeshua's brothers. The one who had been curious during Alexander's first visit.

The Hebrew chuckled quietly. "My brother and I thought you might return." He pulled Alexander into an embrace.

When the rabbi's brother released him, Alexander said, "This is my brother Ptolemy."

"I'm James." He pulled Ptolemy into an equally gregarious hug. "Come. Yeshua will want to see you."

Another man at the fire leapt to his feet. "They're Roman! How can you trust them?"

"My brother trusts this one, Peter." James gestured at Alexander. "And he vouches for Ptolemy's behavior." James grinned at Alexander. "Don't you?"

"I can vouch for my own good intentions," Ptolemy grumbled.

James laughed. "Spoken like a true believer." He clapped both Alexander and Ptolemy on each of their shoulders. "Come. Yeshua will want to speak with you."

As they followed James through the throng sleeping on the ground, Alexander asked, "Who is this Peter?"

"A fisherman who believes in the new way." James glanced behind them before he lowered his voice. "Peter can be a bit prickly at times."

"A bit?" Alexander quipped.

"If he gives you a hard time, call for my sister-in-law Miriam." James grinned. "She has no problem putting him in his place."

They approached another campfire set apart from the mass of humanity on the shore. A woman sat on Yeshua's right along with his irritable brother from Alexander's visit to the rabbi's home. Two other men Alexander didn't know sat to Yeshua's left.

"Brother!" James ran the last few paces. "Look who came to visit!"

Yeshua rose, a broad smile on his face, but it was the man sitting on his immediate left who drew Alexander's attention. The man stiffened as if he expected some retribution from Alexander.

The rabbi noticed the odd looks exchanged between the two. "Matthew? Is there a problem?"

This Matthew looked up at the rabbi and back at Alexander. "I don't question your wisdom, rabbi, but I find a Roman patrician by Lake Galilee highly . . . unusual."

"Matthew!" the woman snapped. "That was rude!"

His face reddened at the rebuke, but he glared defiantly at Alexander.

"I don't consider myself Roman," Alexander replied evenly. But damn, if the man's words didn't raise his ire.

Which meant his eyes would start glowing if he didn't get himself under control.

Yeshua merely laughed and hugged Alexander. "I'm afraid it's the nose that gives you away, my friend."

Alexander's laugh was bitter. "Obviously, you never saw my mother's."

"I'm sure your mother was as lovely as my Miriam." Yeshua gestured at the woman by the fire. "May I present my wife?"

Once again, introductions were made. Yeshua invited them to join their group, and places were made for the newcomers.

"Ptolemy, has your brother told you about my ministry?" Yeshua asked once everyone was settled.

"A little. The rest I've heard from others." Ptolemy cocked his head. "You have the right idea, but I think you underestimate the dark side of humans."

"Maybe the real problem is no one encourages the light." Yeshua patted Matthew's shoulder. "When someone only sees hate from others, it's much easier to take that hate into your heart. It takes the strength of the Lord and the strength of your belief in Him to drive that darkness from your soul."

"What did Rome do to you?" Alexander asked Matthew.

Yeshua's student sighed. "They only offered me a job. I'm a publican."

Alexander schooled his face, but from the corner of his eye, he saw Ptolemy wince. No doubt, the locals gave Matthew a horrible time for working with their oppressors. The people of Numidia resented Selene's husband for submitting to Rome's rule. Juba had done so to keep his people safe, but in the end, they died for their resentment of their king's Romanization. The Hebrews had never seen Rome's retribution when a vassal state rebelled.

"What if there were an alternative to working for the Governor of Syria?" Alexander said.

"No," Miriam said, but there was steel beneath her gentle tone. "My husband told me of your request last winter. I have no great love for Rome, but your idea is suicide, Prince of Kemet."

"There was a time when our peoples were allies, my lady," Alexander replied.

Miriam cocked her head. "And there was a time when we were only vassals to your empire, much like we are to Rome today." She laid her left hand on Yeshua's arm, but her gaze remained locked on Alexander. "My husband is correct in his philosophy that what is the emperor's is the emperor's and what is God's is God's. Rebelling against Rome because a Kemet princeling wants revenge makes no logical sense."

"It's not revenge—" Ptolemy began hotly.

Miriam's expression grew sad, and she asked softly, "Then why do you seek to kill the descendants of Augustus Caesar for the sake of parents you barely remember?"

Instead of pouting or shouting, Ptolemy started laughing. "I wish my sister had half your sense, my lady."

"Rabbi—" Alexander began.

"No, my friend." Yeshua shook his head. "Even your brother recognizes my wife's wisdom. I told you before. I have no wish for my ancestors' throne. My kingdom is not of this world." He tapped his chest with his right palm. "My kingdom is of the soul. My work is to help my people find peace. In time, Rome will fall, just like every tyrant who has subjugated my people, but our souls will continue on until God decrees otherwise, for we are his chosen people."

The other Hebrews around the fire murmured their agreement to the rabbi's statement.

"Very well." Alexander rose. "I had hoped circumstances might have given you a different perspective. Farewell, rabbi."

"Do not fear, my friend." Yeshua smiled his secretive smile. "We will meet one more time. And it will be my turn to ask you a favor since you are so concerned about the line of David and Solomon."

His statement sent a quiver of worry down Alexander's spine. "What do you mean?"

"War isn't the way, my friend." Sadness filled the rabbi's eyes. "Your alliance is doomed to fail. Some day, you will understand."

Alexander shook his head. "It's you, dear rabbi, who doesn't understand. Rome will crush your people just like they have crushed Kemet." He turned on his heel and walked away from the campfire before he said or did something he would regret.

Ptolemy rose and followed him. "What if he's right?" he asked softly when he caught up to Alexander.

He stopped and stared at his youngest brother. "You think our parents, our brothers, don't deserve vengeance for what was done to them?"

"With the blood sickness, we could live for decades. Centuries. Maybe even millennia." Ptolemy's eyes gleamed like gold under the sun's rays. "How long are you going to carry this grudge? The odds are we could outlive Rome itself."

Alexander whirled away and headed toward the spot where their guards and horses waited. But both the rabbi's and his brother's words gnawed on him. Why was he carrying this grievance when he was the one who had actually killed their mother?

December 25th, 32 A.D.

For the third year in a row, Alexander found himself on a road in Galilee. Except this time, he rode south from Damascus. Phillippa had accompanied him on his travels east over the past twelve months. His attempts to rouse the tribes, kingdoms, and empires were only partially successful. Rome's reputation had grown well past its borders.

However, a large number of the peoples he contacted simply wanted to continue trading with Rome. He couldn't convince many of the rulers Caesar Tiberius would and could take what he wanted. But many of the outlying territories didn't believe they would be annexed by the empire.

The road south from Damascus was just as dusty as the road north from Jerusalem. This year, however, there was no moon to light the way.

"I could use a bath," Phillippa commented. "So could you. Or are you planning on washing yourself in the Sea of Galilee?"

"Maybe."

She sighed. "I have to agree with Selene and Ptolemy. You are obsessed with a backwater teacher."

"He has a great following."

"Which already has Tetrach Antipas bothered," she said. "He did execute Yeshua's cousin John after all. If you convince Yeshua to claim the ancient throne of Israel, you're putting a price on the man's head. And his family's as well. It won't matter if it's Rome or his own people coming to collect."

Alexander shot an annoyed glance at Phillippa. "Just because you refuse—"

"My sisters are dead, and my people are scattered across the four winds," she snapped. "Chasing a war to fill some demented wish for power or vengeance won't change that." Her tone gentled. "Any more than it will for you."

"You don't understand," he murmured.

"You're right. I don't." She sighed again. "I also don't understand why you seek to sacrifice an innocent man on Adrestia's alter."

"If you feel that way, why are you here with me?"

Phillippa fixed him with a haughty look. "Because I'm letting my own pride get in the way."

"You made your promise to Mother, not to me," he growled.

"My promise was to keep you and your siblings safe."

"And a fine job you did, too," he bit back.

And immediately regretted his words. With Octavian's fleet entering Alexandria's harbor, Mother had sent Caesarion away against Phillippa's advice. None of Mother's other advisors would stand up to her.

His older brother died by the hand of one of those same advisors.

Phillippa's visage turned to marble at his insult.

"I owe you an apology, my lady. I am sorry."

She sniffed. "If you were truly sorry you would heed my advice, and let the man be, Alexander." She spurred her horse into a canter.

One of their guards pulled alongside Alexander. "Should I follow her, my prince?"

"No." He shook his head. "She's rightly cross with me. Let her work off her anger alone."

"Yes, my prince." The guard and his horse slipped back in the ranks with an air of relief. The Amazon princess in a snit was not a pretty sight. And she had a tendency to take her anger out on the nearest object.

Or person.

———•———

Once again, Alexander found Yeshua by a campfire on the shores of the Sea of Galilee with his wife and his closest followers. The rabbi rose and beckoned Alexander.

"Come, my friend." The old glint of humor in Yeshua's eyes was far duller that before, though his smile was welcoming. "We need to speak privately, my friend."

Phillippa stepped forward, her hand on her sword hilt. "That is not wise."

Alexander smiled at her. "You yourself said he has more to fear from me than I do from him."

Her disgusted expression said she wasn't happy he threw her words back in her face. No doubt, he'd pay for that and his earlier insult the next time they sparred.

"Do not worry, my lady." Yeshua chuckled. "I'll keep him within rescuing distance."

She snorted. "Men." But she turned back to the campfire while Alexander and Yeshua walked up the dark hill.

Once they were out of human earshot, the rabbi stopped and turned toward the lake. "I told you I would see you one more time."

"Only to tell me no one last time." Alexander wasn't sure whether to laugh or rage. He settled with chuckling.

"And to ask you a favor." Yeshua exhaled and raised his eyes to the stars. "I ask that you guard my wife and child after my death."

Alarm trilled through Alexander and he seized Yeshua's elbow. "Are you ill, rabbi?"

"No." Yeshua looked at Alexander and smiled. "Nor has my wife conceived yet. But the time for the conception and my death are fast approaching, and I cannot trust some of my followers to watch out and care for Miriam. It saddens me that I will not be with her through her trials, that I will never see my daughter, but alas, that is the fate My Lord has decreed for me."

No hint of ginger came from Yeshua, only the odor of fresh apples below his natural scents. He wasn't a witch, but a normal human. Yet, this wasn't the first time the rabbi had predicted the future.

"Why don't you and your family come with us?" Alexander said. "We can take you with us to Kemet. Mauretania. Even back to Damascus, if that is what you wish."

"I know you mean well, my friend—"

"There is no reason for you to die," Alexander protested. "If you foresee dying in Galilee—"

"Don't the Greeks tell stories of people attempting to avoid their fates, only to have that fate follow despite their best efforts?" Yeshua shook his head. "This is not something I can escape. However, there is hope for my family." He held up his index finger. "But only if you escort them to safety."

"Why me?" Alexander asked.

"I only know it is part of your greater destiny." Yeshua smiled. "You will bring together the elements to deliver a cure for your people."

It felt as if Alexander's heart stopped. "There is no cure."

"Yet." Yeshua's gaze dropped to the hillside where most of his followers slept. "It will be some time from now. I cannot tell you exactly when. But caring for my family will be the start of your journey."

"That's how you'll convince me?" Alexander mocked. "Tell me I might be human again someday if I do this favor?"

"No. This is why the Lord gave us free will." The rabbi shrugged. "It is your choice on whether to take responsibility for my family. It is Miriam's choice whether to accept your protection when I am gone."

"Yeshua—" Alexander searched for the right words to convince his friend. His friend.

Even though they had only met three times, there was a strong connection between them. "Please come with us. Don't stay here. The world needs men like you. Men who truly believe peace is the way."

"Free will, remember?" The rabbi clapped Alexander's shoulder. "There are some things that must be. Oh, and there is a message I need you to deliver when you tell this story."

"A message?"

"Tell Sam the reason Azrael did not take her when she died was because she said no."

"Sam? Who in Hades' name is Sam?"

"You'll know when you meet her."

Out of all the things Yeshua had ever said to Alexander, that was the most confusing.

"Go to Jerusalem on the first night of Passover." The rabbi's countenance no longer held the jovial air from their previous meetings. No, this time, sorrow tugged at his eyes and lips. "Miriam will be ready to hear the truth then."

THE FIRST NIGHT OF PASSOVER, 33 A.D.

Alexander had heard the procession as it passed the White Dove Inn, Jerusalem's safe house for those with the blood disease. At the noise, Selene and Ptolemy joined him in his quarters beneath street level. Their ashy fear tainted the small room. One could never be sure what an angry mob might do or in which direction the fury might be aimed next. Part of him wanted to race outside, but he couldn't risk his brother and sister's lives. Not when their mother's last command was to protect them. Instead, the three siblings huddled together as they had when they were children, and they waited.

He wasn't sure whether it was cowardice or acceptance of the inevitable that filled his soul. If the sun didn't strike him down in a foolish attempt to aid Yeshua, the crowd certainly would have ripped him apart. Not even a single vampire could stand against such a frenzy.

The innkeeper had informed them of the trial when they arrived in Jerusalem during the night. Alexander cursed himself for not coming to Jerusalem sooner. If it hadn't been too close to dawn, he could have pretended to be his nephew Ptolemy of Mauretania, demanded an audience with the Roman governor of Judea, and pressed for Yeshua's release.

Near sundown, the city had calmed with the start of the Passover observance, and Alexander and his siblings left the inn as soon as the sun dipped below the horizon, knowing they were too late. The guards at the city gates made no move to stop them. Their horses picked their way up the trail to Kranoin, the place where Jerusalem's executions were held. When they reached the top of the hill, imperial guards were removing the last two bodies from the crosses.

The only other people were two weeping Hebrew women by the center cross, a young man Alexander recognized from Yeshua's inner circle, and two other men he did not know. As Alexander approached, the jingling of the horses' tack drew everyone's attention.

"Hey, now." The tesserarius approached them. "What are you—" He recognized Selene's accoutrements as those of a Roman matron and bowed. "I beg your pardon, lady—"

"I am Princess Drusilla of Mauretania," Selene said, identifying herself as her own daughter in the haughty tone only those of royal blood could develop. "I came to render aid to the widow of Yeshua."

"I-I, uh, of course, your highness." The tesserarius bowed again and backed away from their horses.

Alexander and Selene dismounted and handed their reins to Ptolemy before they approached the party surrounding the prone form on the ground. The youngest man stepped forward.

"I am John." He gave a tremulous smile as grief warred with manners on his face. "I don't know if you remember—"

"I do." Alexander reached out and clasped the young man's hand.

"Why are you here, Roman?" a quavering voice, husky with tears, said. Yeshua's mother, who could barely stand even with Miriam's help.

Alexander swallowed hard. "I came as I promised him." He glanced down at the two men performing Yeshua's final rites. Myrrh filled his nose. He faced Yeshua's mother once again. "I'm sorry we were too late. What can we do to help?"

One of the other men tied off the final linen strip and stood. "I am Joseph, also a friend of Yeshua's. If I could borrow your horse, we could get him to my tomb before the light fades. It will give the rest a chance to get home before true dark."

"Your tomb?" Selene asked.

Joseph shrugged. "It's going to a better cause than my old carcass, your highness."

"Escort the family back to the inn and get them rooms," Alexander murmured to his sister. "I'll assist Joseph."

Selene's lips parted as if she were about to protest. Instead, she closed her mouth and nodded. Maybe the weeping women touched her more than she would ever admit. She and Ptolemy insisted Miriam and her mother-in-law ride their horses back to the city gates.

As Miriam passed Alexander, the scent of citrus penetrated the myrrh and other spices the men had used on Yeshua's body. The rabbi was right. His wife was now with child. This could make getting her out of Jerusalem more difficult, especially if any of his followers knew of her pregnancy.

"This is Nicodemus." Joseph gestured toward the third man who had also stood. "Thank you for assisting us."

Both men's clothing was of a much finer quality than the rabbi's family and his usual followers, but now was not the time to ask such questions. Surprisingly, the tesserarius stepped forward and assisted them in placing the corpse across the saddle of Alexander's horse.

Stars appeared to the east. They didn't have much time. The imperial soldiers were already lighting torches to make their work easier. Alexander led his horse down the road, but the clinking of metal behind him made him pause and turn around. The tesserarius and three of his men followed.

Alexander frowned. Josephus chuckled.

"I assure you the rabbi is quite dead, Tesserarius," the Hebrew said. "You yourself stabbed him in the heart to confirm it."

The tesserarius lifted his chin. "The governor issued orders that Yeshua the Nazarene's tomb was to be guarded at all times. He doesn't want any more trouble, in Jerusalem or outside its gates." He looked at Alexander. "I am sorry to treat any citizen of Rome this way, sir, but the governor was quite adamant."

"I'm sure Pilatus was." Alexander pursed his lips before he added, "Especially since he executed a Galilean, who should have been remanded to the governor of Syria."

The tesserarius's skin heated. The smell of his blood was so delicious, it was all Alexander could do to keep his hunger under control.

"Governor Pilatus tried to, sir." The tesserarius gulped. "The governor of Syria is a Hebrew in the city for their religious week. He refused to accept the case, and sent—" He inclined his head toward the corpse draped over Alexander's horse. "—back to Governor Pilatus."

Alexander groaned. Politics. It always came down to shortsighted politics.

———•———

Luckily, Joseph's tomb wasn't far. Alexander pretended to help roll a boulder over the entrance once Yeshua's body was safely ensconced within. The tesserarius and his men settled in for a long night of guarding a dead man.

The White Dove was fairly empty when Alexander returned with Joseph and Nicodemus in tow. The Hebrew Passover observance had started.

"We will leave you to your rituals." Alexander caught his siblings' attention and inclined his head. Selene started to rise, but Miriam grabbed her arm.

"No. Stay. Please," she begged. "I do not wish to be alone tonight."

Selene's attention flicked from Alexander and Ptolemy, back to Miriam, and finally settled on the Hebrew men. "As long as you don't mind my cousins staying. My brother would be most vexed if something should happen to any of us women."

Appalled expressions appeared on John and Nicodemus's faces that they would dare think of harming Yeshua's wife, his mother, or Selene. However, Joseph seemed to find the insinuation amusing.

So the surviving children of the last pharaoh of Kemet spent the first night of Passover with the widow of a rabbi and her friends.

THE SECOND NIGHT OF PASSOVER, 33 A.D.

Alexander gently lowered the Roman guarding the tomb to the dirt. Ptolemy did the same for the other soldier. Between the blurring of the two mortals' memories and the blood loss, they would assume they'd merely fallen asleep on duty. At least, that's what Alexander hoped.

Together, the three siblings rolled back the boulder from the entrance of the tomb. Selene slipped inside, retrieved the corpse, and laid it on the grass.

"Don't roll the stone back," she ordered.

Ptolemy gaped at her. "Why not? These fools will think the rabbi rose from the dead and moved the stone himself."

"Exactly." Selene looked at Alexander, obviously expecting his support. "It would serve them right for what they did to the last of the line of David. What say you, brother?"

He stared at the bound corpse of the rabbi lying on the grass. Yeshua deserved better. He was a kind man who truly believed peace was a better way.

Alexander met Selene's gaze. "He's not the last of the line of David. However you are right. The confusion of leaving the tomb open would buy us some time."

"And that's assuming Miriam will go along with her dead husband's mad plan." Ptolemy shook his head. "Women with child aren't exactly known for their logical thinking."

"I beg your pardon?" Selene snapped.

Ptolemy made a disgusted expression. "Case in point."

"She will," Alexander said. "It may take her some time to come to terms with her husband's death."

"How long are you planning on staying here?" Selene stared at him.

"As long as it takes."

He carried his friend and laid the corpse in another tomb. His sister and brother placed additional stones over the second tomb. Neither Yeshua's friends or his enemies would be able to use him against his family.

—— •◦• ——

A month and a half later, Alexander stood with Miriam on the deck of a ship bound for Mauretania. A gentle wind filled the sail, giving speed to the rowers below the main deck. Light from the nearly full moon flashed silver on the waves of the Mediterranean.

"I never thought Peter would turn on me so," the widow murmured. "That he would dare claim my child is not Yeshua's."

If it weren't for Alexander's increased hearing from the blood disease, he wouldn't have heard her. "He understands the power your husband wielded. But unlike Yeshua, Peter desires that power for himself."

She rubbed the slight bulge of her abdomen. "I only wish my husband was here to meet his son."

"Daughter," Alexander corrected.

"What?" Her eyes widened as she looked up at him.

"He was quite certain the last time we met that your child is a girl."

"B-but I wasn't even . . ." Miriam gulped and stared at the dancing silvery waves. Finally, she chuckled. "He always knew things. Why am I even surprised?"

Alexander chuckled along with her. "Why don't you get some sleep, my lady? You need to take care of yourself for your daughter's sake."

She nodded and carefully made her way to the foredeck where the captain had provided bedding for the women and their guards.

Ptolemy slipped from the shadow of the mast and took Miriam's place by Alexander's side. "We can't keep her in Mauretania. Not with what you're planning."

"Plans have changed."

"What? Why?" Ptolemy leaned away and regarded him. "You're not going to marry her, are you?"

"No. I'm simply realizing I'm dragging innocent people into an unnecessary war."

"And when did you become so philosophical?"

"It took a carpenter from the Levant to make me see reality. We can do a greater good, but it will need to be from the shadows we now inhabit."

"Whatever you say, Alexander." But Ptolemy had a skeptical expression.

Things were about to change. He would never be pharaoh of Kemet, but it didn't matter anymore. "Alexander Helios Antonius is dead." He turned to the horizon. "Long live the new Caesar Augustus."

PRESENT DAY AGAIN

Caesar waited for Sam to say something. Anything.

She poured a shot of tequila. In quick succession, she licked her hand, shook some salt on the spot of her skin with saliva, licked the salt, and tossed back the shot. She finished by sucking on a lime wedge.

Sam spit out the rind and licked her lips. She stared at Caesar with a grimace. "I wish I could actually get drunk."

"I remember that feeling." He smiled. "I'll never have it again, will I?"

She sighed while she wiped her fingers daintily on a snow white linen napkin. "I can see why you never told anyone that story."

He stared at a family sitting at a nearby table. His confession hadn't brought the relief he assumed it would. He regarded Sam again. "Do you send me to your version of Tartarus now that you know the truth? Now that I've delivered Yeshua's message?"

"What? No!" She gestured wildly. "To both of your questions. I meant I could just picture how Duncan, Alex, and Anne would have reacted to that little tale. They were all raised in the Christian faith."

"So were you," Caesar pointed out.

"True, but my circumstances changed when I died." Sam frowned and propped her chin on her fist. "I take what I said back. Alex would be able to handle it, but don't tell Duncan for a few centuries. He's still getting used to talking to angels."

Caesar had to laugh. "It took me a little time to accept Phillippa after she told me who she really was."

"I get your penchant for strays now." A wry smile crossed her face. "If I didn't say so before, thank you for taking me in and helping me get adjusted to my new reality. Mary Magdalene was lucky to have you in her life."

"You're welcome." He saluted her with his goblet before he took a sip. The wine really did taste as good as he remembered it.

Sam's smile turned positively wicked. "As for the drunk thing, that's totally up to you."

"What do you mean?"

"You'll see." Her smile widened into a full-fledged grin. "We dock in a few minutes."

———•———

When Caesar and Sam reached the gangplank, he found he no longer wore an early twentieth-century suit. Instead, his clothing had been replaced with tan Bermuda shorts and a red and white Hawaiian shirt. On the dock, people in a festive mood gathered to see the new arrival. Like him, they were all dressed in current day tropical vacation wear.

"I suppose I should be grateful you didn't put me on the *S.S. Minnow* and leave me on a desert island," he muttered.

Sam chuckled. "Why does everyone assume I have an obsession with American pop culture?"

"Because you do," he retorted.

"Alexander! Alexander!" The shouts sounded so familiar he knew they were meant for him though it had been over two thousand years since anyone had called him by that name.

A dark-haired woman shoved her way through the crowd. She wore the single thick braid she had when they were children and a white chiton hiked to just below her knees. Her feet were bare as if she'd been running through Mother's palace in Alexandria. Most of all, her eyes no longer carried the resentment and madness of when he last saw her.

"Selene?"

His twin leapt into his arms and peppered him with kisses. "I'm sorry. I'm so, so sorry." She hugged him tight. "I was so awful to you, but I'm so glad to see you again."

He looked over his shoulder at Sam and mouthed, "How? Why?"

"I took a page from your book." She grinned. "I've started collecting strays. This one was on the shores of the River Styx, right where Ptolemy said she would be. There's a little bar that way." She pointed to a path leading to the left. "I think you might like it."

"But—" Caesar started.

"Get reacquainted with your sister. We'll talk more later."

"Come on!" Selene tugged his hand. "This way."

"But—" However, the crowd had already shifted around him, hiding Sam from his sight. People welcomed him as Selene dragged him through the throng. Some of them he even knew.

His sister chattered like she used to when they were both young and Normal. When she paused for breath, he said, "I'm glad you found your peace."

Selene leaned her head against his shoulder. "You know something? Your friend Yeshua was right all along. Too bad I had to die to learn that lesson."

He kissed the top of her head. "I think we have all of eternity to soak in that truth."

Suzan Harden transitioned from writing information technology manuals for companies and legal articles for a law enforcement magazine to her first love, fantasy and science fiction in all their forms. She's the author of the Bloodlines, the 888-555-HERO, and the Justice series.

www.ingramcontent.com/pod-product-compliance
Lightning Source LLC
Chambersburg PA
CBHW070521100726

47907CB00004B/928